Books by Alexa Milne

The Call of Home

Choosing Home
Returning Home
Staying Home

Single Titles

Sporting Chance
Comfort Zone
My Highland Cowboy

My Highland Cowboy

ISBN # 978-1-78686-198-6

©Copyright Alexa Milne 2017

Cover Art by Posh Gosh ©Copyright 2017

Interior text design by Claire Siemaszkiewicz

Pride Publishing

MY HIGHLAND COWBOY

ALEXA MILNE

Dedication

This story is dedicated to my family, who didn't bat an eyelid when I told them I'd started writing gay romance. To my mum, my brother, my sister-in-law, who reads all of my stories, his family, and Cath, I'd like to say a big thank you. For many reasons, the last twelve months have been hard. All we can do is hope that, like in my stories, there will be some sort of happy ever after for us all.

Chapter One

"You promised you'd tone it down."

"What?" Drew exclaimed. "This *is* toned down." He examined his skinny jeans and long T-shirt. All right, letting it hang off one shoulder might be considered provocative.

"I wouldn't normally ask…"

"Yeah, yeah, I get the picture. At least I'm not wearing jeggings and this top is plain white—not a rainbow or motto in sight. I'm even wearing riding boots."

"The shiniest ones *I've* ever seen. They're brand new, aren't they? You do realize you're going to a real ranch with cows and horses. You might get a little dirty."

Drew fixed his sister with a Paddington stare that men throughout London had retreated from. It had no effect whatsoever. "May I remind you, I was brought up in the same place as you? Just because I live in Civilization rather than this godforsaken part of the universe doesn't mean I've forgotten what an animal looks and smells like, or what they produce in seemingly endless quantities. I simply choose not to spend time with my hand up their arses."

Jenna's mouth twitched. "No, little brother, I'm sure you're used to dealing with arses a lot smaller."

Drew grinned and nudged her. Finally, Jenna gave in and a hint of a smile reached her mouth. He stretched out his arms, turning them at the wrist. "Not usually with my whole hand. Though, with these slim long fingers, I've been asked."

She laughed out loud this time. "Well, *that* conversation deteriorated quickly. I'm sorry. You know I don't usually care."

"I do, and that's why I'm not taking offense."

The car bumped along the dusty track. "Won't be long now we're off the main road. Remember, best behavior, please. For me. Duncan's doing us both a favor."

Drew checked himself in the mirror. Should he lose the glasses? He'd never got on with contact lenses and these provided him with a certain urban chic. "You make him sound like an ancient homophobic prick. I know he's Craig's best friend, but why on earth did you choose here for me to stay?"

"It's convenient. And Duncan's just old-fashioned. He isn't homophobic. As a matter of fact…"

Drew sat up in his seat. "What?" She turned away too quickly and Drew's senses tingled.

"Nothing—just he isn't homophobic. I like him. Anyway, here we are."

Drew reached to the back seat, pulled on a blue jacket then checked the view as they drove under the sign for *McLeish's Highland Experience* into a huge gravel-strewn courtyard. To the right stood a large stone house, behind which several log cabins lay dotted along the riverside. To the left were several outbuildings, stables, paddocks and a view down the glen so glorious it took his breath away. Whenever he returned to this part of the world, Drew was reminded of its simple beauty, with its glens, mountains and lochs. Jenna parked the Land Rover in a space at the front of the house.

"Now, for the last time, please be nice. Duncan's an old-school gentleman, always polite, using sir and ma'am. The visitors love it, but he doesn't put it on just for them. It's who he is. I don't think I've ever heard him say anything rude about anyone, even when he's sorely tried. He doesn't cuss or swear, either."

Drew couldn't wait to meet this paragon of virtue.

He didn't believe people like that really existed outside American films from the fifties.

The door to the house flew open and an Adonis strode out, accompanied by a large dog that walked obediently to heel. Whoever Drew had expected, it wasn't someone who'd seemingly stepped out of...*The Magnificent Seven*... he thought, searching his memory for a Western film reference.

Duncan stood tall, dark and impossibly handsome — Jenna hadn't warned him about that — dressed in a gray and white plaid shirt tucked into jeans held up by a belt with a buckle which looked suspiciously like a Highland Cow. The outfit was finished off with real cowboy boots and he carried a Stetson in his huge and calloused hand.

"Fuck me." The words escaped Drew's mouth before he could stop them. He'd always had a soft spot for cowboys and he had no doubt he could give this one the ride of his life.

"Drew, put your tongue in. You're staring."

He adjusted his jeans, wishing for the first time he'd worn something with more room, then wafted his hand in front of his face like some Southern lady sitting on a porch in New Orleans.

"But you didn't warn me. From what you said, I thought this Duncan would be some old guy, not...*him*. Why haven't I had an introduction before? I mean, come on, sis, look at him. He's beefcake on legs, and those thighs. Oh, my, a girl could swoon and fall into his arms."

"No. Absolutely no swooning. Don't even think about it. He's being kind letting you stay. Maybe you should have visited me more often, rather than insist you were too busy and make me come to London."

Drew fixed his expression into what he hoped was something neutral. *Man, I could have a million fantasies based on that body and face.* He attempted not to scan the gorgeous frame again. He willed his cock to behave, glad his T-shirt had a diagonal hem that covered his groin. Jenna had already exited the car.

Drew checked his face in the mirror once again. He'd arrived *au naturel*, but he still looked good. His cheekbones didn't need blusher and his blue eyes were striking enough not to need liner or shadow, unless he felt so inclined. He nudged his black-framed glasses up his nose, pushed a hand through his hair, sweeping it to one side, and climbed out of the other side of the Land Rover.

Jenna hugged his host and stepped back. "Thank you so much for giving Drew a room. It's kind of you."

Drew didn't sashay and instead ambled toward Duncan, hand outstretched. "Yes, thank you for giving me somewhere to lay my head. It's good to meet you."

Duncan gazed, wide-eyed, up Drew's body until he reached his face. Drew shivered as the hair on his arms rose in response to such scrutiny.

Finally, Duncan spoke. "It's no problem as long as you don't mind being here among the visitors and the animals, although there's only us in the main house. The cabins have their own facilities." Duncan took Drew's hand in a firm grip and shook it for a fraction longer than Drew expected.

Drew's libido ratcheted up another level at the sound of Duncan's voice. He was sure his insides had turned to mush. He wanted to wrap his body around the man and climb him like a sturdy oak tree. He had a thing for voices, particularly deep manly ones. *Ol' Man River*, sung by a great bass, could have him squirming in his seat. He needed to pull himself together. They'd be sleeping—just them—in a house—together—alone. *Oh, hell.*

Duncan smiled. "I'll get your bags, sir."

Drew fanned his face with his hand once again until he noticed his sister's death stare. *Maybe being here is going to be fun after all.*

Jenna opened the boot. Drew had left his sample cases at her house, so only his own bag remained. Duncan picked it up as if it weighed nothing and placed it on the floor. Jenna mouthed something, but he wasn't paying enough attention while Duncan rolled back his sleeves, picked up the case once more and strode off.

"This way," he called.

Drew followed up the couple of steps and into the hallway, unable to tear his gaze from Duncan's arse until the man turned at the foot of a large wooden staircase. His dog sat patiently next to him.

"Do you want to see your room first? There's a bathroom next door with a decent shower or bath if you want to get cleaned up from your trip." Duncan dropped the suitcase at the bottom of the stairs. "Or perhaps you'd like some tea. Carrie made a lemon drizzle cake when she brought the supplies earlier. That's if you eat cake."

"He eats cake." Jenna leaned over and patted the dog. "He has hollow legs and the appetite of a horse. Don't let his slim frame fool you. He's one of those annoying people who can eat anything."

Drew raised his eyebrows. *Oh, yes, I can eat all sorts, and I have eclectic tastes.* "Tea and cake would be lovely. And do I get an introduction?" he said, nodding at the retriever.

"This is Misha," Duncan said, rubbing the top of the dog's head. "Don't worry, she's well-trained."

"So I see," Drew said, kneeling in front of the dog whose tongue lolled as she panted in the heat.

"You are beautiful, aren't you? Don't you turn those brown eyes on me, though." He leaned in and lifted a floppy ear. "I'm a sucker for brown eyes." At Jenna's cough, he rose. "Lemon drizzle cake, then?"

Duncan led them into a large kitchen. Nothing matched, but that only increased its charm. A large red Aga stood to one side. At the other end of the room, double doors stood open, covered by a screen. Misha settled onto a bed in the corner, ever alert for any instruction her master might give.

"The midges get in if you're not careful," Duncan explained. "Especially when it's warm like now. The summer has been good so far. Lots of visitors." Duncan placed the kettle on the stove top and pulled three mugs from the shelf.

"Is there any chance you could have a quick look at Megs while you're here, Jen? She threw a shoe this morning and seems out of sorts. You know how placid she usually is."

"Sure, I'll give her the once-over for you. Is Carrie over at the cabins?"

"Yes. She and the girls are cleaning before the new lot arrive this afternoon, although we've a German family who've been here a week already."

Tea made, Duncan placed the mugs on the table in front of them. "I guess this is different from what you have back in London."

Drew thought of the steel units which filled his tiny kitchen, and the many gadgets he'd used only once. His flat was in a great location, but small. Business was good, so perhaps he should consider a move. Then again, he didn't spend a lot of time there, anyway.

"It suits the house," he said. "There's no point in having something out of character for a place like this. And you look exactly right in here, too. That shirt is perfect. Have you considered growing a beard? They're all the rage now." Drew picked up his mug with its Highland Cow logo.

Duncan stroked his face, as if giving the idea serious consideration. "It would be easier. I need to shave so often. You don't even have a shadow."

Drew ran a finger down his own cheek. He'd noticed. "No. Family trait. We don't have much hair, except for Jenna. She's the one who has to shave every day."

Duncan stared at the vet.

"He's kidding," she said. "His so-called sense of humor is an acquired taste."

Drew sipped his tea. "Jenna told me you've transformed this place. Who'd have thought you could have round-ups and learn rodeo skills in Scotland. It's very *City Slickers*."

"That's where I got the idea from. I saw a gap in the market, bought in some more cattle, built a few cabins and people came. Now we get visitors from all over the world.

We have over a hundred head of cattle—a mixture of Aberdeen Angus, Belted Galloways and Highland Cows. Every foreign visitor wants to see the coos. We also have horses trained to take all levels of ability, even disabled visitors, so whole families can visit. There are sheep and goats, as well as the dogs and cats and a couple of donkeys we rescued. We're thinking of getting more alpacas, or maybe some llamas."

"You have alpacas?"

"Yep, and wild deer roam the hills. It's a bit of a menagerie. The other dogs help with the round-ups and are out with Lachlan and Lenny. Oscar and Grouch will be mooching around somewhere chasing mice, or more likely asleep in the sun. Luckily, we have Jenna to look after them all now Jock has semi-retired and just deals with the pets."

Drew licked the cake crumbs from his lips. "And Jenna told me you didn't talk much."

A blush of red swept up Duncan's face. "She's right. I don't."

"I'll consider myself honored then. I hope you'll show me around."

"Jock's decided he's going to fully retire." Jenna interrupted their mutual gaze and both turned to look at her.

"We need to advertise for a new vet, or I'm never going to get a honeymoon. Talking of which, I'd better get going and check Megs over. You're still okay for dinner later, aren't you, Duncan?"

"Sure, I'll be there. I believe they've live music tonight. I'll take you up to your room, Drew, then leave you to it. I'm taking the Mullers out for a short trek this afternoon. You could join in if you want."

Drew glanced at Jenna. "It's been a while since I rode a horse. Maybe another time, though. I'll be at Jenna's tomorrow with my assistant, Joy. You'll meet her tonight. Wedding and bridesmaid dresses don't design and make themselves."

"No, I suppose not." Duncan stood up and collected the mugs.

Jenna handed over her plate on her way out. "I'll get off to the stables and check on Megs. I'll let one of the lads know if there's anything to worry about, and leave you to it. Say hi to Carrie for me."

"I'll see you later, Jen. It's been a while since I had a night out." Duncan waited as Jenna left the room via the French doors.

"You'd better follow me then."

Drew once more enjoyed the view as Duncan led him upstairs and along the landing. He opened a door to reveal a bright room with pale blue walls and polished wood flooring. In the center stood an old-fashioned metal-frame bed, covered with blue cotton bedding. Duncan placed Drew's case next to a chest of drawers.

"There's a wardrobe for anything you need to hang up," Duncan said, opening the door, "and you've a great view down the glen. My room is opposite and the bathroom is next door. We'll be sharing, if that's all right. Carrie sometimes stays in the annex at the back of the house if the weather is bad, but she lives in the village the rest of the time with her husband, our local policeman."

Drew bounced on the bed, which creaked under him. "It must get lonely here all by yourself."

A patch of red expanded across Duncan's throat once more and spread up his neck. "I'm used to it, and I'm not completely alone. Lachlan and Lenny have rooms over the stables and there are the guests."

"Lachlan and Lenny work here?"

"They're Carrie's sons. They take care of the horses and help with the visitors all year round. We have other people to help during high season—often students from agricultural colleges looking for experience. So, I'm seldom by myself and I like quiet. I couldn't live in a big city like you do with all those people and the noise and dirt. Here I can ride out and breath clean air."

"Bit difficult to order pizza, though," Drew said.

"I make them myself. I have an oven outside next to the barbecue. Carrie does some cooking when I'm busy, but I mostly manage on my own. Lachie and Lenny sometimes drag me into the village to eat. There's a great inn where we're having dinner tonight. It serves good food and they have music sometimes as well as karaoke and quizzes." Duncan smiled and Drew's cock stirred, or at least tried to, given its lack of room to grow.

"Everyone has to join in."

"Is that so?" Drew said, grinning. "Maybe I'll give you my special rendition of *I Am What I Am*. What's your specialty? I'm guessing *Rhinestone Cowboy*. Do you have chaps and everything? I bet you look good in them." Well, Jenna wasn't there to tell him off.

Duncan shifted from foot to foot and dug his hands into his pockets. "I'll leave you to it. There's hot water if you want a bath. I'd better get over and see if Jenna's had a look at the mare I mentioned. Lots to do." Duncan turned and hurried out of the room.

Damn, I've scared him now. Drew couldn't imagine why there weren't women fighting over this man. But then maybe Duncan was a bachelor through lack of opportunity. It had to be difficult to find single women who were prepared to live out here. Being single at forty didn't imply anything, but Drew certainly liked what he'd seen.

It had been a while since he'd split up with his last boyfriend, and he wasn't getting any younger, either. He could have fun shocking the locals, if nothing else. He stood and picked up his case, pulled the zipper and began to unpack. He grinned at the leather kilt he'd designed himself, which he'd team with a black shirt. He did love to make an entrance.

Chapter Two

"Argh." Duncan reached to pick up the deodorant he'd knocked onto the floor. Why had he agreed to host the wedding, as well as to be Craig's best man? Yes, the event was months away, but he'd have so much to do. He stood and examined himself in the mirror, turning from side to side, letting the kilt swish around his knees. Trust Jenna to insist everyone wore Highland Dress so she could see how good they'd look for the wedding itself. With the warmth of the day, he finished the outfit with a plain black waistcoat rather than a jacket. Thank goodness the colors of his clan tartan weren't too garish.

Downstairs, he waited for Drew to appear. Jenna had warned him her brother might be rather — how did she put it — outlandish. But then, she had no knowledge of the exact nature of Duncan's visits to clubs in Glasgow and Edinburgh. Duncan expected Drew to push boundaries — he *was* a clothes designer and gay.

He fidgeted with his sporran, making sure he'd positioned it correctly. In a way, he'd been looking forward to meeting Drew. As a teenager, Duncan had messed around at boarding school, though never with Craig, but that wasn't unusual when boys and girls were shoved together away from home. Experience, even his limited amount, had shown him that he leaned more toward men than women. Female visitors had attempted to get to know him better on occasion, but despite their many, and in some cases, obvious charms, he'd resisted any involvement. His visits to the capital, or Glasgow, had been few and far between. He'd been to clubs and had fumbled sex in dark corridors and brightly lit toilet stalls, or once, when too much alcohol had made him brave, in his hotel room. He'd enjoyed the sensations well enough, but he'd felt disconnected during those anonymous encounters. He'd gotten release, but nothing else, and frankly he could have achieved the same result with his hand.

In the end, he'd decided he could live without another person in his life. He had his horses, his land and his friends. Anything else was too complicated to contemplate. He poured a wee dram of whisky and swallowed it in one go. When the door creaked, he swiveled on the spot.

"Crivens!" He didn't ever swear, conditioned as he'd been by his grandfather, remembering the cuff around his head for even thinking a bad word, but seeing Drew Sinclair, standing in the doorway dressed in black leather, almost made him break his rule.

"There's a word I haven't heard for ages. I assume you're impressed with my outfit," Drew said, beaming. He twirled around. "My mother says that to me all the time. She doesn't swear, either, well, except for the time she found me wearing one of her dresses."

"You wear dresses?" The words came out before Duncan could stop them.

"Not usually." Drew stepped nearer. "But I'm not averse to putting one on to show a model how to wear it. I'm blessed with a great figure."

"Oh." Words refused to move from Duncan's brain to his tongue.

"You'd be amazed how many of them need to be taught how to walk in heels," Drew continued.

Duncan spluttered. "You wear high heels?"

Drew placed a hand on each hip. "I don't *wear* heels, cowboy. I *rock* heels. I can walk any distance in five inches." He bent over and rubbed the back of his legs. "I have strong calf muscles."

He stretched out a limb and turned slightly. Duncan found himself staring at the white crisscrossed laces wound around the sturdy calves. He needed to change the subject and regain control. He swallowed to wet his throat and clutched the back of the armchair to steady himself. "I've never seen a leather kilt before. Isn't it uncomfortable?"

Drew stepped forward into Duncan's personal space. "I designed it myself. The leather is so soft. See. Touch it for yourself."

He took Duncan's hand and lifted the leather flap for him to feel. Not knowing what else to do, Duncan stroked the material between his fingers. It *was* soft and warm. He glanced down, not daring to look up and meet Drew's gaze now they were close enough to touch each other. His cock stirred under his own kilt as his fingers sent messages to the rest of his body. He stepped back.

"You're right. It is soft and that's an unusual...sporran." He must sound like such a bumbling idiot. He raised his head and found blue eyes scrutinizing his face.

"You look good yourself," Drew said. "Nothing as handsome as a man in a kilt and I love the white shirt on your tan skin."

Duncan placed a hand on the back of the nearest chair, affecting a nonchalance he didn't feel. "It comes from a combination of genes and working outdoors a lot, especially in this weather."

"Well, it suits you. Makes you look all rugged and sexy. I expect women can't get enough of you. I wouldn't say no."

Duncan's mouth fell open. Without warning, Drew placed a finger under his chin and pushed his jaw upward, closing his mouth again.

"Come on. Haste ye away, or we'll be late."

Duncan watched him pivot and stride across the room, unable to move.

Drew glanced over his shoulder. "Come on, big boy. Don't dawdle. I assume you're driving."

"Um, yes." He glanced at the whiskey bottle on the sideboard, wanting nothing more than to take another dram. Jenna had warned him about her brother's tendency to flirt with everyone, men and women. It was his way. It meant nothing. So, why, with every fiber of his being, did Duncan want his words to be true?

He pushed down the rising panic, attempted to swallow the lump in his throat and still the butterflies performing somersaults in his stomach. At the front door, he halted and peered into the mirror.

"Pull yourself together. Why would the likes of him want the likes of you? He's just messing with your head, stupid." Duncan straightened his waistcoat and ran his fingers through his hair then followed Drew out to the car.

Throughout the forty-minute drive to the village, Drew jabbered on, but Duncan only heard a few words as he concentrated on negotiating the route to the road. He needed to fill in a few of the ruts caused by the dry weather. He made a mental note to speak to Lachie.

"What the...?" A sharp pain caught him unawares.

"Have you heard a word I'd said?" Drew sounded annoyed.

"You shouldn't poke someone so hard when they're driving." He stopped at the junction and indicated left, glad to be on the road. "You might have caused an accident."

"I'd asked you about the ranch, but you were miles away, so I poked you. Believe me, some people would be ecstatic to get such attention from me."

Duncan decided to take the bull by the horns. "Is that another example of your innuendo? Is there some reason why you keep attempting to embarrass me? I'd prefer it if you didn't in front of the others. These are my friends, and I work with them, so I'd rather not be the butt of your so-called witticisms. No doubt you think it's funny to tease the country man. I may not have lived in London, but I've traveled and met people from all over the world, including monarchs and presidents. Just because I'm not a sophisticated intellectual like you." Duncan stopped, having divulged more of his past to Drew than he'd revealed to anyone in a long while. Next to him, he sensed

Drew backing away, his shoulders slumped. Regret quickly followed Duncan's sense of triumph. No one had flirted with him so outrageously in a while, at least no one who his cock found interesting, and now he'd slapped the other man down. "I'm sorry."

Duncan glanced at Drew's hand on his thigh.

"I didn't mean anything by it," Drew replied quietly. "It's how I am. And you're a good-looking man, Duncan McLeish. I sometimes forget."

"I'm sorry, too. You're…different from most people I meet."

Drew jerked his hand away, and Duncan wanted to slap himself, knowing how his words must have sounded.

"I apologize for my gayness," Drew said, folding his arms. "I guess there aren't many people in touch with their feminine side around here."

Duncan had no idea how to answer, so remained silent. Ten minutes later, he pulled into the car park. As soon as he stopped, Drew opened the passenger door and stepped down from the Land Rover. Before Duncan could apologize, he'd set off walking to the door. Duncan climbed out, then hurried after him. Now there would be an atmosphere that Jenna and Craig would notice.

Drew didn't hold the door open for him and it nearly slammed in Duncan's face. He pushed it and followed Drew into the familiar room with its blazing fire at one end, dark wooden chairs and settles and tartan wallpaper, unsurprised to see the man receiving wolf whistles and twirling around to show off his outfit. Duncan stood like a spare part behind him. Seated at the table were Jenna and Craig, along with Mhairi, her assistant at the vet's, Carrie and her husband, Sandy, and another woman who must be Drew's assistant, Joy. He moved around Drew and strode to the table.

"What's everyone drinking then?" Duncan made a mental note of all the orders, and turned to face Drew. "Could you give me a hand?"

"I suppose so."

Several others in the inn stared at Drew, but he appeared not to notice or not to be bothered by the attention. He stood at the bar next to Duncan as he ordered from Ned, the owner of the establishment.

"I'm sorry. You know, about what I said. I don't always get my words right."

Drew stared at him and he wanted the ground to open up and swallow him. Was the hurt in those amber eyes real?

"It doesn't matter. I'm only around for a couple of weeks maximum. I can find somewhere else to stay and to go to my parents' once the dresses are sorted. I haven't been home for a while."

"There's no need for you to go. Jenna and Craig wouldn't be pleased." He placed a hand on Drew's arm, but the other man shrugged it off. Duncan glanced around the room in case anyone had seen them touch.

"Craig's your best friend, isn't he?" Drew asked.

"Yes, we went to boarding school together. He's a good bloke. With Craig, what you see is what you get. He's kind and a great listener, but he won't hold back if he thinks you need telling. The surgery here was lucky to get him, but he loves it."

"There you go, gents." Ned placed the drinks in front of them on two trays.

"Ned, this is Drew Sinclair, Jenna's brother."

"Oh, ay, the designer from London come to sort the dresses." He winked at Drew. "Well, I hope you'll not be planning to have them in leather. I'm sure oor Mhairi has her heart set on something with lace."

"Mhairi is Ned's daughter," Duncan explained.

Drew grinned. "I'm partial to a bit of lace myself, so I'm sure I can work with her on something glorious. She will be beautiful on the day. Just maybe not *as* beautiful as the bride."

Drew picked up the tray and Duncan followed him to the table with menus tucked under his arm. He took the spare seat opposite Drew and listened as Jenna introduced everyone. Craig sat to his left, nudged him.

"You're quiet."

"I'm choosing what I want to eat."

"You're all tense. I'm a trained member of the medical profession, and your best friend. I can tell something's wrong. Is it Drew? He can be a bit full-on, but he's a fun guy when you get to know him."

"It's nothing." He needed a reason or Craig would be like a dog with a bone. "You know how busy it is at this time of year. I worry about leaving Lachie and Lenny in charge even for a short time."

"They'll be fine," Carrie said, interrupting them. "I've warned them to be on their best behavior. Even you need time off every so often, Duncan. I mean, when did you last have a holiday?"

"It's been a while, but the job keeps me busy. Animals need looking after all year round, even if we don't have any visitors."

Joy leaned forward. "It must be rewarding, though. I love London, but the views here are to die for. I wish I was here longer than a few days."

"You should come on one of our treks if you've time, or bring your family for a visit. We have horses suitable for every level of rider even if you haven't ridden before. I said the same to Drew. Maybe you should both come on Monday. Drew said you were busy tomorrow."

Joy smiled and her face matched her name. She had long blonde hair tied back in no particular style, and blue eyes. Her strappy summer dress revealed freckles over her shoulders. She nudged Drew next to her. "You ride, Drew? You told me you'd grown up in the countryside. We've time to do some holiday stuff, haven't we?"

"I'm not sure. It depends how things go tomorrow. You should go if you want." He gazed pointedly at Duncan and for a moment everyone stayed silent.

"I'd like you to come," Duncan said.

Drew fixed a grin on his face. "Then as you've asked me so nicely, I will. Now, let's order some food. I'm famished with all this country air. I'm going to have the biggest steak they do because, as Joy will attest, I do love my meat as large as possible."

Jenna leaned forward. "I suggest the T-bone, then. That's what Dunc always has. He's a man who loves his meat, as well."

If looks could kill, Drew's sister would have disappeared in a flash of smoke and fire immediately. He swallowed hard, desperate not to blush at the implication of her words. What had she been thinking? She'd made it sound as if he…

Drew turned toward him. "Do you, Duncan? I suppose you like it practically mooing, all oozing with blood. I'm more of a medium man myself. I might have the pheasant, though. I do like meat that's well-hung, don't you?"

Duncan willed the heat away from his neck and hoped it wouldn't spread up to his face. He grabbed the jug of water and poured a glass, taking a sip or two before replying. "You don't know everything, it seems. I'm not a fan of game birds and as far as steak goes, I'm more of a medium man myself, too."

The waitress appeared at the end of the table, pen and pad in hand. "Are you ready to order?"

As each of them made their choices, Duncan glanced over to Drew and caught him staring in his direction, as if scrutinizing him. Automatically, he wondered if he had something on his face, or, even worse, in his teeth or up his nose. He ran his fingers through his hair then across his mouth, Drew followed his movements until Joy leaned in and whispered something in her boss's ear. Duncan couldn't hear her words above the general chat in the room, but straight after she, too, glanced in his direction.

Chapter Three

As he tucked into his steak, Drew kept his head down. Duncan had said hardly anything to him since Drew had teased him earlier. Had he gone too far? While Jenna was in full flow discussing possible styles for wedding dresses, Duncan and Craig talked quietly to each other. Drew had the feeling he might be the topic of conversation, considering the number of times both men glanced in his direction. He pretended not to notice.

"So, Sandy, what sort of crime do you have to deal with around here?"

Sandy looked grateful to be rescued from talk of dresses. "You'd be surprised. We have the usual robberies and burglaries, drug dealing in a small way and thefts of machinery and animals. Domestic abuse can be an issue, as well, with people being so isolated and farming such a difficult profession."

"Ever had to deal with a homicide?" Drew let the steak melt on his tongue, waiting for an answer. They'd been right. It was tasty — as good as anything he'd eaten in fancy London restaurants.

"Thankfully, no. We've had a few accidental deaths, mostly climbers or idiots who went out in poor conditions inappropriately dressed. Duncan and I are part of the mountain rescue team. Craig helps, as well. We get a few every winter around here."

"I would imagine winters can be hard if the snow is bad."

"You have to be prepared. Duncan's place has its own generator for backup, as do most of the farms around here."

"Let's hope the romance of a winter wedding isn't

overtaken by the reality of real winter snow, then." Drew nudged his sister.

"What will you do if the weather is bad for the wedding?"

Jenna shrugged. "It won't be. And we've four wheel drives. Guests are going to stay at the ranch. We're going to kit out the demonstration area with a dance floor, and Ned is doing the catering. I'm not going to listen to anyone who says things will go wrong, so there."

"Fair enough. You'd better plan some thermal underwear, then, for under the dress. I'm sure I can rustle up something for Craig from my men's collection."

Drew waved his fork at Craig to get his attention. "How do you feel about thermal lace underpants for the ceremony, as you're having a winter wedding and it might get cold in your kilt?"

"I'm more of a boxers man, myself," Craig replied, grinning. "Though maybe something in satin. Can you do tartan? I'll leave the lace to my intended. She looks better in it than me, that's for sure."

Drew considered revealing his own underwear for the sheer fun of it, but maybe this crowd wasn't ready for black lace 'manties' as some people called them. He'd designed them himself and they encased his cock and balls perfectly. Women especially loved them for their men. He just loved them for himself. Why should he deny himself the feel of something soft and sexy against his skin?

The waitress removed their empty plates and some ordered desserts and everyone chose coffee. Drew decided to try to engage Duncan again.

"So, how did you end up owning a ranch in the Highlands of Scotland?" he asked.

Duncan shifted in his seat and the others stared at him. What had he said? Surely, it wasn't an unreasonable question to ask.

"I inherited it from my grandfather. My family have farmed around here for hundreds of years, even before the Massacre."

"The Glencoe Massacre? The one they sing the songs about? Are you descended from the MacDonalds?"

"A long way back. My ancestors managed to keep hold of the land during the Clearances and kept out of trouble. But when my grandfather died fifteen years ago, the place was on its last legs."

"Duncan's done an incredible job to make the place popular and profitable, coming up with new ideas. Our wedding is intended to be a run through to see if the place is suitable, then other people will be able to get married in these gorgeous surroundings and have their honeymoons here."

"Sounds lovely. I might even consider it myself."

"Yeah, little brother. If you could ever find a man willing to marry you."

"Will you be having same-sex weddings now they are legal in Scotland?" Drew asked, sticking his chin out.

"I would have to," Duncan replied. "There are anti-discrimination laws."

Drew straightened up in his seat as Jenna touched his arm. He understood a warning when he felt one. He decided not to challenge further.

"So, why didn't your parents inherit the land? You haven't said much about them." A nervous hush descended once more.

Duncan's hold on his large mug of coffee increased. "My parents are dead. They were killed in a plane crash in South America a few months before my grandfather died."

Drew covered his mouth with his hand. "Oh, my God, I'm sorry. I had no idea." Why hadn't Jenna warned him?

"There's no reason why you should."

"That must have been such a hard time for you back then." *Nothing like stating the bleeding obvious. Why don't I keep my mouth shut?*

"It was." Duncan pushed his chair back. "Now, if you'll excuse me, I need to go to the gents'." He hurried through the crowd before Drew could say any more.

"I'm sorry," Drew said, glancing around. "How could I have known?"

"It's all right," Craig said, patting his arm. "It was awful at the time. When a job came up in the local surgery soon afterward, I grabbed it. I'd planned to go into emergency work but… Anyway, water under the bridge. I'd better go after him."

"No," Drew said, pushing his own chair back. "I'll go. I need to pee."

Before anyone could stop him, Drew eased his way through the tables to the other side of the room following where Duncan had gone. The sign to the gents' said to go through the door by the bar. He barged open the entrance, but there was no sign of Duncan. He used the facilities then checked for an exit off the corridor. Moving quickly, he pushed through the fire door into the open air.

The sun shone longer on summer days in Scotland, but now it was late enough for moonlight to glint off the loch in the distance, and the clear sky was full of stars. A dark shape sat on a bench about twenty yards away overlooking a babbling brook. The sound of voices drifted from the front of the inn where tables were set outside, but at the back all was quiet. Drew crossed the grassy area. When he reached the bench, he trod on a stick. The cracking sound made Duncan turn around to look at him.

"I came to check you were all right. Can I sit down?"

"It's a free country."

Duncan didn't exactly sound happy to see him.

"I can leave you if you prefer. The others were worried, that's all. I didn't mean to upset you." He sat next to Duncan, leaving as much space as he could between them. Without speaking, Duncan slumped and buried his head into his hands. Drew waited in silence.

"You reminded me of a bad time in my life. Losing my parents, then my grandfather and inheriting the ranch—I nearly lost myself. If it wasn't for Craig and Carrie and Sandy I might have gone under. Carrie became like a surrogate mother to me. I stayed with them for a while until I got my head together. Sandy's always loved the film *City Slickers*, especially the old cowboy character, Curly. We watched it one night and the idea came to me about doing something similar so people could get the cowboy experience without having to go to America for it. Mum and Dad had left me a good amount of money, and granddad had left me the land. I did some research and spent time literally learning the ropes, then started the ranch."

"That's amazing. You must be so proud of what you've achieved."

"I am. And I'm glad your sister and my best friend's wedding will be the first of a new venture. And, just so you know, I'm totally for same-sex marriage. Everyone has the right to be happy. My parents adored each other and would have been lost if one of them had gone before the other."

Drew reached over and placed his hand on Duncan's arm. Duncan didn't move away.

"We'd better go back in before they send out a search party. Thank you for coming to find me. It must seem like I'm set in my ways to you. I spent a long time either with my grandparents or at school. I was taught to be tough, to be a man. The sort of man who doesn't cry or show his feelings. Being that man nearly broke me back then. I'm still a work in progress."

"You make yourself sound ancient," Drew said.

"I'm more than ten years older than you."

Duncan rose and ambled back to the inn. Drew walked silently at his side. He wanted to ask Duncan so many questions, but, for now, they would have to wait.

* * * *

Talking to Drew had been oddly comforting. He hadn't told him everything. He certainly hadn't told him about his grandfather's attitudes to sissies, or 'big girls' blouses' as he'd called them, and that was the tamer term of abuse he'd used. He'd loved his grandfather, who'd taught him to appreciate the countryside and nature, but his ideas about what constituted a man had infected Duncan's psyche.

One day, on a hunting trip, he'd refused to shoot a huge stag standing on the hillside. Duncan had stared in awe at the glorious creature and had to hide his tears when his grandfather had killed the beast. All right, people did say if you were prepared to eat something, you should be prepared to kill it, and he'd seen animals die in a slaughter house, animals he'd raised and sent to market. He wasn't a hobby farmer. He kept animals to sell for meat, but he made sure every animal was treated well.

Back in the main room of the inn, everyone else at the table stared in their direction. He sat next to Craig again, who slung an arm around his shoulder.

"I've been telling Joy tales of our schooldays," he said.

Drew leaned forward. "Oh, please, tell me, too. Were you naughty boys? Did you get up to bad things? I've heard what boarding schools can be like. All those boys together."

"I hate to disappoint you, but we had girls, as well. Ours was this strange mixture of old-fashioned values and modern views. There was a lot of emphasis on outdoor pursuits and teamwork — character-building stuff, preparing one for leadership. We camped and walked and climbed until we were too exhausted for anything else." Craig shivered. "It was always so bloody cold. I hated living in a tent and having no toilet. My family live in a large town house in Perth. Don't get me wrong, I loved the sport, but I also wanted to read and investigate. I collected all sorts of creepy-crawlies for science lessons."

"Not only for science." Duncan sniggered.

"They never proved it was me who put a grass snake in Matron's drawer. Anyway, all she did was pick it up and take it outside."

"You must have done something you shouldn't," Drew said.

Craig chuckled. "We did get caught smoking weed. Or

we thought it was. I'm not convinced it wasn't oregano or something. We thought we were so badass."

"You bad boy, Duncan."

Yet again, he had to admit to being the good guy. "I didn't smoke the stuff. I was just there. I can't stand smoking. My grandfather smoked a pipe and I hated the smell."

"But you grabbed the joint from me and said I wasn't involved," Craig protested.

"I didn't need to stay in the sixth form like you. You were going to be a doctor. Farming didn't need qualifications back then. It was only my parents insisting I go to school that took me away from here and from my grandfather's influence. They said I needed to meet a bigger variety of people and experience more of the world."

"Maybe you should tell everyone about your antics in school, Drew." Jenna winked at him. "Locking a class in a room and the time you led a conga through the staffroom. Oh, and the drawings."

"Drawings?" Carrie asked. "I hope these weren't pornographic."

Drew sighed. "No, I drew caricatures of all the teachers and pinned them up around the building."

Jenna grinned. "They were bloody brilliant, especially the one of Mr. Hargreaves, the PE teacher, in drag."

"Served the bloody homophobic bastard right," Drew said before swallowing the last of his coffee. "He always wanted me to fail, but I wouldn't give him the satisfaction. I ran, jumped, and played football and rugby."

"So how did he know you were gay?" Duncan asked, then realized what he'd implied. "I'm sorry. I didn't mean to suggest gay men can't do sport."

"I came out when I was thirteen. I told everyone and waited for them to kick the hell out of me. I flounced, I sashayed, and even wore a sarong on non-uniform day, like a certain footballer. The girls loved me and their boyfriends hated me. Most of the teachers shook their heads except for Mr. Arden, the art teacher, and Ms. Gregory, who ran a craft club at lunchtime. She taught me about materials, pattern making, shape and design. I owe a lot to her. I wasn't the easiest of kids, but I thought the best form of defense was attack. My parents simply shrugged and loved me."

Duncan digested all that Drew had said. He admired the bravery of the man. As a boy, Duncan hadn't even wanted to admit his actions to himself, let alone anyone else. Those occasional fumbles in the dark with other boys, or the time when one of the older girls had 'initiated' him like she had so many others, by giving him a hand job in a stockroom at break remained secret. He hadn't felt shame because he hadn't felt anything. None of them had mattered, and yet, when Drew had touched his arm he'd wanted... No, there was no point. Drew was here for a short time. He glanced at his watch.

"We'd better get a move on. The track can be tricky in the dark. Are you ready to go, Drew?"

Drew swallowed the last of his beer. "Yes, absolutely. I'm knackered. With all this fresh air and good food, I expect I'll sleep tonight. I'll see you ladies tomorrow. Come on, Duncan, lead on. My carriage awaits."

In the car park, Duncan climbed into the Rover with Drew beside him, inches away. He didn't say anything before switching on the engine and setting off.

"It really is dark out here, isn't it?" Drew said, breaking the silence. "And bumpy."

"I need to get the boys out to fill in some of the ruts before the visitors complain."

Drew yawned and leaned his head back. Within minutes, small snores sounded next to him. Eventually, Duncan turned into the ranch and stopped at the house. He nudged Drew who jumped at his touch. "You fell asleep."

"I'm more tired than I thought," Drew said, rubbing his eyes. "Straight to bed for me, I think."

Duncan locked the door after they'd climbed out of the Rover.

"I'll go up now, if that's all right?" Drew asked, standing

on the bottom stair.

"Sure. Give me a shout when you've finished in the bathroom."

"I was going to shower, but I'm too tired. It'll wait until the morning. Good night and thanks again for putting me up."

"It's no problem. I'll try not to wake you up in the morning. I'm out of bed early to sort out the animals."

"I have to be at Jenna's by ten, so don't let me sleep in."

Duncan waited until Drew reached the top of the stairs. He didn't follow him. Instead, he walked down the small hallway and stepped into the main room. He picked up the whisky bottle and poured out a small measure, glad to see there were no messages on the phone. The visitors must have settled in. Tonight, Drew would be sleeping in the bedroom opposite his. He had no idea what made this man different to any of the others he'd encountered, but something did. Maybe it was his utter belief in himself, his confidence and certainty. Duncan had worked hard to feel proud of all he'd achieved, and come out from under the shadow of his grandfather's and his parents' successes, but Drew merely showed there was more to be had if he was prepared to go after it. He swallowed the whisky, letting the heat flow down his throat, and hoped he'd be able to sleep despite the maelstrom of thoughts whirling around his head.

Chapter Four

Drew forced open one eye and glanced at the bedside clock. *Bloody hell.* He'd slept like the dead. His bladder screamed at him for relief when he stretched, attempting to bring life back to his limbs. He had an hour before he needed to be ready. Carrie had said she'd give him a lift to Jenna's once she'd done her usual checks and prepared the meals.

Drew's own mother had sat him and Jenna down at the kitchen table in the big house and taught them how to cook, what ingredient went with what. He'd been able to rustle up virtually any meal, sew, iron and keep a house clean as well as chop down a tree and use a rifle before he'd reached sixteen. Joy often teased him by saying he'd make someone a great wife because he bustled behind the scenes at fashion shoots and shows, ironing or doing last-minute repairs.

His bladder reminded him again of its urgent need and he listened to see if Duncan was about. He couldn't have cared less about pissing in front of someone else, but this was Duncan's home. He decided to take the risk and, clad in his sleeping shorts, hurried to the door. Seeing no one, he rushed across the landing—to be greeted by Duncan emerging from the bathroom with a towel wrapped around his waist. Water droplets glistened on his skin and caught in the dark hair adorning Duncan's chest. Wild horses couldn't have stopped Drew's gaze following the trail of hair downward.

"Drew," Duncan said, keeping his gaze leveled at Drew's face. "You were snoring so I figured I'd get a shower first."

Drew hunched over, strangely reluctant to reveal his

boney hairless chest to the man in front of him. He'd never experienced such self-consciousness before. "I woke up desperate for the loo."

Duncan stood to one side. "I'm sorry. I'll let you get on with it. There's plenty of hot water and spare towels. I'll see you downstairs. Bacon and egg do you? You'll need a decent breakfast, facing a day sorting out dresses. I imagine trying to make sure everyone is happy can be a big task."

Drew moved forward, accidentally touching Duncan's arm. "Yes, it is. I'm sorry, I've got to go." He grabbed the door handle and shut it quickly behind him before breathing a heavy sigh of relief as he finally got to the toilet. *Bloody hell.* If the man looked good in plaid, he looked better out of it. Big shoulders, strong arms, just the right amount of dark hair on a muscular chest, a narrower waist, but not too narrow—a regular man used to exercise and outdoor living. Drew's cock stirred in his hand and he glanced at the shower. It wouldn't hurt to ease some tension under the warm water and fantasize, would it?

Thirty minutes later, after a relieving shower, a shave and spending some time working out what to wear, Drew walked into the kitchen to find Duncan and Carrie, along with two other strapping men—what did they feed them around here?—who, judging by their similarity to their father, must be Lachlan and Lenny. He nodded to everyone and went to switch on the kettle. He needed tea. Carrie beat him to it.

"You sit down, Drew. You're a guest here. Tea, bacon and egg? Do you fancy a few mushrooms and toast, or fried bread? I've some black pudding, as well."

"I can't remember the last time I had fried bread or black pudding. My mum used to make those sort of breakfasts. Lined your stomach for a busy day, she said."

"I'll get you sorted, then. These are my sons, Lachie and Lenny."

Drew put out a hand. "Bloody hell. You've some grip there," he said after Lachie grunted a hello. Lenny did much the same.

"They're not the most talkative pair in the world," Carrie added. They grinned at their mother.

"You always said we followed Dad."

"You do, Lachie."

"Nothing wrong with being the strong, silent type," Drew said. "It seems to work for Duncan here. I guess throwing around straw bales and mucking out makes big shoulders a must, judging by you three. I feel like such a wee thing next to you strapping fellows."

Carrie tittered from in front of the stove as she placed the food on a plate. "Jenna tells me you ran the London marathon in three hours last year."

Drew flung his scarf around his neck in an exaggerated fashion. This morning his T-shirt sported a rainbow-colored unicorn worn with beige cargo pants and canvas shoes. "Busted," he said. "How am I supposed to get away with needing a big, strong man if my sister gives away my secrets?"

Duncan spluttered his tea and Lenny slapped him on the back. "Something go down the wrong way, boss?" he asked.

Drew shoved bacon, egg and fried bread onto his fork. "You need to be careful. A good gag reflex helps."

Lenny leaned forward with a glint in his eye. "I guess it depends on whether you're a spitter or a swallower, doesn't it? So, which are you, Drew?"

Duncan spluttered again. "I don't think that's an appropriate question for the breakfast table, Lenny."

"Oh, come on, he started it. I'm not having him think we're country yokels, afraid of the gay."

Drew nodded as he chewed then swallowed. "Sorry. Lenny is right. I was teasing. But it depends. As the Internet meme from *Beauty and the Beast* says — both are good."

"Enough, boys," Carrie shouted. "Eat up, Drew, and we'll get over to Jenna's. You two need to get the horses ready. There are ten people booked in for the trek today. Everyone was happy with the cabins this morning, Duncan, and looking forward to you taking them out. There's the usual demonstration of roping and lassoing this afternoon, so you'll need to get the cattle in."

"Yeah, yeah, Mum." Lenny stood, toast in hand, and tapped his brother on the shoulder. "We have worked here since we left school."

Duncan placed his cutlery on the plate. "Thank you, Carrie. Enjoy your day. I'll see you later, Drew." He stood. "When you're ready, you two."

Drew hid a chuckle behind his hand as the brothers hurried to finish, kissed their mother and followed Duncan out of the door. Drew swallowed the last of his tea.

"Don't mind them," Carrie said.

"Oh, I don't. I give as good as I get."

"Jenna told me you didn't always have it easy in school. I guess you learned to fight your own battles."

He wanted to roll his eyes but refrained. What had Jenna said this time? "You do. I made no secret of my sexuality. I was ten when I told my parents and thirteen when I came out at school. My uncle is bisexual so he'd sort of paved the way in my family. Mum says she never knew who he'd be out with one week to the next. He lives with his partner, Alain, in Strasbourg, but they're hoping to be at the wedding if they can get away. Mum doesn't see him very often."

Carrie picked up the empty plates and filled the washing-up bowl. "I'm looking forward to meeting your parents again. Such down-to-earth people. Duncan got on with them *really* well when they stayed here the last time they visited Jenna."

Was there an inflection in the announcement? Did Carrie want him to know his parents had liked Duncan? Did she know something significant about the taciturn cowboy? After all, she did spend a lot of time with him. He decided to fish.

"Duncan seems like a nice bloke. A bit shy, maybe."

Carrie finished washing and drying the plates and stacked them in the cupboard. She turned to face him. "He's made a great success of this place. He's a hard worker and expects others to be the same. His parents were too wrapped up in each other most of the time and his grandfather was — how shall I put it — not the easiest of men. He didn't suffer fools and had no truck with emotions. Animals were food or worked for you. Duncan learned to shoot, hunt, fish. To be a man in the same mold. His parents flitted in and out of his life then left him alone with that old grouch."

"What happened to his grandmother?"

"Cancer in her thirties. She was the one person who softened the old man. I'm not sure he ever smiled after her death. And school was the same — lots of outdoor stuff. Oh, it was academic, as well, and at least Duncan met Craig there. But he's not experienced much outside his home and school, well, not since he reached eight years old. He's never been abroad since then, surprising considering what his parents did, and he doesn't do holidays because he doesn't like to leave his animals."

Cards on the table time. "I get the feeling you're trying to tell me something, Carrie."

"Maybe I am. I'm not blind, Drew. I saw you glancing at him last night, and he at you. Just be kind to him, that's all I'm saying. He's a good man. Now, we'd better be off. And before we get there, I'm going to tell you this right up front. If there is a hint of pink, or peach, or a flounce, I will *not* be wearing the dress."

Drew grinned and waved his arm in an exaggerated gesture. "Right, no flounces, then." He followed her to the car.

* * * *

By mid-afternoon, a few bottles of wine had been downed and tongues wagged. Quiche and salad hadn't quite managed to soak up all the alcohol. Drew, needing to keep

35

his head clear, had stuck to water, unlike his sister, her bridesmaid and her matron of honor. At least they'd settled on heather as a color for the attendants.

"Everyone gets shoulders," Jenna said. "It will be winter after all."

Drew stared at her. "And why you had to decide to have a winter wedding, I've no idea."

"Because it's romantic. Mum and Dad are coming to stay for a couple of weeks before. Luckily, the Laird is away in Monte Carlo for Christmas, so they aren't needed to work as long as dad can get someone to take care of the birds. That means we can pick any day for them to come here. And this side of Scotland isn't like living near Tomintoul where the snow gates are closed all the time in winter. We've all got vehicles designed to be driven in snow. Duncan even has a sleigh."

Drew put down his pencil. "A real sleigh. Does he have reindeer to pull it, as well?"

"There are red deer on the mountains," Carrie said. "Beautiful creatures—incredible in the mating season during the rut. You see them fighting, antlers crashing together to get the best females. Sadly, I don't think they would pull a sleigh. Duncan dresses up as Santa, though, for the kids in the village and gives out presents."

"I'd love to see that," Drew said.

Jenna ginned. "I told you. He's a wonderful man."

"It's a shame he's never found anyone to be with," Mhairi added. "Lenny loves working there. He wouldn't work anywhere else."

Carrie, with more than half a bottle of wine consumed, grabbed his arm. "He'd make someone a wonderful partner. Does anything for anybody. You should see him with the visitors. Nothing is too much. People come back year after year. There's one family with a disabled little boy who'll be here next week, who've been for five years now. The boy calls him Unc Dunc. It's so cute. If ever a man was made to be a father, he was. Such a waste, but even though some have tried…"

The look Jenna gave him after Carrie's speech suggested she knew more than she was saying. "So, how's your love life, Drew?"

He finished his sketch with a few strokes of the pencil and laid down his pad. "My love life is nonexistent — the proverbial wasteland. Or, more aptly, a desert, as this is my longest dry spell ever. Oh, don't get me wrong, I've had offers. I mean, look at me. Who wouldn't want this body?"

"You could do with putting on a few pounds," Carrie said.

"I'm naturally thin. I eat like a horse. Jenna and I are fortunate with our biology. Now, sis, what do you think to this? It gives you full shoulders and sleeves made with a lacy fabric, has a corseted bodice with laces up the back. The full skirt will flow out, but you'll be able to lift it over the snow —"

"To reveal my white Doc Marten boots."

"Yep, and I can make a cloak with a fur collar — faux, of course. Dying the fur the same shade of lilac might be a problem, but the other dresses can have the same shape, with or without the corseting. You could have some tartan, a sash, or maybe a bow at the back if you wanted, picking out the green and purple colors. Do you agree, Joy?"

"Should be possible. I've some material swatches here for you to feel. It'll need to be warm enough but not too heavy to carry."

For a while, the women gathered, heads down over the materials, feeling each piece while Drew thought idly of Duncan. He needed to find out what his sister knew, or suspected. First her, and now Carrie. If he didn't know better, he'd think his sister had planned this whole visit as some sort of matchmaking attempt between him and the quiet cowboy. But really, how realistic was he being? He lived in London. His work was there, his flat, his life. Yes, he missed the Highlands and his home, but there wasn't a future here. Maybe, Jenna had other ideas — a simple fling to boost Duncan's confidence with someone who knew their way around a man's body and how to pleasure someone, and Drew certainly knew how. Was that it? Was he supposed to be Duncan's gateway experience to the great big gay world? He wasn't sure if he should be annoyed or flattered. And he had to admit the thought of a roll in the literal hay with the big burly cowboy wasn't exactly anathema to him. A hand shaking his arm brought him back into the room.

"Drew, you were off with the pixies."

"Sorry, just thinking about something."

"Something, or someone?" Jenna asked.

"Not telling. Now, have you made a decision?"

"This one," Jenna said, holding up a swatch. "And this lace. You're sure you can dye the fabric the right shade of heather?"

"We've done it before," Joy said. "You are going to look sensational."

"Mum wants to wear green, so that will go with the purple and white."

"Suffragette colors. We learned about them in history." Mhairi glanced around the room. "Seems appropriate."

"I like it," Jenna said. "I'm not sure about Craig's mum, but we'll let her see the colors we've chosen. When are you going home?"

"Next week," he answered. "Joy's flying back tomorrow, after all, to get the ball rolling and check on things. Then you can all come down for a fitting and have a weekend in the big city."

"I've never been to London," Mhairi said, rubbing her hands together. "Been to Majorca and Turkey, but not to London. That's daft, isn't it? I'd love to see a show and go to the Tower."

"Then we'll do that," Jenna said, picking up her glass. "So, how's it going with Lenny?"

Mhairi sighed. "He's very attentive, but I'm not sure I'm ready to settle down yet. I'm sorry, Carrie."

"It's all right. But I warn you, Lenny has a tenacious streak like his father. Sandy wore me down, eventually."

"A policeman always gets his man, or woman, in this case," Drew said.

"Why don't you come to dinner next week, Mhairi? We'd love to have you."

"I'd like that," Mhairi said.

Drew sat back on the sofa. He supposed in a place like this, everyone knew everyone. Jenna had explained to him how Carrie had taken her under the family wing when she'd first arrived on her own. Obviously, Duncan wasn't the only person Carrie mothered. So when Jenna had needed a Matron of Honor, Carrie had been the obvious choice.

"That's a plan, then," he said "Joy and I will get the designs made up, and you can visit for the fittings. I assume the men are sorted."

Jenna winked at him. "After seeing your leather kilt last night, I did consider dressing the men in the same. What do you think? Could Craig and Duncan wear the same thing? I reckon they've both got the legs for it."

"From what I saw of Duncan, I would say so. I'm not sure about leather, though, unless he has a pair of chaps. Then I might be persuaded."

"He is a handsome man," Jenna agreed once more. "Not as handsome as my fiancé, but he fills a pair of jeans."

"I am not going to discuss the relative merits of Craig and Duncan's arses in front of you," Drew protested.

"You looked, then."

"Damn. Caught bang to rights. Must be the riding firming them up."

"And did you notice his thighs?"

"I might have done. I said I hadn't seen much action lately, but I'm not dead." He held up his hands. "Okay, I'll say it. Duncan McLeish is a good-looking hunk of a man, and if he batted for my side, I'd go there." The women laughed.

Jenna rose from her seat. "I'll get us another bottle and I have chocolate brownies." She leaned over, close to his ear.

"Don't give up, little brother. I'm not sure Duncan knows which side he bats for."

Chapter Five

Drew leaned over the fence, staring at Duncan showing off his roping skills like some cowboy who'd escaped the Wild West. He even wore a Stetson. Visitors stood around in the sunshine, watching the demonstrations of lassoing posts, before they tried it themselves with various degrees of success. In the large paddock, the horses had been turned out to enjoy the freedom of the open field. Duncan himself sat on a stunning chestnut mare with a white blaze down her nose. Holding the reins in one hand, he maneuvered her with ease as they worked as a team. Drew waved when Duncan glanced his way and steered the mare in his direction.

"You look good up there," Drew said as Duncan pulled the horse up next to the rail. He gave the man his best smile, and Duncan rewarded his attention by blushing furiously.

"Did you get the dresses sorted?"

"Yep, hopefully everyone will be satisfied by the final designs. Jenna will bring Mhairi and Carrie to London when they're ready to try on. You should come with them — see the sights. I'd love to show you around. You must be able to leave this place occasionally." *Wow, that came out of nowhere.*

Duncan stroked the horse's mane. "I don't know. I'm not one for big cities. All those people in so small a space and no countryside."

"We have parks and there are trees and grass. It's not all concrete and skyscrapers." He found himself wanting Duncan to agree, without knowing why. "Your horse is beautiful. Such a stunning color. What's her name?"

"Blaze. I've had her since she was born. We make a good

team. I'd better get back to helping Lachie and Lenny with the visitors. Why don't you have a wander around? The alpacas are over the other side, and there are Highland cattle and some Belted Galloways. The calves are so cute. Maybe tomorrow you'd like to go out for a ride. You do ride, don't you? Jenna said you did. We take the visitors out on Thursday again, herding the cattle from one set of pastures to another once they have more riding experience. Tomorrow would be just us. There a lake up the glen where you can swim, and the views are wonderful."

Drew peered from under his hand, shielding his face from the sun. "Sounds wonderful. It's been a while since I was on the back of a horse, but I'm sure it's like riding a bike. I'll go the long way to the house, before I settle in front of my computer and sketch out some designs. A cool drink would be lovely round about now and I'll need to get out of the sun. My pale skin does suffer in the heat."

Duncan lifted his hat and plonked it on Drew, who moved it backward.

"It's too big, but it'll cover you," Duncan said.

"What about you?"

"I've a spare hat."

"Duncan." From over the other side of the fenced area, Lachie waved.

"I'd better get back to work. I'll see you for dinner, though, won't I?"

"Sure, I'm looking forward to it. Carrie said she would leave something in the fridge."

"She usually does, even though I can cook, but often I'm too tired to bother after a long day. I don't know what I'd do without her. She's been a second mother to me. Craig will be over later. We can have a few beers on the terrace and watch the sun go down."

"It's a date, then." Drew walked away, strangely annoyed because they wouldn't be alone. He shook his head and strolled in the direction of the house.

* * * *

"Where is he, then?" Craig strode into the kitchen as Duncan closed the oven door.

"Upstairs, I assume. He said something about making a start on the dress designs for the wedding. Seems odd, a bloke designing women's clothing, but I suppose he's not the only one."

"He designs more than dresses," Craig said, taking a beer from the fridge.

"I wouldn't know. It just seems an odd profession for someone who was brought up in central Scotland on a huge estate. I mean, his father's a gamekeeper. How on Earth do you go from there to designing frocks in London?"

"Talent. Jenna said he got a bursary to study fashion and design and even while he was at university, his work was picked up by a design house in London. After a few years, he went into business for himself, and now shows all over the world. He has a sideline making manties."

Craig's smirk caught Duncan's attention. His friend beckoned him to follow him out to the terrace at the back of the house. It gave a great view down the glen as the sun set.

"What the hell are manties?" Duncan asked as he sat on the bench, noting the smirk appear again. "Do I even want to know?"

"Panties for men, hence manties. Underwear made to hold men's bits properly, but with ribbon and lace inserts, and in different colors."

Duncan crossed his legs under the table, conscious of the stirrings in his cock.

Craig fiddled with his phone and passed it to him. "Look, here you go. This is the website. Some of them are all right, like Y-fronts but with lace."

Duncan stared at image after image, all the colors and shapes from thongs to boxer briefs. A vision of Drew modelling his own wares flashed into his mind. Suddenly, aware he was gazing at the phone, he handed it back.

"I'm more of a boxers man myself." He picked up his beer and swallowed half of it, letting the cool liquid flow down his throat before he wiped the chilled glass across his forehead. "And lace looks better on women."

He gazed at Craig, daring him to disagree. His best friend was all too aware of what had happened at school, but, despite their closeness, Duncan hadn't shared his doubts about his sexuality. Craig wouldn't care if he was gay or bisexual, he had no doubt. But what was the point? He didn't want to talk about it. Merely thinking about talking, even to Craig, made his stomach churn. He didn't need that sort of confusion in his life and what man would want to live as he did, out here? In bad winters, he could get snowed in for weeks. And even though Lachie and Lenny had their place over the stables, he didn't socialize with them all the time. After all, the nearly twenty-year age gap made him old enough to be their father. In winter, when there weren't visitors, Duncan spent a lot of evenings on his own. He had his horse and his dog. Misha, as always, lay by his side. He didn't need love or sex complicating his life.

He turned at a noise behind them. *Oh, God.* Drew stood in the doorway with one arm raised, peering down the glen. His lower body was encased in skinny black jeans with open-toed sandals. As he stretched his arms upward, his plain black T-shirt rose to reveal a flat stomach and a hint of black lace. Shit, did he have on one of his own designs? A poke in his side brought him back.

"What?"

"You're staring," Craig said, grinning.

Heat rushed into Duncan's cheeks. He needed to close this down. "Why don't you take a seat and I'll get you a beer. I've some bottles. Or maybe you'd like wine. I have red and white. I wasn't sure which." Could he sound any more ridiculous? He rose quickly but angled so neither man could see the bulge in his jeans.

Drew lowered his arms, walked over and settled on the bench. "It's so beautiful here. I'm not surprised you rarely leave. And a beer is fine. Do I smell lasagna, too?"

"Carrie's left us one, and I've made a salad. There's strawberry cheesecake as well. You're not allergic or anything, are you, because I'm sure I can find something else if you are?"

Drew stared. The heat in his eyes made Duncan feel scorched and totally exposed.

"Carrie's a great cook." God, he sounded like an idiot. He hurried to the kitchen and leaned over the sink, trying to get his breath and calm his racing pulse. What the hell was the matter with him? He grabbed a bottle from the fridge and opened it. Panic rose in his chest. He needed to breathe. He had no idea what was going on in his head or his body. He didn't have a thing for skinny blokes, did he? In the limited porn he'd watched, the men tended to be alpha males with perfect physiques, not twinks, whereas Drew had a whole geeky college look going on. Maybe it was the glasses. Did Duncan have a thing for glasses he hadn't known about? He checked the oven timer. The lasagna would be ready in fifteen minutes. Time to get out there again and face the music.

"Noooo. I'm not telling you anything. Jenna's secrets are safe with me."

Duncan stood in the doorway and listened to Drew laugh. He chose to sit on the bench opposite and placed the beer on the table. Drew ran a finger up the side, scooping up the condensation before sucking that same digit. Duncan's cock leaped at the sight. Next, Drew raised the bottle to those same lips and swallowed. Duncan had to drag his gaze away. *Think about something else. Don't think about sucking on his neck.* He picked up his own bottle.

Drew stopped swallowing and wiped his mouth. "I needed that. Is it a local brew?"

"Yes, there's a microbrewery outside the village. It's good stuff. They do tours, if you're interested."

"I doubt I'll have time. Not here for long, remember, and I've got to visit my parents, as well. So, you've got me until

Friday."

A few strands of hair fell across his face. Drew blinked then looked out from underneath the fringe. "Better make the most of me."

"I thought you were here to see Jenna," Craig said, unable to keep the smile from his face as he glanced between the two men.

"She's working tomorrow, and Duncan has volunteered to take me trekking up the glen for a picnic and a swim. Will I need trunks? I haven't packed any. I don't suppose it matters as we're all boys together. I imagine it's quite a secluded place."

Heat flushed Duncan's cheeks again. The buzzer sounded from the kitchen. "That's the oven," he said, grateful for the interruption. He jumped up. What had he been thinking, offering to take Drew to his special place? He didn't take the tourists there. It was off the track, a perfect little glacial lake, deep enough to swim, private enough to not be seen.

As he removed the dish from the oven, his hands shook. "Craig, get in here and give me a bit of help, will you?"

Craig sauntered through the door with a great big grin on his face. "He's got you on the ropes, hasn't he? He's playing you like a Stradivarius, but then you're letting him. What's going on, Duncan?"

"Keep your bloody voice down and get the salad out of the fridge. And to answer your question, I've no bloody idea. I've never…"

"We both know that's a lie."

"School doesn't count, and it was years ago. Everyone dabbled, even you."

"And Glasgow? I've noticed the odd bite and bruise. I'm not stupid, Dunc. And I don't care if you're gay or bisexual. It makes no difference to me."

"For God's sake, keep your voice down," he hissed. He wanted to sink down on a chair. Instead he leaned on the counter, unable to face Craig. "I'm nearly forty, set in my ways and isolated. Every so often a visitor has shown an interest, but I've never been bothered enough to complicate things and take them up on their offer. Some of them have been quite persistent and the married ones were the worst. I've even had offers of threesomes. You've no idea."

"But you didn't take them up? I don't like to ask, but has there been anyone serious at all? I thought maybe there was someone in Glasgow you saw regularly."

Oh, God, how embarrassing was this? "No, always anonymous fumbles in dark corners."

"Men?"

"And women—a few—but it was entirely physical. Feeding a craving—a release."

"If you ask me, Drew wants the same."

Duncan shrugged. His encounters had grown more infrequent of late.

"Do you want more? Is that it? Jenna says he hasn't had a serious relationship with anyone. He flits from person to person like a bee collecting pollen and he's over ten years younger than you. I doubt he's ready to settle in the Highlands."

"I'll cancel our trek tomorrow. No point in allowing anything to happen."

"Unless you want a Highland fling for a few days. It might be good for you getting your end away with no strings."

"I thought I'd get another beer."

Duncan stilled. How much had Drew heard? "Can you grab the bowls and cutlery? We can eat outside as long as the midges stay away. They haven't been so bad this year. I'll bring out your beer."

"Sure."

Duncan turned toward the fridge once more and grabbed three more bottles. "Can you manage these and the salad bowl?" he asked Craig. "I'll bring the lasagna."

He followed Craig back out onto the terrace. For a while, they talked films and TV shows, anything other than personal topics. Somehow, he didn't get round to canceling tomorrow's trip. He might be imagining Drew's interest.

After all, why would the man want him? No, nothing would happen, would it?

Chapter Six

Drew woke and stretched his arms. The clock told him it was barely seven, but the sun's rays already streamed through the thin curtains, lighting up the east-facing bedroom. His morning wood pushed at the fabric of his lace briefs and he reached for it absentmindedly, his thoughts filled with memories of the rather pleasant dream he'd been having before the sound of noisy cattle had woken him from his slumbers.

He opened the drawer next to his bed and pulled out a bag. The perfect way to start the day. He lowered the zipper and removed his Fleshlight. Yes, exactly what he needed to lose himself, in imagining Duncan's arse tight around him. He pulled out his cock, prepared and eased himself into the foam inner. With eyes closed, and a fist full of cotton sheet, he slowly moved his most faithful companion up and down.

"Mmm." There was something about the big square cowboy which brought out the top in him. Having all that strength under him, begging him for more. He shuddered at the thought and sped up his hand. With his head laid on the soft feather pillows, he arched his back, chasing the familiar tingle as his orgasm built. He grabbed more material. *That's it. Just a little more. Nearly there.* He forgot everything, letting out a long moan as he chased the conclusion he needed.

"Oh, God."

Drew opened his eyes and grabbed the duvet, ready to cover himself then changed his mind seeing Duncan's wide-eyed stare. Neither man spoke. Drew continued, exaggerating every movement, every moan, thrusting into the Fleshlight until his orgasm ripped through him. He couldn't remember one so powerful as he laid the sex toy to one side and lay panting, his now deflated cock on display against the dark lace of his briefs.

"Haven't you ever heard of knocking?" he said, struggling to keep a straight face, and not in the least embarrassed.

Shaking loose his hand, now white from gripping the door handle, Duncan found his voice. "I'm sorry. I didn't think. You said you slept through alarms so I thought… I thought I'd better wake you."

"Well, as you can see, I'm awake. If you give me a few minutes, I'll be down after I've washed and dressed."

Duncan straightened. His bringing together of his hands over the zipper of his blue jeans confirmed Drew's certainty that the bulge in Duncan's jeans had grown.

"I'll be downstairs." Duncan turned on his heel, closing the door behind him.

Interesting.

Drew stripped off his briefs, quickly washed and dressed then hurried downstairs to an empty kitchen, empty except for a bacon sandwich and glass of orange juice. He swallowed the tangy liquid and grabbed the sandwich. He guessed Duncan would be in the stable. Maybe after his display, their trek was no longer on the cards. Sometimes, he was his own worst enemy.

He strolled across the yard, eating the bacon roll. Already, the air was warm and a film of sweat broke out on his forehead. He'd need a hat and factor fifty for his skin, or he'd burn. Lenny and Lachie waved from the display area where they appeared to be shoveling horse dung, a smell which filled the atmosphere. In the stable, the horses nickered from their stalls. As he walked to the tack room at the end, there was no sign of Duncan. Drew stopped and ran his hand down the nose of Duncan's horse with its prominent white blaze. "So where's he hiding, girl?"

A noise from behind the slightly open tack room door told him he'd found his quarry. He swallowed the last of the roll, brushed his T-shirt and ran his fingers through his still damp hair. This morning he'd chosen to wear his contact lenses although his glasses remained in their steel case in his pocket just in case. He pushed open the door and found Duncan perched on the edge of a counter, cleaning a bridle. All around were saddles, bridles and other tack, along with curry combs and brushes of every variety,

"Hello," Drew said, sidling through the door. "I thought I'd find you here. Thanks for the sandwich."

Duncan's face flushed red once more. "I'm sorry about earlier. I should have knocked. You're a guest, after all."

"Yes, you should have. Nothing like being interrupted to spoil a moment. Not that you did. I hope you enjoyed the show."

"I... I... I've no idea. I've never seen one of those before."

Drew stepped forward a few paces, lessening the distance between them, determined to bring the shy man out of his shell. The reddening patch spread up his neck and over his cheeks. Dark stubble covered the lower half of Duncan's face, with its square jaw, long straight nose and broad mouth, which made him more attractive in Drew's view.

Duncan glanced up meeting Drew's gaze for the first time. "What was that...thing?"

The question surprised Drew. He hadn't expected Duncan to be so direct.

"It's called a Fleshlight or Fleshjack. They come in several varieties, according to your preferences. It's used for—"

"I saw what it's used for."

Drew took a step closer. From here, he noticed Duncan's brown eyes had green flecks and were framed by long lashes. Now, they stared at him with curiosity and... Was that *interest*? This situation needed further investigation.

"You can get them on the Internet, along with lots of other interesting items. I'm sure they'd deliver even this far north."

Duncan lowered the bridle in his hand. "I wouldn't know."

Drew waited as the silence stretched between them. Duncan glanced up at him and down once more at the thin strap of leather in his hand. Drew desperately wanted to know what was going through his mind. All Duncan did was rise from his perch on the edge of the counter and reach to place the bridle back on its hook. Drew shifted his weight from foot to foot. What the hell was wrong with him? He hadn't felt this nervous in so long. His heart beat faster and his palms and forehead felt damp with perspiration. He rubbed his hands on his jeans then, without thinking, lifted the edge of his T-shirt to wipe his brow. Even across the space in between them, Duncan's sharp intake of breath was clearly audible. Drew teased, keeping the shirt up longer than he needed.

Duncan moved to one side and sank down on a bale of straw with both hands on his thighs. The rolled-back sleeves of his plaid shirt revealed strong forearms covered in downy dark hair. Drew could stand the quiet no longer.

"Is there something you'd like to ask?" He placed a hand at his waist and stuck out a hip like one of his catwalk models striking a pose.

Duncan raised his gaze. "I don't know. I was surprised, that's all. I didn't expect you to... I thought you'd be..."

Drew had a lightbulb moment. "What? Oh, you thought I'd be the girl?" He chose his words deliberately. The red spreading up Duncan's neck told him he'd hit home.

"Even if I did enjoy the feel of a man's cock fucking my arse, I wouldn't be the... No, I'm not even going to go there. Do you think because I design dresses and wear lace, I'm somehow less of a man than you with your wide shoulders and thighs and your plaid shirts and cowboy boots?" He put out of his mind how much those boots turned him on.

Drew strode across the room until he stood in front of Duncan. Without warning, he grabbed Duncan's hand and placed it on his zipper. "Feel that. Do I feel like a girl? Or do you want me to take one of those guns locked in the safe and fire off a few rounds? Would that prove how much of a man I am?"

Duncan didn't remove his hand, or lift his head. He simply continued to stare, being eye level with Drew's midriff. Finally, he looked up and said, "You were the one who used the word girl insultingly, not me. I didn't mean anything bad. I don't have the vocabulary." He paused, as if trying to find the right words. "I certainly didn't mean to demean you in any way."

Drew sighed. Duncan had a point. "You didn't, and you're right. There's nothing wrong with being fucked, believe me, or with being a woman. I work with women, and I consider being called a girl a compliment. My mother, sister and granny are the strongest people I know. Jenna spends half her life with a hand up a cow's arse."

"Technically, it's not their arses." Duncan smiled at him and took his hand away. "I've seen her handle horses, too. I'm sorry, but I haven't seen a man dressed in lace before, either."

Drew angled his head and smiled. "Did you like what you saw?" He dug in his jeans and pulled out the blue lacy cotton. "I design them, and you'd be surprised how popular they are. They're made to cup a man's cock and balls snuggly, but not too tightly. I don't imagine you wear those long combinations with the flap, like they do in all the cowboy films. Shame, really. I've always liked to think they use those flaps to get better access and shag each other stupid around the camp fire every night. I can see you now, bent over a bale of hay, flap open, revealing your gorgeous round arse. Is it tan like the rest of you or paler?"

His cock stirred. Boy, did he want that vision to come true. In the silence, it was obvious their breathing had increased.

"Are you deliberately trying to goad me?" Duncan asked.

"Maybe, or perhaps tease you a little. Most people would have closed the door and left straight away, but you stayed and stared. A man could read something into that." This was getting out of hand. He needed to rein the conversation back.

"Look, I don't want there to be any difficulty between us, and I've no right to make you feel uncomfortable in your own house. It was never my intention. I thought... I don't know what I thought. I can go to my parents and get out of your way, if you want."

Duncan clutched his arm. "No. Don't. Besides, we're going riding this morning, and I've a picnic all prepared. Nina is waiting to be saddled up for you to ride. She's a plodder, but yours for a carrot."

"You still want to go riding with me even after?"

"Why shouldn't I? I've always known you're gay. You don't exactly hide it."

"I don't consider it as something I should hide. If people have a problem with me then fuck 'em. I get heterosexuality shoved in my face all the time – it's everywhere."

Duncan's chortle brought a smile to his face. Those soft brown eyes stared up at Drew like Puss in Boots. Duncan's hand remained on his arm.

"Yes, I suppose when you look at it that way, you're right," Duncan replied. "I should warn you, though. Those posh boots you're wearing might get dirty. With all this dry weather, the path will be dusty and, even though it's sunny, you might need to take a jacket. The ride to our destination takes about an hour and it's off the main track, but worth it. If you want to swim, you'll need trunks."

"And if I don't have any?"

"The water can be cold even at this time of year." Drew couldn't miss the implication of his smirk.

"I'll take my chances." *Alone and naked in water with you. I'm up for that.*

Voices from the stables made them both lift their heads.

"I'll go and get the picnic panniers," Duncan said. "Lenny or Lachie will bring out the horses."

"I'll go and fetch my jacket and a towel." Drew hurried past the two men. This trip out could prove to be just as interesting as he'd expected.

* * * *

Duncan waited on the bales of hay for a while. No way could he go out and face Lenny and Lachie with a bulge in his jeans. Instead, he slipped out of the back door and jogged to the house. By the time he returned to the stable, Drew was already there, batting his eyelashes at both men, feeling their biceps and commenting on how such physical work had made them big and strong. A bolt of jealousy shot through him watching Drew tease. Obviously flirting was Drew's usual pattern of behavior, not something just for him. He coughed and all three men turned.

"There you are," Drew said, striding toward him. "I thought you'd got lost. I was telling these two how popular they'd be in certain clubs in London."

"So I see," Duncan mumbled unable to keep the growl out of his voice. Drew raised his chin and winked at him — he bloody well winked.

"We'll bring out the horses, boss," Lenny said, glancing between the men.

Duncan strode outside. The mid-morning sun already high in the sky would burn the unprepared. He placed his Stetson on his head and made a mental note to warn Drew to cover his exposed skin.

Drew emerged, walking next to the horses and men and already wearing a hat. When the horses stopped, he took the reins from Lachie, put his left foot in the stirrup and threw his body over in one graceful movement. For all his city demeanor, Drew looked right on a horse as he adjusted his hat and took a secure hold of the reins. Duncan grabbed Blaze's reins and swung the panniers over her back. Lifting himself up, he, too, mounted and tied on the bags.

"Ready?" he asked Drew.

"Yep. Lead on, McLeish."

Duncan nudged the chestnut mare with his heels and guided her out of the graveled area. She knew her way to their destination.

"Come on, Nina. Let's not let them get too far ahead of us." Drew trotted alongside him then slowed to a walk.

"You haven't forgotten how to handle a horse, then," Duncan said.

"Like riding a bike. Jenna and I rode ponies on the estate when we were little."

"You and Jenna are close."

"We don't see as much of each other as I'd like, but I guess we're a close family. My parents are great. They've never had a problem with who I am. I didn't need to come out with some dramatic announcement. My mum said I was born out, but I can still shoot and fish, and even chop down a tree should you need one felled. I watched my father, and although I couldn't shoot anything, I helped with the grouse chicks and learned my way around a gun. Mum taught me how to cook and sew. Jenna wasn't interested. I hope your friend Craig can cook because otherwise they will starve, or have to live on tinned soup and sandwiches. Jenna once thought she'd kill two birds with one stone and boiled eggs in the kettle. She fused half the house, but she was the clever one. Me, I loved to paint and draw. I made clothes for her dolls and my teddy. My Action Man got some interesting new outfits, as well. I was happy amusing myself. School and me didn't always have the best relationship."

"Me, neither." Duncan surprised himself with his admission.

"I'd have thought you'd have been right at home at boarding school with all the outdoor stuff. Isn't Shoon known for its extra-curricular activities?"

Duncan nodded. "But it's not such a good place if you're shy and weedy. I started there when I was eight and was a late bloomer. I hated it to begin with. I rarely saw my parents because they were always away."

"What exactly did your parents do? I'm guessing they worked abroad."

"My mum was a diplomat. She and my father lived mostly in South America because mum was bilingual, being half-

Spanish. I traveled with them until I was old enough to go to school, and spent holidays with my grandfather."

"I can see how that would have been tough."

"Sending kids to school at eight wasn't unusual."

"And your grandfather owned this place?"

"Yes, he did. Living with him wasn't easy, either. He threatened to take a belt to me when I cried after falling. 'Men don't cry.' I can hear him now — those deep Highland tones. I learned to keep my views to myself at home and at school. Craig helped. I was eleven when he arrived. One day, he saw these older lads having a go at me and punched one of them. Said he didn't like bullies. He was captain of the rugby team, popular with staff and students and clever, as well. The name-calling and bullying stopped. Craig didn't mind if I wanted to talk about books and comics, or how I loved old black and white musicals." Duncan glanced sideways to discover Drew's reaction to his admission.

"Ah."

"See, even you have that same expression on your face, and you *are* gay."

"Sorry. But you don't look like the sort of man who'd appreciate Fred and Ginger movies."

"Mum loved them. On the rare occasions she was home, we used to snuggle up on the sofa together and have a movie fest. I guess watching them made me feel closer to her. Though I haven't watched one since they died."

"That must have been tough."

"It was. Then grandfather left this place to me. Most people thought me mad using my inheritance to bring it into the present and try to get tourists in, but I did a lot of research online. It took a while, but now we're doing well. Word of mouth and reviews on TripAdvisor help. We get the same people coming back year after year. Those are our cattle over there." He pulled Blaze up. Drew stopped next to him.

"There are more than I expected."

"We have around a hundred head altogether. We bring

visitors to help move them from place to place, and we do sell them for meat. This is a commercial farm, as well. We breed them and sell the cows to dairy farmers. Milking is too complicated and not always profitable." He pulled on the reins and motioned Blaze to turn left up the slope. "We go up here now, off the path. It gets steeper in places, but the horses manage. We can get off and lead them if you feel safer."

"I'm fine, although I'd guess my arse and thighs will feel sore in the morning. Still, been there and done that, and I'm looking forward to seeing this place you obviously love."

Duncan avoided rising to the innuendo. "We'd better get on, then."

They rode in silence except for making encouraging noises to their horses. Eventually, the landscape opened to reveal a corrie fed by water from the mountain with a stream flowing in a more orderly way down the glen.

"Bloody hell. You were so right. This is…beautiful. There's no other word for it."

Duncan's heart warmed and tiny butterflies fluttered in his stomach. He realized for the first time how much he'd wanted Drew to love his secret place as much as he did.

"We're above the tree level here," Duncan said, "so there isn't much shade other than the shrubs and gorse bushes, and you don't want to get too close to them. The run off from the mountains feeds the lake. It's deep in the center, so stick to the edges. You do swim, don't you?"

"Yes, the estate I grew up on had a loch, so we were taught as soon as possible."

"I did life-saving training when I set up the ranch, and I keep a float up here just in case." Had he always hoped he'd find someone to bring? He nodded at the post with the orange ring attached. A rail stretched between it and another post. "We'll tie up the horses there."

Drew dismounted and led his horse to the rail. Duncan checked they were securely fastened, although neither horse would go far, being well-trained. He pointed to a flat spot partly shaded by bushes. "It should be dry enough to sit on the grass as long as you don't mind the stains."

"I brought a towel with me," Drew said. "I'll put it under me. I didn't bring much to change into."

Duncan sat and stretched his legs. "You'd better put on some sunscreen." He reached into one of the bags and pulled out the tube. "I would have thought a designer would have brought lots of clothes, or are you like the builder who never gets around to finishing all those little jobs at home, and you slouch around in jeans and T-shirts all the time?"

Drew spread the cream on his arms and face. "I mostly design for women. Men's clothes aren't my forte. Women like to have something different, unlike men."

"But you design men's underwear."

"I design what I like to wear, briefs and vests. I make corsets for women so I'm researching into designing them for men, too."

Duncan stared. He couldn't quite get his head around what Drew's words "Why would men wear a corset? I can understand women wanting to pull in their waists and accentuate their hips and breasts, but men... Unless they were chubby?"

"You'd be surprised. Some men look good in panties, stockings and high heels. A corset takes the look to another level."

Duncan crossed his legs. "I'm going to sound like a complete idiot here, or offensive. I get wanting to feel something soft next to your skin, and I know some people like to cross-dress or wear drag. In school, we did plays, but..."

"Don't knock it until you try it. Not everyone wants to wear plaid shirts and a Stetson. Each to their own, I say."

The words tumbled out of Duncan's mouth before he could stop them. "Do you look good dressed like...? Well, like that? You said you rocked heels."

Drew put down the sun cream and swung to face him.

"Why? Would you be interested in seeing me?"

"Isn't it like playing the girl?" Duncan asked, raising his eyebrows.

"Touché. Do you really want me to answer?"

"I guess I don't live around sophisticated people like you do. Up here in the Highlands, people are pretty much what you see."

Drew stared at him, sending shivers down his spine. "In my experience, people are rarely the same in public and private. We all play roles, in and out of bed. That's why certain books sell. They allow us to indulge in a walk on the wild side. Naughty clothes, naughty toys, naughty dreams. A little indulgence here and there to relieve the dull boredom of life. Some people like to dress up. Some like pain. Others go further. I've known straight men who get their girlfriends to fuck them. A man's arse is a sensitive place, made to be pleasured. You must have fantasies... secret desires."

Every drop of liquid drained from Duncan's mouth and he attempted to swallow as he squirmed, his cock half-hard. "I'm going to have a swim." Never had he been more thankful he'd worn his trunks under his jeans. He needed to cool off, and fast.

Without waiting for an answer, he stood and pulled off his boots, shirt and jeans then ran to the water and waded in. Bloody hell, it was cold even with the sun blazing down. In seconds, he was waist-deep. He turned and almost stopped breathing. Drew stood totally naked at the edge of the water, peering at him.

"I'm not sure about this. It feels cold to me."

He needed words. "You get used to it." He also needed to stop staring at the faint smattering of hair on Drew's chest, and his small pinkish nipples.

"Come on in. I'm warming up now." And how. If the water hadn't been so cold, his cock would have been fully erect, begging for attention. And talking of cocks, Drew had no reason to worry. The man might be skinny, but he sported a decent-sized cock with low-hanging balls surrounded by neatly trimmed dark-blond curls.

"All right. I'm going to sink down quickly and get it over with." Drew disappeared under the water. For a moment, Duncan worried, until he emerged right in front of him and shook water droplets from his body like a dog caught in the rain.

"Bloody hell, that is refreshing." Drew pushed back his hair. Duncan stared rooted to the spot. Finally, he reached out and cupped Drew's smiling face in his hands, hoping he'd see the question in his eyes. When Drew gave a small nod, Duncan closed the distance between them and kissed him.

Chapter Seven

Drew melted into the kiss, angled his head perfectly and pressed his chest against Duncan. Opening his mouth, he pushed his tongue forward to explore, and met no opposition. After a minute of kissing that threatened to turn his mind and body to mush, Drew sucked on Duncan's lower lip, until he reluctantly let it go. Despite the cold of the water, his cock wanted more. It was all he could do to stop himself grinding against Duncan's more than ample thigh.

"I didn't expect…"

Duncan smiled and the skin around his eyes crinkled in the bright sunshine. "I'm not sure I did, either." He glanced around. "Maybe it's being here, surrounded by all this beauty and majesty. Maybe this is my fantasy come to life. It's always been a special place for me — magical even. I not exactly sure why, but I wanted to share it with you."

Duncan's eyes shone as they gazed at Drew. But they were also questioning and fearful.

"You didn't mind, did you? Me kissing you. I didn't ask out loud first, but you did nod."

Drew considered the number of times someone had launched themselves at him, or he at them, but here stood a man worried he'd overstepped a line. Drew closed the distance between them and brushed his lips against Duncan's in the briefest of kisses. "No, I didn't mind. It's nice to be asked. Anyway, didn't my tongue tell you, or the way I grabbed your arse and rubbed against you?"

Pink bloomed on Duncan's cheeks. Drew sighed. *God.* The man was adorable.

"They were good clues," Duncan agreed.

"So what are we going to do?" Drew asked. "Seems we're both in agreement here."

"Perhaps we should get out of the water." Duncan wrapped his arms around Drew and lifted him. Drew hooked his legs around Duncan's waist. *Wow, is he strong.* His cock pressed against Duncan's stomach as he carried him out of the water and laid him on the towel. Drew held his hand over his eyes and peered upward, taking in the gorgeous sight in front of him, from strong calves and thighs, past a good-sized cock, judging by the obvious bulge, to the broad chest with a covering of equally dark hair onward to a face with the strong jaw, straight nose, dimpled cheeks and damp hair. Water droplets shimmered in the heat. Drew lifted himself onto his elbows.

"I'm a little exposed here and you're overdressed."

Duncan lowered his trunks and stepped out of them.

Drew couldn't stop the gasp that escaped his lips. He wasn't a size queen, but, bloody hell, Duncan was packing, and all his shyness seemed to have disappeared with his trunks.

"Like what you see?"

Drew nodded and wetted his lips. "I've no complaints so far." He patted the towel.

Duncan lay down next to him and pulled Drew over until he was positioned on his chest. "I need to kiss and touch you."

"You'll get no argument from me." Drew pressed his mouth to Duncan's. This time, Duncan met him open-mouthed and their tongues explored as they changed angles, deepening the kiss, not wanting to part. Drew had been kissed plenty of times before, but never like this, never so perfectly.

Duncan grabbed Drew's arse and pulled him closer. He moved, grinding their pelvises together, and leaned forward. With this kiss, Duncan claimed him and held him tight, until a break for breath allowed Drew to ease down and place kisses along Duncan's jaw then his neck, while the Duncan arched his body nearer. The kisses became nips and bites as each man-made contact as best he could. Drew turned his head to kiss Duncan's shoulder, then moaned when Duncan's lips and teeth enclosed his earlobe and sucked hard.

"Oh, God, yes," he yelled, knowing there was no one to hear them. He'd never made love in the outdoors. If they kept this up, he'd come from the friction alone, but Duncan didn't seem inclined to stop. Drew had little doubt he'd have bruises on his hips and arse from the way Duncan was holding him close and digging his fingers into his flesh. Duncan's moans got louder.

"Need you. Need to come. Yes, that's it. Just there. Move but don't move. Sorry, do what you're doing. I'm not making sense?"

Somehow, their bodies knitted together and their cocks aligned as if they'd been made especially for that purpose. Drew's orgasm roared in from nowhere. He reared up, throwing his head back while his climax ripped through him.

"Yes," Duncan cried as he thrust upward. "Yes, Drew. Don't stop. I'm nearly…"

His words disappeared as he joined Drew, sending more warmth between them. Drew urged his body forward until his arms gave way and he collapsed, breathing heavily, his heart full, with tears threatening to fall. He couldn't remember ever feeling like this. Strong arms enclosed him, holding him in place as he lay with his head on Duncan's shoulder, panting into his neck.

"I don't want to let you go," Duncan said. "This is real, isn't it? I'm not dreaming, am I? Ow." Duncan rubbed his arm. "What was that for?"

"You wanted to know if it was real, so I pinched you. I'm not sure I've felt anything more real in my life, but I need you to let me go now so I can breathe."

"You won't disappear?"

"Not yet."

Duncan let go of him and Drew rolled off and sat up, staring down at Duncan's body. He reached out a hand to make certain he wasn't dreaming, either, and ran his finger through the sticky mess already drying in the heat. He wanted to taste, but common sense prevailed.

"I haven't been with anyone for over a year," Duncan said, as if he could read Drew's mind. "I get tested regularly. I was stupid once and it scared the hell out of me, but you shouldn't take my word for it."

Drew stuck out his tongue and tasted. "You don't strike me as a liar."

He stood and held out his hand. "Come on, let's get cleaned up and swim. Then we can eat. I've built up quite an appetite, and maybe later we can scare the horses again."

Duncan reached out his hand and allowed Drew to pull him into his arms and kiss him. It felt so good standing there, skin to skin, the slight breeze on his flesh, surrounded by mountains, separated from the rest of the world. Duncan was right. This place was magical. Holding hands, they raced back into the still cold water, swam up and down and splashed until they were too tired to continue. With no embarrassment whatsoever, they sat cross-legged on the towel with hats on their head and sun cream slathered all over their bodies as if it was the most normal thing in the world. Drew bit into a sandwich as Duncan did the same and chewed slowly, pondering his question.

"Does anyone know you're gay?" he asked.

Duncan stared at him. "Even I'm not sure about that one. I'm not keen on labels."

"So you've slept with women, as well?" Drew asked.

"Slept might be pushing the description a little far. I've had encounters with a few people, but it's never bothered me not to have sex all the time."

Drew let Duncan's words sink in. He'd always been certain where his interests lay. He didn't want the situation to get complicated. *I've got to leave here in a few days.* Maybe they could simply have a fling if he didn't let his emotions get the better of him. He'd had sex with people whose name he hadn't discovered, but there was something different about the big cowboy in front of him.

"So do you think you'd like to, you know, do this again, or something more? No strings. Just two people enjoying their time together."

"I don't see why not, as long as we keep it to ourselves. There's no point in being obvious if it's only a few days, now, is there?"

What was the matter with him? He'd been thinking the same, but a wave of disappointment caught him unawares. "Suits me, but bagsy I get to fuck you first."

Duncan didn't reply. Instead, he glanced from side to side as if he expected someone to overhear the conversation and he reached for his clothes.

Have I gone too far? What if he's never... Drew grabbed his jeans and dressed hurriedly without adding anything to the conversation. A shadow passed over them as the sun disappeared behind a cloud. Other more substantial indications of a possible shower heading their way shrouded the top of the mountain.

"It looks like we might get some rain," Duncan said, as he packed away the remnants of their picnic. "Maybe even some thunder and lightning. We'd better get a move on. Don't want the horses spooked."

Drew placed a hand on Duncan's arm. "I'm sorry. Did I push too far just now?"

"No. I'm just not used to speaking about sex. I expect you and your city friends don't have those sort of boundaries."

He supposed in some ways Duncan was right. He'd held hands with other men walking down the street, though you still couldn't do so everywhere without worrying someone might take exception to a public display of affection. But up here, where Duncan hid his sexuality, such matter-of-fact conversation might be out of place. "We don't have to do anything you don't want to do. As you said, there's no point in opening a can of worms if we're simply two ships passing over a few nights."

Drew strode over to the horses, grabbed the reins and lifted himself onto Nina's back. She raised her head and whinnied as he patted her neck and stroked her ears. Duncan threw the bags over Blaze and soon led the way back down the track. The clouds became as ominous as the silence which stretched between them. All the joy they'd experienced in the magical place had dissipated into nothing.

He let Nina follow while his mind wandered and worried about what he'd found and could have already lost. Duncan's shout and Blaze's whinnying as she reared and deposited Duncan on the stony ground brought him rushing back to reality. Nina pawed the ground and shook her head but didn't bolt. Instinctively, Drew reached for Blaze's reins to stop her making a run for it while Duncan moaned on the ground. The reason for the horses' reaction stood in front of them, magnificent and massive—a red stag. It stared at them but made no move to attack, holding up its head, which was a good sign. A fully-grown stag like this one could rip open a horse's chest all too easily. Drew remained seated, not wanting to surprise the animal with any sudden shift. The only noise came from Duncan, whose groan was almost a whisper. Then, as suddenly as he'd appeared, the stag turned and disappeared into the bushes once more.

With his knees still shaking, Drew dismounted and rushed to Duncan's side. "Are you injured?" He couldn't see any blood, but Duncan held his left arm and something wasn't quite right.

"I've dislocated my shoulder," he said, still trying to get his breath under control. "Don't worry, I've done it loads of times before. Craig will be able to pop it back in for me. Do you have a signal on your phone?"

Drew dug into his pocket and was happy to see one bar showing. "I'll text him and ask him to get to the ranch. Okay?"

"Fine."

Drew pressed the keys and crossed his fingers the signal would last. "We'd better not wait for a reply. He could be at the surgery. We need to get you back on Blaze. Those clouds are gathering, and I don't want to get caught up here."

He helped Duncan get to his feet then stood by as the big man scrambled onto Blaze's back. Drew took off his T-shirt and replaced it with his jacket. He maneuvered Nina alongside Blaze and fashioned a sort of sling to give Duncan's arm some support. "It's not perfect, but it will do."

By the time they reached the courtyard in front of the house, large droplets of water had started to fall and faint rumbles of thunder sounded across the darkening sky. Lenny ran toward them as Duncan slid off Blaze's back, clutching his arm.

"What the hell happened?" he asked, taking hold of the reins.

"A stag jumped out of nowhere and spooked the horses. Blaze reared and dumped Duncan on his arse."

"You should have it looked at properly."

Duncan shrugged then winced. "Don't just stand there staring. Take the horses and sort them out. Craig should be on his way."

Drew's phone beeped to let them know Craig had set out and would be there soon. "Let's get you inside and pour some hot sweet tea down you."

"Mum's in the house," Lenny shouted. "Lachie has the Spanish visitors in the indoor court, showing them how to lasso and stuff. Could have done with you there, but their English is good."

"You speak Spanish?" he asked Duncan as they walked back to the house.

"My mum taught me. I also speak French and a smattering of Italian and Portuguese. When I was little, I picked up languages like a sponge. It's been useful with tourists."

"There's more to you than meets the eye."

Duncan stopped briefly and stared at him. "I would have thought you'd have been the last person to judge a book by its cover."

"Guilty as charged. Now, come on, we need to get you inside."

"Ouch. It hurts."

"Well, stop moving it, then, you idiot."

They entered via the kitchen door. Carrie turned and immediately rushed toward them. "Don't tell me. It's your shoulder again. When are you going to stop being such a stubborn idiot and get it fixed?"

"I told you. I haven't got time to have surgery. It's put back in easily enough. Though doing it now isn't exactly convenient. No doubt Craig will insist I get it X-rayed, which means a trip to Fort William."

Carrie glared at him, and Drew guessed there was a story behind the injury. "Could you make us some tea?" Drew asked, taking a seat at the table with Duncan. "Is it all right to have some?"

"I'll put the kettle on. Craig usually manages to put it back, even though it hurts like hell while he does."

"He's on his way," Drew said.

* * * *

"I'm not going to argue with you. Yes, I could put it back now, but you know I don't like doing it. This time, I'm taking you to Fort William to get it put back, and you'll have to rest it, which means using the sling and keeping your movements to a minimum."

"But it's the height of the season," Duncan protested.

"And we're wasting time. It's going to be bad enough being out there in this weather, without listening to your complaints."

"I'll come, too, if you want," Drew said. "I've nothing else to do."

"Fine. I'll have to stay with you, anyway, to bring you

back. You need to be more careful."

"I couldn't help it if the stag spooked Blaze. It jumped out right in front of her."

"Good job Drew knew what to do and didn't panic. At least it's not rutting season. Then it might have been a completely different ball game. Come on. Sooner we get there, the better."

Drew helped Duncan get in the jeep. By now the big man seemed smaller and he was certainly paler. "Are you all right?" he asked, placing his hand on Duncan's thigh.

"I don't like hospitals."

"Does anyone?" Drew replied. "I hurt my arm once when I was little. Only a green stick fracture, but I had to have a plaster cast. It was kind of cool getting people to sign it. From what's been said, I gather the shoulder has been a problem for a while."

Duncan winced and Drew wasn't sure whether it was his shoulder or the question.

"Might be best to leave him alone for now," Craig said from the front. "And I need to concentrate."

Drew stared out of the window as the sky flashed and a fork of lightning lit up the mountains. A crash of thunder followed soon after. The windscreen wipers did their best to deal with the volume of spray, but Craig had to slow down to avoid skidding in the large puddles which had formed on the main road.

After fifty minutes, they pulled into the car park. Craig put his doctor's badge on display and they hurried into the A & E department.

"I'll wait here," Drew said. Fortunately, the waiting room had few occupants that afternoon.

"Get me a hot chocolate, please," Craig said. "It's the one decent thing in the machines. I'll deposit him and come and wait with you."

Drew nodded, uncertain as to why Craig didn't stay with Duncan, but he knew best, and the doctors would need to put the shoulder back. He found the machine and waited for the chocolate to pour into the plastic cups. He could read on his phone if they were allowed. He didn't see a sign, settled into the plastic chair and waited for Craig to reappear.

Chapter Eight

Drew rose when Craig entered the waiting area. "How is he?"

"He's fine. They've sedated him and put his shoulder back. He'll have to keep it strapped up, but he bounces back from these things. They'll let us know when he's ready to go. It shouldn't be long. I suggest we sit and wait. Is that my chocolate?"

Drew handed over the plastic cup.

"Good, it's still drinkable, unlike everything else in these places. I swear the liquids those things produce are part of a government experiment about what sick people and their relatives can tolerate under stress."

"I'm glad he's all right. It could have been much worse. I've seen red deer in the wild and that was a large male. Luckily, I think it was as surprised as we were."

"You did well not to panic. Not everyone would have reacted so calmly."

Drew shifted in his seat and blood rushed back into his numbed leg. "Jenna and I *were* brought up on a laird's estate, and our father *is* a gamekeeper."

"Yeah, but I figured you wouldn't have had a lot of interaction with the animals."

Drew's hackles bristled automatically, and he curled then unfurled his fingers. "Why? Because I'm gay and we don't like tramping about in mud and the great outdoors?"

Craig gave him a weak smile. "Shit. No."

A woman stared at them both and nodded at her daughter who, as she had her iPod plugged in to her ears, was unlikely to have heard Craig's exclamation. He mouthed an apology then turned back to Drew. "I'm sorry, my assumption was lame. It's just looking at you…"

Drew frowned.

"I'm digging a bigger hole, aren't I?"

"You could say that. And I'm experiencing déjà vu. Put a man in skinny jeans and a tight T-shirt and he automatically becomes an urban kind of a guy? I love my home country, but my job means being where the action is, and I love London, too. I've traveled all over Europe and elsewhere with shows. My designs have become more well-known. I've even had a couple worn on the catwalk at the BAFTAs this year. I like making people feel and look good. The Comfort and Joy label is my baby — or mine and Joy's."

"Where does the Comfort come from? I'm guessing your assistant is the Joy part."

Drew recognized Craig's clumsy attempt at changing the subject and went with it. "I thought Jenna would have told you. My middle name, and my mum's maiden name, is Comfort. Hence the label. And it works. We want women to have comfortable clothes that bring them joy. Anyway, I wanted to ask you something. Duncan's had a shoulder problem for a while, hasn't he? I get the feeling there's a story behind it."

"I don't suppose it would do any harm to tell you. It first happened at school. Duncan wasn't always as big as he is now. In fact, when I first met him, he was skinny and the victim of constant bullying. I hate bullies, and after I came to his rescue one day, we became friends. My size, and the fact I was the captain of the under thirteens rugby team helped. However, I wasn't there all the time and the Easter after I arrived, his grandfather was ill, so Duncan had to stay in school along with a few others who took their frustrations out on him. They lifted him up and put him on a bar in the gym, hanging by his hands — one of those on frames which pull out of the walls. They raised it so if he fell he'd hurt himself. Duncan was a stubborn bugger. He held on until his shoulder gave way. They let him down so he twisted his ankle when he dropped, but he'd pulled the bone out of the shoulder socket. He didn't grass on them, even then."

"Nasty. I had some bastards in my school, but my dad had taught me how to box since I was six, so when I decked one, they laid off the physical stuff."

"Sadly, they didn't give up on Duncan. They were like animals searching for any weakness, and rugby tackles can be fierce. His growth spurt came late, but when it did, he filled out in all the right places. But old habits die hard, and he still gets annoyed with himself — sees himself as weak because he couldn't stand up to them on his own. Maybe that's why he likes you. You wear who you are literally on your sleeve, or on your chest. He's never been able to."

Drew turned to face Craig. "Are you trying to tell me Duncan's gay?" he whispered, conscious of the woman and her daughter.

"I'm not sure. I don't know if *he* is, either. Perhaps he's bisexual, or pansexual, or whatever label is appropriate these days, but I've seen the way he gazes at you and I think you're interested in him. I'll just say one thing. Don't hurt him. A highland fling might seem like an interesting diversion for a few days but…"

Drew placed a hand on Craig's arm. "Duncan is a grown man, capable of making his own decisions. I haven't hidden who I am, and what happens between us, if anything does, frankly, isn't your business."

"I—"

"There you are. Get me out of this place."

Drew looked up to see Duncan standing next to them with a face like thunder. Had he overheard anything? He stood.

"Sure, Dunc." Craig added, standing beside Drew. "I see they strapped you up good and tight. Let's get you home."

* * * *

Drew had to admit Carrie's pizza tasted better than the stuff he ordered in London. With salad and homemade coleslaw, he was in food heaven. However, he and Duncan weren't alone enjoying their meal, so there was no chance to talk or reflect on what had happened between them. The whole thing seemed so long ago now and almost unreal.

Craig stayed and Lachie and Lenny joined them for their feast. The storm had passed now and the sun sent out pink and orange hues as it set down the glen. They ate outside with a patio burner helping to take the slight chill from the air. Lenny suggested poker, so they played and ate with Duncan taking them for all their money.

"Always the quiet ones you have to watch," Drew said, as more of his cash transferred to Duncan's pile.

Lenny slapped his brother on the shoulder. "Lachie's quiet, as well, but he doesn't have a poker face like Duncan. Good job you've never been to Las Vegas, boss. They'd think you have some sort of system."

"I'm just good at remembering cards. If Solitaire was an Olympic sport, I'd be a gold medalist. And I've a one-hundred-percent record on FreeCell. I like figuring patterns."

"Well, I've run out of money, and we've got to get up in the morning," Lenny said, gathering the cards back into one pile. "Don't worry about the round-up party tomorrow, boss. Lachie and I can handle moving the cattle with the visitors. I'll give Des a ring. He'll have some mates who want to come and see the horses. Mum can pick them up on her way here. They'll be glad of a few pounds, even if they have to shovel horseshit to get it."

Craig pulled on his jacket. "And I'd better be off home, as well, or Jenna will get annoyed with me. You'll be over tomorrow won't you, Drew? Or I could take you tonight so you two can get an early start on your shopping and cinema trip. Jenna's been dying to see her heartthrob play Macbeth, even if it is only on a screen."

No way did Drew want to leave Duncan after what had happened between them earlier. He had plans for Duncan's body even with his injury, if he still wanted him and, judging from the odd glance from the other man, he was certain Duncan was having similar thoughts. Obviously, he kept his poker face only for playing cards.

"I'll pass, if that's all right. Jenna's going to pick me up early, and I couldn't leave this wounded soldier all alone in this big old house tonight, now, could I?"

Duncan's cheeks flushed rather beautifully and the others exchanged glances. Lachie's mouth fell open until his brother reached over and shut it. "Time for us to go, Lachie. Two's company and four's a crowd."

Drew checked Duncan. Was he cross? Had Drew gone too far?

"Take care of your arm. Remember nothing strenuous, all right?" Craig said. Drew caught the wink as his future brother-in-law turned and bowed his head, making a chuckle into a cough.

"I hope you're not getting a chill, Drew," Craig continued. "Maybe the both of you should get an early night. Don't worry. I'll let myself out and see you tomorrow."

Once Craig had disappeared around the building, Drew eyed Duncan. "Perhaps we'd better follow doctor's orders, then. I could give you a hand in the shower if you like." *Nothing ventured, nothing gained.*

"I'll have to leave off the shower with my arm strapped up. It's easier not to take it off, but I will need some help with my clothes." Duncan glanced at him with the trace of a smile.

Drew beamed his approval of this suggestion. "I can certainly do that for you. I'm sure the washing up can wait until the morning. You go on up and I'll tidy everything away and turn off the burner."

Duncan stood. "I'll be waiting in my room if you're sure. We can work around this." He swung his arm. "See, it's already on the mend."

"Oh, I know exactly how we can get around your injury," Drew said, piling the plates on top of one another. "Will you be able to pee on your own? You won't need someone to hold it for you?"

"I'll manage," Duncan said. "But it doesn't mean I don't want you to hold it for me."

He strode off through the kitchen. Lenny was right. It was sometimes the quiet ones who surprised you the most.

After tidying downstairs, Drew waited in his bedroom until he heard sounds on the landing. Duncan had returned to his room. In the bathroom, Drew cleaned his teeth and stared at himself in the mirror. Should he shave or leave the stubble? He decided on the latter and pushed his glasses back up his nose. Should he have left them off? He'd taken his contact lenses out so needed them. He examined his chest with its smattering of down, his pink nipples and the slight padding covering his ribcage if he didn't stretch. He wasn't ripped. He had no six-pack. Thin, he might be, but he wasn't a gym bunny, just lucky with his metabolism. He and Jenna had that much in common. He glanced down at his briefs. Should he have stuck with the more conventional sort? These weren't quite a G-string, but with his junk now encased in deep-purple stretch lace and his arse mostly on display, he hoped he'd get a reaction out of Duncan. *Time to face the music.* Butterflies beat their wings in his stomach. He drank water from the tap, hoping to still them. He hadn't suffered from stage fright in his life, yet here he was, mouth drying despite his attempt to moisten it.

"For fuck's sake. Stop overthinking things. We've already rubbed our junk together in the open air. He wants this. You want this. So get out of here."

Duncan wiped his eyes as if he couldn't believe what they were showing him when Drew entered the bedroom. "I thought you'd fallen down the loo or something," he croaked out.

Drew found Duncan sitting up in bed with a sheet covering his bottom half. He failed to disguise the wince of pain when he patted the bed. Drew did a twirl.

"Like what you see?" he asked.

"I'd be lying if I said no. There's something so intriguing

about a man wearing glasses and sexy underwear. Come here."

Drew eased himself into bed next to Duncan. "Have you taken your painkillers? I couldn't help noticing how you winced. We don't have to do anything, you know. I don't want to hurt you."

Duncan picked up Drew's hand with his good one and dragged it under the sheet. "I need some help with this."

Drew rested his fingers on Duncan's erection. "I think you started without me." He ran his hand over the silky flesh to the leaking tip.

"You wouldn't leave a man with that, would you?" Duncan asked.

"I suppose not, but maybe nothing too strenuous." He leaned over. Keeping his hand on Duncan's cock, Drew licked around one darkening nipple then sucked. Duncan moaned and shifted beneath him.

"You like that, don't you?"

"Mmm."

Drew continued to lick and nip, losing himself in making Duncan feel good as he eased down his chest, leaving a trail with his tongue, each nip and lick connecting him further to this man, until he pressed into Duncan's belly button.

"No," Duncan said, squirming beneath him. "Tickles."

Drew stopped then pulled down the sheet. Duncan's erection lay on his stomach now. He'd planned to ride the hell out of such a beautiful cock, but maybe not yet. Taking a firm hold of the base of Duncan's shaft, he stroked up and down, feeling every vein until he moved close enough to lick the bitter clear liquid from the tip. Still, he wanted more, to be closer, to connect, something undefinable.

"Please," Duncan moaned.

Drew turned, lifted his leg and straddled him. Dark-brown, almost black eyes gazed up at him. He resisted the temptation to pepper kisses over Duncan's face, in his desire to maintain the closeness. Instead, he pivoted around and wiggled his arse.

"I wish I could reach to bite those cheeks of yours," Duncan said. "I'm not sure I've ever seen an arse so smooth and creamy." He ran a nail down one side, no doubt leaving a red trail as Drew moaned. "Makes me want to lick your hole. Oh, God. Did I really say those words? See what you do to me, Drew Sinclair?"

Drew glanced over his shoulder. "I love it when you talk dirty. Have I ever mentioned that your voice make me want to do bad things and, believe me, one day I'll demand you reciprocate? But for now, I have something I need to get up close and personal with."

He struggled to encase Duncan's whole shaft in his mouth, but it was worth the effort. Moving back, Drew wrapped his hand around the bottom of Duncan's erection and licked around the tip and in the slit. Duncan gasped and his cock hardened further on Drew's tongue. Every so often, he squeezed Duncan's balls and rubbed along his taint, trailing his fingers back to circle Duncan's hole before returning to grasp the shaft again. He had no qualms about shaking his arse in Duncan's face. He'd received enough compliments in the past to know that it was one of his best features. All the same, Duncan running a finger down his crack took him by surprise and his arse clenched instinctively at the thought of where that finger might go. Drew tried to concentrate on his own actions. Didn't Duncan understand that distracting the man with his cock in his mouth might have dangerous consequences?

"Your arse is so pale. I want to leave my mark on it."

Drew sucked harder and Duncan lurched up, almost hitting the back of Drew's throat,

"Sorry, but the things you do to me. Your tongue is a lethal weapon. I need to touch you."

Drew was totally on board with that suggestion.

When Duncan freed his cock from the lace covering, he moaned and hummed with pleasure, knowing he was dripping onto Duncan's chest.

"Don't stop. So, close now." Duncan wrapped the fingers

and palm of his free hand around Drew's cock. Drew closed his eyes, letting sensation overwhelm him as his nerve endings tingled with anticipation of what was to come. He fought to concentrate on all the feelings clashing together—the weight on his tongue, the girth of Duncan's cock stretching his mouth, the smell of Duncan's body, the pull of Duncan's hand on his own body guiding him ever closer. It was intoxicating.

His own orgasm gathered pace, sending tingles down his spine until it burst like a dam seconds before Duncan's shout warned him and spurts of hot spunk filled his mouth. He swallowed, trying to concentrate while his own orgasm slowed down as Duncan milked him, covering his chest with sticky stripes. He pulled off Duncan's cock with a *pop* and moved until he lay at Duncan's left side with his head propped up on one elbow, his smile as wide as the Cheshire Cat's.

"You okay?" he asked.

Duncan nodded, still breathing hard. "I'm good—more than good, although somewhat messy." He ran his finger through the cooling liquid and put the finger in his mouth. Drew's cock lifted again. Why did this man have such an effect on him? He wanted to curl up as close as possible and be surrounded by his feel, his scent, like a cat curled on a lap. He shook his head as if to clear it of such nonsense.

"Do you have any wipes? I'll clean you up. I hope you didn't get any on the sling. Might be difficult to explain."

"There's some in the drawer."

Drew wiped Duncan's chest. "Are you okay if I go?" he asked. Not that he wanted to leave, but something about the strength of his reaction to this man unnerved him.

Duncan grabbed his hand. "Don't go. I want you to stay. I might need help in the night, or something."

Drew breathed in. Despite his question, he had to acknowledge that he couldn't run away, even if every bit of his common sense told him to.

"Okay. You roll over on your good side, and I'll tuck in

behind you. It'll stop you rolling back and hurting yourself."

He could argue with himself that he was simply staying to help, but when he pressed his chest to Duncan's back and placed his hand on his hip, Drew recognized the lie for what it was. He wanted to be there. He wanted to feel the warmth of Duncan's skin next to his. He wanted to hear him breathing slowly and steadily in the darkness as he fell asleep. He'd worry about these feelings in the morning, but for now...

For now, Drew allowed the happiness of being so close to this particular person to wash over him and lull him to sleep.

Chapter Nine

"Thank you. Shakespeare isn't exactly Craig's thing."

Drew threaded his hand through Jenna's arm as they strolled along the path beside the River Ness back to the car.

"You're welcome, sis. At least cinemas show plays live now. It's such a great idea. And truth be told, I don't go often myself. I love a musical, but I've only been to the Globe once, and I don't watch dramas. I haven't even been to many of the tourist spots in London. We don't always see what's on our doorstep, do we? Growing up, I took where we lived for granted, hated it even. All that countryside, mountains and lochs on our doorstep and all I wanted was the city, and not living in some cottage with dubious heating being collected by a bus every day to go to school. I suppose at least we could do that. I can't imagine having to be sent away like Duncan."

He stopped and leaned over the rail. All around people walked, some obviously tourists and others locals on their way home from the city center, having crossed the bridge from the town.

"Let's sit for a while." The warmth of early evening brought out insects that buzzed around them. Bees wiggled in flowers contained in troughs. At least the midges that Scotland was famous for weren't as much of a problem here as they were on the west coast. The Ness flowed wide at this point on its way to the sea and Drew gazed at the buildings on the other side, large houses, most likely converted to flats and hotels. Farther up, on the opposite side on the hill, Inverness Castle stood proud, dark against the sky. He pulled out his phone, took a few photos of the view then held his arm away and leaned toward Jenna.

"Smile."

She grinned as he took the selfie.

He showed her the photograph. They shared features in common—the same dark-blond hair, pointed chin, blue eyes and longish nose, though hers had been broken when a horse had kicked out and caught her a glancing blow. Luckily, it hadn't been full on, or the damage would have been much worse.

"You're going to make a beautiful bride," he said. "I hope Craig knows how lucky he is."

"He does. I tell him often enough. We had some good news yesterday, as well. Craig's brother, Cormac, has been in Australia studying the coral reef for three years, but he's returning home to stay and has a job at Glasgow University come January. He's hoping to be here in time for the wedding. I hear he's a bit of a character. He certainly tells some tales when he Skypes. He's not bad-looking, either. Shame he and Duncan don't get on."

Drew ignored the obvious insinuation and forced himself not to ask what had caused the animosity. "That'll be fun for you. I should travel more. I've been abroad with shows, but sometimes it feels like all I see is the inside of hotels, and catwalks. Coming here is different and it doesn't take long to fly. Joy will be back home already or, if I know her, already at work buying the material for your dresses. Jonty and Ben think I'm mad stopping even for a few days. They shiver at the idea of animals and dirt and not being able to buy a skinny hazelnut latte on every corner."

Drew had been to university with the pair who now lived in the same block of flats. Jonty worked as a pattern maker and Ben was a buyer in a high-end store. He'd brought them together. "They're looking forward to meeting you again when you come down for a fitting. Funny how Scotland seems so far away when I'm there."

Jenna nodded. "It sometimes feels as if we're in different

worlds and not on the same small island, with me up here in among the mountains and lochs and you down there surrounded by skyscrapers. I couldn't live in London. Here, I sit on my deck with a view of the water and breathe in the air while Hamish races around like the mad dog he is. Craig and I can drink a chilled glass of white, as long as we aren't on call, and all's well with the world. I have a great life, a job I love and someone to share all it with. I'm so lucky. I wish you had it, too, baby brother."

Drew sighed. He loved his job. He loved creating clothing that made people feel and look good, and most days, he enjoyed the hustle and bustle of London, but, sitting here, watching the water flow past them on its way to the sea, he realized he didn't miss that life half as much as he'd expected. He sighed. Jenna turned slightly to face him.

"Are you all right? Usually by now you'd be telling me I'm mad letting myself be stuck up here in the middle of nowhere. I don't suppose this might have to do with a certain handsome cowboy currently sporting a poorly shoulder?"

Drew stared straight ahead, not wanting to meet his sister's gaze. How much did he share? She nudged him.

"I'm not prying," she said.

"Aren't you?"

"All right. I suppose I am, but you're my baby brother and I want you to be happy. How long is it since anyone mattered to you? You getting nearer thirty now."

"Thanks for the reminder."

"What? Thirty's nothing. Craig will be forty next birthday."

"You and he have spent a lot of time dithering."

"I needed to be sure, but I want kids while we're young enough to enjoy them. I'd love it if you had someone, too, and Craig worries about Duncan."

This time Drew did turn to smile at his sister. "Are you two matchmaking? You're making a big assumption about Duncan, aren't you?"

"Are we? We'd have to have been blind not to notice you both checking each other out. And he took you to the lake — his lake. We may not have lived together for some years, but I know that look in your eyes. You were twelve the first time I saw it, and staring at the fifteen-year-old son of Sir Machie's friend as though he was an ice-cream cone you wanted to lick all over. So, come on, spill. You and Duncan. I'm not wrong, am I?"

There was little point in denying it. Jenna would dig and dig until she hit her target. "All right. I'll admit I like him. I mean what's not to like? He's tall, he's handsome and he wears a cowboy hat, but there's no future in it. We live in different worlds. I'm a fling. We'll have some fun together. He'll learn some new skills, but nothing more. That's all it can be. Anyway, he's bisexual, so I imagine if he ever settles, he'll choose the path of least resistance, get married and have babies to pass his land on to. I'm only going to be here for another three days. We'll have some no-strings sex, or as much as his injury allows. I'll go off to visit Mum and Dad, and he'll stay here with a few memories of the best sex he's ever had."

"Is it really so simple?"

Drew wanted to scream that it wasn't, but there was no point. He'd known the man precisely four days. They'd had sex twice. He didn't believe in love at first sight — lust, yes. He'd fallen in lust at first sight far too many times and been disappointed. Having sex with someone who was more interested in how they looked than satisfying him was something he could live without. Duncan had been interested in him, whether he felt good, not if his arse was too thin or too fat. He supposed a certain amount of self-obsession was necessary for a successful male model, considering all the pressure they were under to fit certain criteria, but he couldn't imagine living with such self-centered behavior all the time.

"It doesn't matter, Jen. This is the real world. My life is in London and his is here. Best to have some fun and gain a few pleasant memories of a lovely break in gorgeous surroundings. Things don't work out because we want them to and a few days aren't enough to make life-changing decisions. After all, you've been engaged to Craig for two years and known him for three years before that. You've hardly rushed headlong into matrimony. And Duncan is ten years older than me and no doubt set in his ways. Can you imagine how people would react if he took up with me? I don't hide who I am, and I'm not going to change out of my skinny jeans or lower my voice and keep my hands off my hips."

"I don't think Duncan cares if you are camper than a row of tents."

"Maybe not when no one knows about us, but I couldn't pass for straight if I tried. Take me as I am or not at all--lacy knickers and high heels included. No, we'll, play around, have some fun and get out before things get awkward. And now, sister dear, let's get back to your car and back to the ranch. I hope the food we left in the trunk is okay. The deli was so good, and I wanted to give Duncan a treat to make him feel better."

"Yeah, yeah. You don't care at all."

As they hurried to the car, Drew didn't let himself think too much about the man waiting for him, or what they might do that evening. Three more days and he'd be gone. If he kept telling himself this was a fling, then maybe he'd believe it.

* * * *

"Blast. This is hopeless." Duncan collapsed onto the bale of hay, curry comb in hand. "I'm sorry, old girl." He'd managed one flank but kept knocking his arm on the other. Blaze continued eating feed from her bag, oblivious to his frustration.

"Here, boss. Give me that and I'll finish her off for you."

Duncan handed the comb over to Lachie. "Thanks. I'm

next to useless at the moment. I'm sorry you and Lenny have to do all the work."

"It's okay. It can't be helped, and Lenny's got the lads cleaning around the place. I've never seen a pair who enjoy shoveling shit the way they do just to get free riding and roping lessons. They'll be here until they return to school in a couple of weeks."

"How did the round-up go this morning?" Duncan watched as Lachie finished up grooming Blaze.

"Great. We had six guests with us. The youngsters stayed with Carrie, collecting eggs and feeding the chickens and ducks. The cattle cooperated with being moved to the higher pasture and everyone had a good time. Both the teenage girls kept staring at Lenny and he flirted like mad. You know what he's like."

"What about you, Lachie? Any girl caught your eye?" Now, what the hell had made him ask? True, Lachie was the quiet one compared to his confident brother. It couldn't have been easy growing up under such a large shadow.

Lachie led Blaze into her stall, closed the gate and sat opposite Duncan, staring at the floor.

"I'm sorry. I'd no right to ask. Your social life is none of my business."

"I'm gay."

Heat rushed into Duncan's cheeks. He'd had no idea. Did Carrie and Sandy know? What the hell did he say? "Oh, I see." How lame could he be? *Pull yourself together. The boy is reaching out to you. Does he know? Stop it. This isn't about you.* "Have you told anyone else?"

"I think Lenny suspects something. I keep meaning to tell Mum and Dad. They'd be all right about it, but it's not as if I'm involved with anyone, so why rock the boat?"

"Why tell me then?" *Foot in mouth again, idiot.* "Not that it's a problem."

Lachie pushed his hair back from his face and glanced sideways at Duncan. "Jenna's brother, Drew. He's so open about his sexuality, and...you and he went off together yesterday. I mean…you took him to the lake. You don't take the tourists there. And I've not known you have a girlfriend, so I thought…"

Duncan clutched the edge of the bale of straw which crumbled in his hand. Butterflies rushed into his stomach. He wanted to run—fight or flight—as the adrenaline pumped around his body, sending his pulse rate into overdrive. His shoulder ached in sympathy.

Lachie leaned forward. "Are you all right? You've gone as white as a sheet. Do you need a drink? I'm sorry. You and Drew are none of my business. I didn't want to step on your toes if you and he… Shit, this is coming out all wrong."

Duncan wanted to smile at the irony of those words. "It's okay, Lachie. Don't get your knickers in a twist. Drew and me—it's nothing serious. It can't be. He's leaving in a few days. And I'd appreciate you keeping this to yourself. I don't want gossip. Not even Lenny. My private life is—private."

Lachie jumped to his feet. "Yes, of course. I won't say anything to anybody. He is good-looking, though, isn't he? I'm not sure he's my type, but there aren't many opportunities around here."

Duncan chuckled. "No, you're right there." His panic had subsided. "But there are probably others like us, hiding in closets, or not shouting it from the rooftops."

"I guess. There was a German guest we had here last year. Me and him—we had some fun. Nothing serious. He was sexy and good to me."

"You mean one of the bikers? I remember them."

"Yeah, the tall one with the long hair and tattoos. He took me out on his bike one day—so strong."

Duncan noted the wistful look in Lachie's eyes. The visitor had been nothing like Drew with his styled hair and slim frame. Lachie stood at six feet in his bare feet, but the German had been bigger and more than a little intimidating in his black leathers. He and his friends had been archetypal bikers on the surface, but no problem, and as interested in riding the horses as their bikes.

"Interesting group of guys," he said.

"Yeah. Definitely not what you expect investment bankers to be like." Lachie stood. "I'd better get off. Lenny will be wondering where I am. We're at the pub quiz tonight if you and Drew want to join us, although I'll understand if you want some time to yourselves."

A car skidded on the gravel. "That might be him back now. I'll ask him about the quiz. It's been good to talk. You know I'm here if you need to unload and if you want me for anything."

"Yeah, thanks. And the same if you ever...you know."

"Might have guessed I'd find you in here."

Duncan turned to see Drew, standing with his hands on hips and with a huge smile plastered on his face. Glancing back at Lachie, who'd gone bright scarlet, he grinned. "Thanks for helping me with Blaze. Maybe we'll see you later."

Lachie scurried off past Drew, who faced Duncan again, looking puzzled. "Something up?" he asked. "And what's later?"

"There's a quiz at the Highlander tonight. Lachie asked if we'd be going, although I can't drive, so I'm not sure how we'll get there."

"I can drive," Drew said, moving forward now they were alone.

"But I thought..."

"I don't like driving. Took me five times to pass my test and there's no need in London, but I can manage if I have to and if you're not too scared to let me take control of your precious Land Rover." He closed the distance between them and Duncan raised his head. Drew leaned over and kissed him as if it was the most normal thing in the world. He tasted of coffee and Duncan's cock rose immediately in response to his touch. Now open-mouthed they continued, adjusting angles, until Drew sucked on Duncan's bottom lip and pulled away.

"Did you miss me?" he asked.

"I might have done. Did you and Jenna have a good day? How was the play?"

"Bloody brilliant, even via a screen. I'm going to have a shower and get changed. You can come and watch if you want."

Drew turned and sashayed out of the stable, wiggling his arse. Duncan grinned and followed him. Watching Drew soaping his body? Oh, yeah, he could get on board with that idea.

Chapter Ten

By the time Drew had finished soaping every part of his body, exaggerating every stroke while Duncan watched, his cock's ability to stand to attention would have passed muster in any military parade. He wrapped his hand around his shaft and stroked up and down, loving the way Duncan squirmed while seated on the edge of the bath. When he swallowed, setting his Adam's apple on a journey, it made Drew want to lick and suck on Duncan's neck.

Stepping out of the shower, he grasped the proffered towel and dried himself off. "Enjoy the show?" he asked.

"What's not to enjoy?"

"I don't have muscles and a six-pack."

"Neither do I—the six-pack, I mean. I'm just an average bloke."

Drew stepped between Duncan's thighs, conscious of his nakedness compared to Duncan, who remained fully clothed. He undid the belt and pulled the plaid shirt out of Duncan's jeans, being careful not to knock the damaged shoulder.

"How is it?" he asked, with an ulterior motive.

"I can get my arm in and out of the sleeve now, but it's still tender. The doctor said no strenuous activity."

Drew slowly undid the buttons on the shirt then fell to his knees. Exposing the tan skin underneath, he ran his fingers over Duncan's chest. "You may not have a six-pack, but you feel good under my hand."

Duncan removed the sling and sloughed off his shirt, carefully allowing Drew to press his cheek to the bare chest.

"I must smell like a horse," Duncan said.

Drew snorted. "Maybe a little." He picked up the flannel, ran it under the tap and squeezed on some bodywash. "Let me," he said, wiping the cloth over Duncan's chest and down his arms.

"Lift." He rubbed the cloth into Duncan's pits, then stood and reached around him to soap his back and wash around his neck, squeezing the cloth over the bath before adding more gel. Somehow, he forgot his own nakedness and how his cock bobbed against Duncan.

"Stand up and undress and I'll do the rest."

"You don't have to."

Drew pulled down Duncan's jeans and briefs and let him lean on his shoulders. He threw the discarded clothes across the bathroom, hitting the laundry basket. Duncan's cock stood hard and proud right in Drew's face. He licked the end once then concentrated on washing Duncan's feet, pressing the cloth between each toe then over the instep and ankle and around each firm calf. Each leg sported a covering of downy hair. Finally, he reached Duncan's middle section.

"Do you want to do this bit yourself?" he asked, hoping the answer would be no.

Duncan shook his head. Drew added more water and bodywash to the cloth, lifted the heavy cock with one hand and soaped Duncan's balls and between his legs, not quite reaching his hole. The other man moaned at the attention, but Drew didn't give into temptation to bury his face in those untrimmed curls. He had other plans.

"Turn around."

Duncan expression changed. "No, it's all right. I can do that."

"You heard me. Turn around and I'll wash your arse."

"But…"

Drew placed a hand on each of Duncan's hips and turned him. He leaned forward and nipped at one cheek, making Duncan squeal.

"What was that for?"

"Because I wanted to. Your arse is too perfect and I wanted to leave my mark on it." He soaped each cheek then ran the cloth between. Knowing how intimate this was, he understood Duncan's nervousness.

"It's all right. Yours isn't the first arse I've been up close and personal with." Hell, that hadn't come out how he intended it to. He placed the cloth in the sink, pulled apart the cheeks again, and ran his tongue down the crack before Duncan could move.

"Oh, God. What the hell?" Duncan lifted his body but Drew placed his hand in the middle of Duncan's back to still him.

"Stay. You mentioned wanting to. Lean forward and brace your hand on the edge of the bath."

"I... I... Are you sure? I've never been..." All the same, he did as Drew instructed.

"Then I can promise you're going to enjoy this." Drew licked at Duncan's hole, deliberately making sounds Duncan could hear. He pressed his tongue, probing farther.

"Feels...so good."

"And so bad," Drew agreed, stopping for a moment. He didn't stop licking, wetting the hole, pushing into the tight space. He had an idea Duncan hadn't been fucked. He didn't want to spook the man, so he shifted back.

"Should we take this to the bedroom?" he asked. "I'm sure we can find a way to have fun and be careful at the same time."

Duncan turned and his cock slapped Drew's cheek.

"We're supposed to be going out tonight, but I'm not sure I've ever been this hard," Duncan said, holding himself.

Unable to resist, Drew kissed him and, even though no one could hear, whispered into Duncan's ear while moving his hand to clasp Duncan's balls. "We've time, and I'll drive quickly."

Duncan shivered under his touch. "You make me want to do things..."

Drew rose and took hold of Duncan's good arm. "Well,

let's not waste your impressive erection. I've a need to ride a cowboy."

He pulled Duncan into his bedroom where he had supplies. "Lie on your back." He stood, admiring the view for a moment.

"You are so beautiful." He grabbed lube and a condom and rolled the rubber over Duncan's cock. He crawled up the bed to settle over Duncan, slathered lube on his fingers and worked himself open while the man below him stared wide-eyed at his every move.

"Are we all right?" Drew asked. Duncan nodded. Positioning himself, Drew took hold of Duncan's now rock-hard shaft and guided it, taking his time, not wanting to spook Duncan.

"You're so tight," Duncan gasped. Drew stopped moving. "I don't want to hurt you. I've not much experience…"

Drew leaned forward and placed a finger on Duncan's bottom lip. "Sshh. Stop worrying and enjoy. This is for you." He hadn't liked to ask if Duncan had done this before. So foolish, not talking when…well, in this position. "And for me. I need to be full of you." He sank down until Duncan was fully encased. He'd been quick and the burn as he finally lowered himself had taken his breath away, but now any pain was simply a memory. He needed this like a plant needed rain. Too much too soon maybe, but he pushed the thought aside. One little touch and that dick rubbed his prostate, sending bolts of electricity through his body. He usually wanted hard and fast, but not this time, not with Duncan.

"Get your arm in a comfortable position. I don't want to hurt you, either."

"Don't care if you do. I never expected… Not in a million years. You're amazing."

Fuck, did the man underneath him just growl? Drew's cock grew even more rigid, if such a thing was possible, and dripped onto Duncan's stomach. He placed his palms on the broad chest, bent over and sucked Duncan's bottom lip before doing the same to his neck. He'd leave a mark, but he didn't care. He wanted Duncan to remember him after he'd gone. Shit, he wanted to leave bite marks down the man's chest. He sat back up, raised his hips then slowly, teasingly, lowered himself. Duncan thrust up to meet him, as if seeking the heat.

"Bloody hell. I love the way you feel around my cock, so hot, like being encased in a velvet glove."

"You getting poetic on me, cowboy?"

"You're every wet dream I've ever had rolled into one. Touch yourself. I want your cum all over me."

Drew took hold of his cock. He smoothed pre-cum all over, knowing this wouldn't take long, despite the slow rhythm he'd set.

"Do you have any idea how beautiful you are? So close, Drew. Faster, please. I need it."

Drew increased his speed, coordinating stroking himself with his rise and fall, until he could hold back no longer. His orgasm burst like a river over its banks, sending streams of sticky white liquid onto Duncan's chest. With one last what could only be described as a yowl, Duncan came, deep within him. When he'd squeezed everything out of Duncan Drew sat back, breathing heavily, while Duncan did the same.

This was supposed to be fun, but when he stared at the man below him, his eyes closed, his hand still clutching the sheet as he came down, Drew experienced an overwhelming sense of loss. He had two more days and it wasn't enough. Even after just four days together, he knew this wasn't an uncomplicated fling. When Duncan opened those soft brown eyes. Drew tried in vain to work out what he was thinking. He reached down to secure the condom as he raised himself and rolled to Duncan's side before removing it, tying it off and throwing it into the bin next to the bed. For a while, neither of them spoke as they stared at the ceiling. What could he say?

"Are you all right? You've gone quiet."

"I'm fine. You've exhausted me, that's all. It's been a long day with Jenna dragging me around the shops and stuffing me with food at lunchtime."

"We could give the quiz a miss if you want and stay here."

Drew sighed at the thought of the two of them cozied up on the sofa watching some old film and snacking on crisps and chocolates.

"Nah, we'd better go. You have the McLeish Ranch honor to defend, and I'll give Jenna a ring. She didn't mention it, but it'll be fun being out together. We've the rest of the night if you want."

Duncan maneuvered himself up and ran his fingers down Drew's chest. "I can't think of anything I'd like more."

"It's a date, then, and we'd better get dressed. I think the shower might have been a waste of time. Still, aftershave can cover a myriad of sins. Do you need any help?" He winked as he asked.

"Not if we don't want to get distracted again. I'll meet you down in the kitchen."

Drew dressed quickly in cargo pants and white cotton shirt. He gelled his hair to smooth it down and dug out the pair of canvas shoes he'd brought in case it was warm. By the time he got downstairs, Duncan was already there, dressed in his trademark shirt and jeans although this time the shirt was pure white and contrasted with his honey-toned skin. His smile took Drew's breath away. Oh, hell, he truly was fucked.

Duncan held out his sling. "I couldn't manage to put it on."

"Give it here." Drew tied it then tested he'd got it right. "Come on, cowboy. Give me your keys and let's get going. I need something long and cool."

A look of concern crossed Duncan's face.

"Don't worry, strictly non-alcoholic, I promise. Not even one mouthful of alcohol shall pass these lips. Anyway, our team is going to win."

The drive proved uneventful after all, and forty minutes

later, they pulled into the car park at the back of the Highlander Inn.

"See, I got you here in one piece, and at this time of year it stays light until late, so we'll be fine. How does this quiz work then? Is it a regular thing?"

"I've been a few times. Usually it's a few rounds of questions with a theme for each round — you know a film round, music and a photograph round. That sort of thing. Teams pay a fiver to enter and the winning team takes the money and spends it on booze, as far as I can see. Each team has a maximum of four members."

"Right, I'll ring Jenna and see if she and Craig fancy making a foursome."

He called her number as they walked in the door. She glanced up at him from the corner table nearest the blazing fire and he grinned. "Looks like she beat us to it. Grab us a couple of stools. What do you want?"

"A shandy is fine and heavy on the lemonade," Duncan replied.

Drew leaned on the wooden counter with one foot on the rail. At one end sat two older men, no doubt regulars, as they'd been in exactly the same position on the last occasion he'd been there. Dozens of whiskies filled one shelf behind the bar. He'd never acquired that much of the taste for it, but had learned Duncan preferred the local brand of Glenlochy. His father had tried to teach him about the differences between malts and blends, but he'd discovered early on his preferences ran toward exotic cocktails. Here, however, he'd settle for a near-beer.

The barman smiled at him when he made his order. Was he being polite? Something pinged. He smiled back but didn't continue the conversation. Lachie and Lenny made their entrance with Mhairi and another girl in tow. Lachie seemed less than enthusiastic when his brother slapped him on the shoulder and ordered drinks at the bar.

"Lachie looks like he's lost a quid and found a penny," Drew said, sitting down next to Duncan.

Duncan glanced over to the bar. "He doesn't appear too happy. I think the girl works at the heritage center."

"Her name's Maggie. She's Mhairi's cousin. Her parents have a shop in Fort William," Jenna explained. "Looks like she's trying to bag a Ross brother."

"From Lachie's face, I'd guess he's either terrified or not interested," Craig added. "Now, has everyone got their piece of paper? Don't shout out the answers if you know them, or others will hear. Write them on your paper and I'll put them on the master card to give in."

Craig's expression, with his furrowed brows, appeared so serious Drew burst out laughing. "Really? Isn't this just a bit of fun?"

Duncan sighed next to him.

"What?" he asked.

Duncan nodded to a foursome over the other side of the room hunched over their table, heads bowed. "Every time either their team or Craig's team wins. It's become a grudge match."

"So, I'm hoping you'll be our secret weapon," Craig revealed. "You'll be up-to-date on music and theater, and people living in London."

Drew didn't like to tell him he spent most of his time squirrelled away in an office with his sketch pad. He'd be fine if asked about dress designers or latest color trends for autumn.

"I can't promise anything. I'll chip in when I can." He glanced at Duncan and mouthed *"Help"*. His plea fell on deaf ears — Duncan didn't react.

"Now, everyone, it's time for the quiz here at the Highlander." Ned, the landlord, announced after ringing the bell at the bar. "The first round this time is films."

After five rounds, there was a break to restock on drinks. "I'm not being much help," Drew said.

"You knew all the music questions and a lot of the others."

"Aww, you're just being nice," Drew said, batting his eyelashes until Jenna smiled at him.

After four more rounds, the last round combined football and photographs. Craig's team were on a level pegging with their rivals, so every point counted.

"Well, I'll be no help. I know nothing about football. Rugby, I might have been more use. I've always had a thing for big men with strong thighs." He grabbed Duncan's leg under the table, making him jump.

"You okay?" Craig asked.

"Yeah, I stubbed my toe on the table leg," Duncan replied, noting Drew's self-satisfied smirk out of the corner of his eye.

Six images appeared on the screen on the wall.

"Concentrate, everyone," Craig said, with some impatience.

"Is he always like this?" Drew whispered in Jenna's ear.

"Only about this bloody quiz. The bloke with the leather jacket is one of his patients and a right pain in the neck. Threatened to report Craig once because he wouldn't give him antibiotics for a cold."

They managed to put names to most of the faces, but Craig didn't recognize the last images the last. Glancing over, Drew saw the other team shaking their heads, too. He grinned and wrote down the name.

"He was at a fashion show I did a couple of weeks ago to support his girlfriend, one of the models. Plays for a London club, but don't ask me which one. He was described as an England prospect. He's so young, he still has spots, love him."

Craig kissed his cheek. "I fucking love you."

"Watch out, Jenna, I think the marriage is off. I've turned your fiancé to the dark side."

As Ned named the player in each photograph, cheering revealed both teams had scored points.

"So with one picture left, two teams have the same points. If one of them gets the next name incorrect then the other team wins. The player in photograph six is…" He beat the counter in a mock drum roll. Ned read the name and Craig leaped to his feet, nearly knocking over his pint, until Jenna pulled him down.

Ned wove through the tables to their corner and handed over their winnings. "Well done. I'd suggest not getting in Jocky's face for now. You know what a bad loser he is."

"This round's on me," Craig said, standing.

Jenna exited to the loo, leaving Drew and Duncan alone. "Well, that was fun," Drew said. "If looks could kill, I reckon Craig would need a doctor now. The bearded bloke over there looks seriously unhappy."

At the bar, the landlord stood his ground, between Craig and the leader of the other team, insisting their Craig's team had had the right answer and the bloke needed to sit down.

"There's going to be trouble." Duncan stood, followed by Lenny and Lachie, who'd been sat across the room, and made his way through the tables to the bar.

The man's friends tried to pull him away, but his rant continued until Sandy Ross appeared out of nowhere.

"Now, don't be an arse, Jocky. You don't want to spend a night in the cells again. Go home and sleep it off. The walk will do you good, or I can give you a lift in my car."

The bloke left, mumbling.

Sandy nodded at his sons. "Good call. Craig won, then, did he? I might ban this bloody quiz."

Duncan returned to his seat. "Let's have this one and get out of here. Are you hungry? We could get a fish supper before we go home. Perhaps park up along the loch. I know a few places."

"Why Duncan McLeish, are you suggesting we go and make out in your car?"

"Might be." Duncan's cheeks flushed red.

* * * *

When they arrived back at the ranch, it was after eleven and dark. Drew yawned in the hallway and peered upstairs.

"Do you want me to go back to my room?" Duncan asked.

Drew shook his head. He wanted Duncan's chest against his back. He wanted to wake up next to him under cool sheets, to have a leisurely breakfast together, maybe go for a walk to see the cattle or the alpacas and have another picnic. Maybe they could share a hot tub and sex in the bubbles when there was no one about. Just spend the day together, touching, laughing, smiling, easy in each other's company. Instead he said, "Do you want to go?"

"No." Duncan's voice was barely a whisper.

Drew took Duncan's hand and dragged him upstairs. Minutes later, they lay naked next to each other, too tired for anything but sleep. Drew shifted on his side away from Duncan who tucked in behind him, letting his injured arm lie on Drew's hip. Such a simple move. A kiss ghosted across his neck and he shivered. Had Duncan said something? He turned his head slightly and was greeted with soft snores. Tucking his arm under the pillow, Drew closed his eyes.

Sixty hours — that's all they had, give or take, before he had to catch the train to visit his parents. He couldn't not go. He'd promised them, and he saw so little of them. Maybe he and Duncan could Skype once he'd returned to London. No — better a clean break. Just make memories before he left. He'd be back at Christmas for the wedding, but there was no point thinking of then. By then, Duncan could have found someone, or he could — anything was possible. A voice at the back of his mind told him to keep saying those words, as sleep overtook him.

Chapter Eleven

Duncan decided waking up next to someone was as good as the feeling he got from galloping across a field with the sun on his back and the wind in his hair, better than the taste of a bacon butty, better than when a calf was successfully delivered—maybe better than anything. Or maybe it was simply better because it was Drew's back pressed against his chest and Drew's arse his morning wood pushed to get closer to. Perhaps that was what was better. He tested his arm with miniscule movements. The pain had lessened considerably, but then it wasn't the first time he'd had to get over this injury and he had a high pain threshold, or so he'd been told. When he kissed the back of Drew's neck, he shifted in Duncan's arms and turned toward him.

"Good morning, handsome."

"Morning, yourself."

Sunshine streamed in through the window right onto Drew's face, showing the darker-blue highlights in his pale blue eyes. His normally controlled hair fell over his face. Duncan threaded the blond locks back and winced.

"Is your arm still giving you jip?"

Duncan nodded. "A little, but I couldn't resist. Your face is too good not to see it all."

Drew flushed and glanced down. "You are such a damned gentleman, aren't you?"

"I was brought up the son of diplomats. I learned what to say and how to say it. Living with my grandfather and going to school also taught me I could talk myself out of a problem if I knew how."

"But what about the bullies in school? You know—your

arm."

"Craig told you." Duncan wasn't sure if he was angry or not.

"Don't be cross with him."

"What else did you talk about?" He had the feeling his ears should have been burning several times.

"He warned me not to hurt you. I don't think your sexuality is much of a secret from him. It appears we've both been obvious in our staring and sneaky glances. Do you mind?"

Did he? He supposed it depended on how this relationship — because it was beginning to feel like one — progressed.

"Not really. I think he and Jenna may have hopes for us both."

"I got that impression, too," Drew said.

Duncan swung his legs over and perched on the edge of the bed. "I'm starving. Let's get dressed and I'll take you out for a walk. We've some Highland Cows in calf due to give birth so I want to check on them. A couple have been born already and they're the cutest things. We can take Misha for a long walk. I've been leaving her to the others to exercise with the farm dogs."

"I love dogs, but it's difficult having pets in the city, and I'm away too often to even look after a gerbil."

"I was brought up not to see animals as pets. The dogs were working animals. When they couldn't work anymore, my grandfather had them put to sleep. The cats were kept to kill the rodents and largely fended for themselves. My grandfather used to breed rabbits for the pot, and chickens, but I couldn't stand it when he killed them. He was always quick, but I can't eat rabbit."

"He sounds like a hard man."

Duncan sighed. "He was. Like the granite these mountains are made of."

Drew moved against his back and wrapped his arms around his chest. "Whereas, you're actually a soppy old thing, aren't you?"

Duncan glanced at his image in the mirror, with Drew's smiling face on his shoulder. "Does it bother you I'm ten years older than you?"

"Not in the slightest. You're not the oldest man I've been with."

"I don't think I want to know." He didn't want to think about Drew with anyone else, not while they were pressed skin to skin, flesh to flesh, naked together without any shame or worry about being so. Every other encounter, no matter if the person had been male or female, had felt wrong, hurried, shameful, but not this. He wrapped his bigger hands over Drew's and squeezed. Drew kissed his shoulder.

"Come on, you're thinking too hard. I might be hallucinating, but I think I smell bacon and my stomach is rumbling. A walk would be great, but I'm going to need a big breakfast to sustain me. And I'll bring my camera this time. Mind if I use the bathroom first?"

"Help yourself. Knock on my door when you've finished."

Duncan found Carrie in the kitchen when he arrived downstairs.

"The post is on the table and I'm making the works this morning. The boys are in the stable mucking out, and I've called Steve to deal with a plumbing issue in cabin five — one of the toilets is blocked. Lenny mentioned you were going up to check on the cows this morning. I assume you'll be going with Drew, so you'll need a decent breakfast. Will he be joining us soon? Sandy said you won last night, but there was some trouble."

The look Carrie gave him suggested she knew everything. Despite being only a few years older than him, she'd been the nearest he'd had to a mother for years and she bossed him about just as she did her own husband and two boys. He had no idea what he'd do without her.

"I don't know where you get your energy from, Carrie, and Sandy sorted the idiot out. He thought we'd brought in a ringer with Drew, and he didn't like losing. Too much drink may also have been consumed. Did the lads take Misha with them?" He'd noted the empty basket when he walked in.

"Morning, Mrs. Ross."

Drew entered the room wearing a pale blue T-shirt and blue jeans with a pair of sturdy boots. "Will I do? I thought I'd better wear proper walking boots today." He ran a hand through his hair pushing back his fringe as it fell over his face. He smiled and Duncan's heart, or was it his stomach — well, something inside him — flipped and fluttered. He needed to pull himself together before Carrie gave him one of her knowing looks.

"I didn't expect you to have walking boots. I thought Londoners took taxis or the Tube. You'd hardly need them."

Drew seated himself at the table. "My Dad's a gamekeeper, remember? He'll have me tramping all over the place checking on his birds before the twelfth. Is it so hard to imagine?"

"I suppose it is. Your accent is so much softer than Jenna's, but you've been down there a while now."

"Since university. Twelve years is a long time, but it still means I spent eighteen years running around on a large estate. Yes, we were near enough to go to high school in Stirling, but during the holidays we ran wild. I told you before, I can shoot, gut a fish and pluck a grouse ready for the pot."

Duncan glanced over to see Carrie chuckling over the stove. He picked up the pile of letters and sorted them into business, personal and rubbish. Carrie placed fully loaded plates in front of them both.

"There you go. That lot will line your stomach. There's tea in the pot when you want it. And yes, Misha is probably in the stables if you're thinking of taking her with you. I'll be getting off to check on the plumbing incident, then I'll change the bedding upstairs. These hot nights make you so sweaty, don't they?"

Heat rushed into Duncan's face? Had they made a mess on the bedding? Drew winked at him, making things worse.

Carrie placed a hand on his shoulder. "Have a good walk, you two, and try not to frighten the cattle."

Before Duncan could reply, she'd hurried out of the back door. Duncan stared at his plate. Now Carrie was making insinuations.

"This bacon is amazing," Drew said, with his mouth full.

"Did we mess up the sheet?" He had time to get up there and remove them. Had Carrie noticed only one bed had been slept in?

"Does it matter? Are you saying you've never had a wank and spilled over the bed? You need a Fleshlight, or a sock."

Duncan sighed. "I'm kidding myself, aren't I?"

"Maybe. I did mention what Craig said to me. It seems Carrie may have an idea about us, too."

"Fucking hell!" He thumped the table in frustration. "Now, look. I don't swear. I'm forty years old, and I'm being treated like a teenager. I should tell them all to piss off."

"Tell them you're bisexual and they'll shut up. Well, maybe they won't shut up exactly. They love you. I think they might be worried the sassy southerner is taking advantage of you and your gorgeous body."

Duncan stood and leaned over, tucking his hand behind Drew's head and pulling him forward until their mouths met. If someone walked in, so be it. When Drew opened up in response, Duncan thrust his tongue forward to be greeted by Drew doing the same. He tasted of smoky bacon and fried egg with a hint of minty toothpaste. Yesterday that tongue had been all over him. Shocked at that realization, Duncan broke the connection.

Drew leaned on the table and it almost looked as if he was steadying himself. "Wow, where the hell did that come from?"

Duncan didn't know about Drew, but he now had distinctly less room in his jeans. He sat back down, amazed at himself.

"You okay?" Drew asked. "You look a little stunned."

"I'm, yeah. I'm good." He needed to get out of there before — bad arm or not — he dragged Drew over the table and fucked him then and there.

Drew took his hand and squeezed gently. "I think we need some fresh air. Come on, eat up. It's a glorious day, and I want to see more of your ranch. A good stretch of our legs will shake off the cobwebs. This is a beautiful place and I want to see some cute animals."

They found Lachie in the stable block. "Have you walked the dogs this morning?"

"Jax and Juno are running around with Lenny. Misha's here. The others are too hyperactive for her. Misha, come here, girl."

The retriever ambled out of the stable and sat in front of Duncan. He kneeled and patted her head and fussed her ears. "I haven't spent enough time with you lately, have I girl? How would you like a walk?"

She bounced around like a puppy, wagging her tail despite the years on her clock.

"Looks like a yes to me," Drew said.

"I'll get her lead in case we need it, then we can set off. I've packed a water bowl for her in my backpack and a few snacks. We're going to check the cows up on the middle pasture and introduce Drew to Angus. A couple of them are due to calve soon so we may need to bring them in, Lachie. You ready, Drew?"

Duncan noted Lachie's shy smile as they left.

The sun beamed high in the sky even mid-morning as they strolled through the fields taking as flat a route as possible. Misha ran on ahead, sniffing everything and sticking her nose down any hole she found.

"Watch out for rabbit holes," Duncan warned Drew. "We don't want you breaking your ankle."

They reached a gate and Drew stopped to admire the view. "I grew up on a beautiful estate, but this is stunning.

I'm not surprised you wanted to hang on to the place. You can see down the glen to the loch with the sun bouncing off the water from up here."

Duncan stood next to him, leaning on the gate. "I never take this place for granted. In the spring, it's covered in yellow with the gorse bushes, then you get bluebells and poppies. In summer, it stays green because it rains and you have to watch out for the thistles. Sometimes snow remains on the mountains, especially Ben Nevis over there in the distance. By autumn, the heather turns everything purple, and in winter we get snow which can be impractical but looks beautiful. People book to stay here for Christmas and Hogmanay, despite the weather, or perhaps that's part of the appeal. We have an old sleigh my grandfather built and once had to use it to get supplies down from the A82."

"I hear you play Father Christmas."

Duncan smiled to himself. He loved handing out the presents to the local children in the small primary school.

"I do, though, I need some padding." He sighed knowing whatever he had with Drew would be short-lived when, if they'd had time—well, there was no point even thinking about that. "I love this place. It's my life, and my home."

He waited while Drew took some photographs, and threw a ball for Misha to fetch. "The cows are farther up the hillside. We follow the track along the edge of the field."

* * * *

Although he'd been brought up on a large estate and was no stranger to great views of the countryside, this place truly did take his breath away, and watching it through Duncan's eyes made it even more special. As Duncan played around with his dog, the joy and contentment on his face were obvious to anyone with a pair of eyes and a heart. This was his element. Misha bounced around her master, waiting for the ball to be sent not too far for her to retrieve. She'd sit in front of Duncan, he'd take the ball and she'd run around him to sit at his side — every time.

"She's well-trained," Drew said.

"They have to be with the animals around. I'll put her on the lead for this section. Angus can get tetchy if she bounces and barks. Come on. Not worn out yet, then?"

"I'm good. Who wouldn't be with this view and all this fresh air? I expect I'll sleep like a log tonight."

Duncan smirked. The man goddamn smirked. "Eventually, perhaps."

Drew pinched himself. No, he wasn't dreaming. He caught up and slipped his hand into Duncan's. He could hardly believe this was the same man he'd met a few days ago.

"Have I corrupted you?" he asked as they strolled.

"Maybe. But I wanted you to. The last few days have been…"

He didn't finish the sentence as a loud mooing noise interrupted his words.

"I'm no expert, but she doesn't sound good," Drew said.

"No. Hold on to Misha, will you?"

They ran in the direction of the noise. At the edge of the field, one of the cows lay on the ground.

"Damn. She's in labor but struggling. Either the calf is breech or too big. She's a first-time mum. I need to get hold of Jenna. Tell her to use the quad bike, or get one of the lads to bring her."

Drew reached for his phone — no bars. "You stay with her. I'll try and find a signal." He glanced around and noticed the phone mast on the hill. If he got nearer… He ran. Finally, one bar appeared.

"Hello, veterinary service."

"Mhairi, it's Drew. There's a cow in labor up in the middle field. Duncan says the calf is stuck. Can you get Jenna here? He says to use the quad bike."

The phone went silent for a moment. "Tell Duncan Jenna is on her way."

Drew returned to find Duncan feeling the cow's side as

it thrashed on the floor, huge horns creating a dangerous situation.

"I think the baby is breech rather than too big. I could try to turn it. I've done it before, but I've no lubrication. I might be able to pull the calf out backward."

"Can you do that?" Drew reached into his pocket. "It's not much, but it might help." He handed Duncan the small sachet of lube he'd brought just in case.

Duncan took the sachet. His brief smile said he knew exactly what Drew had intended. "I'm not sure if that will help. Usually you try and tie the back legs together and pull them out, but you have to get hold of both and do it as quickly as you can."

By now, other cows had gathered around, not threatening, just interested.

"Tie Misha outside the field, will you? I don't want her to spook them."

Duncan rolled up his sleeve and carefully edged his hand inside the distressed animal. Drew watched, fascinated.

"I can't get hold of the legs. It's okay, girl, help will be here soon. I wish I could tell her not to push. I'll try again."

After a while, Duncan gave up. He'd managed to turn the calf, but doubted it would be enough. Finally, the sound of an engine promised relief. Jenna jumped off the back of the quad bike as soon as Lachie stopped. Bag in hand, she hurried toward them.

"I've tried, but I haven't been able to turn it all the way," Duncan said stepping back to let her work Meanwhile, Lachie roped the animal's head and horns to keep one end under control as Jenna donned a long glove and pushed into the cow once more.

Drew remained at a distance, while the three of them helped the cow. He'd never witnessed his sister in action like this.

For what seemed like an age, she felt around. "There, got them. Hand me the rope, will you? Not long, there's a good girl. I'm going to pull the calf out backward. Lachie, try and keep her down, will you? As soon as the wee one is out we need to get both to their feet, but mum is going to be tired."

Drew stared in awe as his sister made a loop, plunged back in then pulled slowly.

"Don't go too fast. We need to ease the calf out. Damn, I wish I'd brought the calf jack. Come on girl. You can do this."

Duncan took over the rope while Jenna checked on the situation, and after a struggle, a pair of legs appeared, followed by a body and finally head and front feet, along with a smattering of blood and amniotic fluid. Jenna checked the mouth and cleared the nose.

"She's breathing. Get Mum up." Duncan and Lachie encouraged the cow to her feet.

"Now, little one, let's get you up and latched on."

For a while, the baby squirmed. Her mother bent and licked her.

"That's it, Mum."

Despite being only minutes old, the calf struggled to its feet and latched on to its mother, sucking hard.

"Yuck," Drew said, as the afterbirth appeared. "I don't know how females do this."

They all sat back watching as the young female fed with her mother, who swiped her coat to start the cleaning.

Drew wrapped his arm around Jenna's shoulder. "That was awesome, sis. You saved them both."

"Thank you," Duncan said, hugging Jenna from the other side.

"She's a beauty. Looks like she'll be fine now."

Drew took out the water bottle from Duncan's bag and handed it around. "Not quite whiskey to wet the baby's head." He picked up his camera and snapped away, taking a few of Duncan as well. When he smiled at him, it was as if they'd become parents themselves for the first time. His proud stance and expression made Drew desperate to kiss him.

Instead, he tried to close himself down and set his face to

neutral, but not before Jenna had caught him staring.

"Will they both be all right now?" he asked Duncan as he cleaned his hands with the wipes Jenna gave him. "You don't have to take them down to keep an eye on them?"

"No need. They're bred to be hardy animals and stay out in all weathers. They'll be fine. Look at her, already so steady on those spindly legs. We can go back if you want, or we can stay up here for a while and I'll take you over to meet Angus."

"Sounds good," Drew said. He didn't want their walk to be over so soon, and he didn't want any company other than Duncan as the clock ticked down on his visit.

"We'll leave you two to it, then," Jenna said smiling at both. "Lachie will take me back on the quad bike." She kissed Duncan. "Let me know if there are any problems."

Drew wrapped his arms around her. "You were amazing."

"All in a day's work. Have fun and don't do anything I wouldn't do."

He glanced over at Duncan. "I think I might be in trouble, sis."

She put her mouth next to his ear. "Judging by the look on his face, I think he might be, too."

Chapter Twelve

When Drew took Duncan's hand as they strolled to the next field, Duncan didn't pull away. Misha trotted at her master's side. Around them, the world went on as normal—the sun shone, the grass and shrubs swayed in the slight breeze, bees buzzed, birds sang and cattle lowed in the distance. He stared ahead, occasionally checking the rocky path under his feet, worn from years of people taking the same route to the fields. Large stones had embedded in the earth, having fallen at some point in the past, and now grass grew between.

"Do you come up here often?" he asked, realizing after he'd said it how his words sounded like some sort of clichéd pick-up line.

"The cattle mostly look after themselves in the summer, unless the weather is bad and we have to bring up extra fodder. We move them around because the round-ups are part of what we offer to tourists, and partly to spread the usage of the pasture. In winter, we bring most of them down, but the Highlands stay out. We've provision to bring in the Belties and the Anguses if needed."

He stopped and Drew gazed in the direction of the field. There stood the largest bull he'd ever seen.

"Bloody hell. He is magnificent. Look at those horns."

"This is Gus. He's nine years old now." Despite the size of the animal, Duncan reached over the fence and patted his head. "We once had a visitor ask if he really was a bull because he was so gentle."

Drew moved to get a better view. "Judging by the size of those balls, I'd say he's all male. Does he get to have fun, or

113

is it all scientific and someone comes to give him a squeeze? Seems a shame to me."

"No, Gus gets put in with his ladies here, and we let nature take its course. He has a great record and is in demand from farmers across Scotland. We do well selling his sperm. Otherwise, we bring bulls in for the other breeds, but I've always loved the Highlands best, and the calves are so cute with their curly ginger hair."

"Can I pat him?" Drew asked.

"Sure, but watch for the horns. He's a gentle creature, but could do you some damage."

Drew rubbed his hand across the bull's head. "They have such amazing eyelashes." He stared down the glen toward the loch.

"I can understand why you love it here. It suits you. You look in place—part of the scenery. I didn't feel at home on the estate. Despite its acreage and the size of the big house, it always seemed so small with nothing to do. I've never told my dad how much I hated the hunting and shooting, but I think he knew when I didn't pick up a gun to fire at anything other than tin cans. When the shooters came in August and we had to beat out the grouse... I know they ate the birds, but it felt wrong. Me and Jenna helped my mum in the kitchen, plucking when she cooked for the visitors, but I couldn't get over how much some of them loved killing things. I think Jenna felt the same. It's why she became a vet."

"But your dad gets to conserve things, as well, doesn't he? It's the only way of life for an estate which hasn't been sold or covered with trees for commercial farming."

Drew nodded. "The family my parents work for have been owners since the fifteen hundreds."

"It's like me keeping this place after my grandfather died. We've owned land around here for hundreds of years, too. Come on, let's sit down. I packed some food and a couple of bottles of water."

Drew chewed the simple ham sandwich. "What about

handing on the land?" he asked. Did Duncan intend to find some willing woman after all to father a couple of kids with?

"I'll be forty in between Christmas and New Year. Terrible time of year to be born as I always got joint presents. I'll admit I've sometimes thought about having children, but if it doesn't happen, and it's unlikely now, I intend to pass it onto Craig's family, should he have any little ones, and if they're interested."

"That's generous of you, but I bet there are women around here who fancy the pants off you, and you're not gay, so it's possible." He unclenched his jaw. What the hell was he doing? He had no claim on this man. On Friday morning, he'd be leaving, and in a week going back to London with its bright lights, traffic noise, twenty-four-hour culture, shops, cinemas, theaters, every type of food he could think of, all within walking distance of where he lived. His work was there, his friends and his life, and still he leaned his head on Duncan's good shoulder.

"I…"

Drew lifted his head and met Duncan's gaze. "What?"

"Nothing. It doesn't matter." Duncan shook his head and stared back over the field.

Drew said nothing, because what was there to say? Maybe he should suggest going to stay with Jenna and Craig tonight and not tomorrow as planned. It would simplify things and remove temptation. After all, he was supposed to be here to see her, not the handsome man sitting next to him.

"I'll pack when we get back and go to stay with Jenna." There, he'd said it and given Duncan a get-out clause. Duncan jerked as if he'd been stung.

"Why? Is that what you want? I suppose I was simply fun for you—an interesting distraction. Or did you feel sorry for me?" He stood and grabbed the bag.

Drew jumped in front of him and placed his palm on Duncan's chest. "Do you think so little of me?"

"I don't know what to think. You come into my life like a tornado, shake everything up then leave."

"But you knew I'd have to go. From the moment you took me up to the lake — your special place — you must have realized what might happen. *You wanted me.* And don't pretend you've never had sex with someone and not seen them again." He swallowed hard, trying to get rid of the lump in his throat.

"What if I want more? What if I have feelings for you even so soon?"

"Are you trying to break me? I can't, Duncan. I have a life and a business miles away from here. We'll get over each other. This will be a lovely memory. You'll be —"

Duncan placed a finger on his mouth. Drew longed to part his lips and suck it in.

"You do care for me, then?"

Drew jerked his head up. "Of course, I do. More than I should. More than is good for me, but not enough for me not to walk away." Who was he trying to kid? He needed to be strong. He couldn't give Duncan any false hope when there was none.

"We should go back."

"Are you…leaving?"

"I think it's for the best. If I stay tonight, we'll end up together and make love again, and nothing will have changed."

"If it changes nothing, then stay and give us our last night together." Duncan took his hand. "I don't want to beg."

Drew dragged his hand away and wiped the tear from his cheek. "I can't. I'm so sorry."

Somehow, he put one foot in front of the other, with no idea whether Duncan was following. He didn't look back at any time until he reached the house. He smiled at Carrie's clear voice, singing in the kitchen, when he opened the door. Glancing over his shoulder, he discovered no sign of Duncan. It took him fifteen minutes to pack. Could he get a taxi out here?

Downstairs, he bumped into Carrie as she entered the hall. She glanced down at the case. "I'll take you," she said. "Is he all right? Are you?"

"I don't think either of us is, but this is for the best."

"You believe what you need to believe. I understand your life is elsewhere, but I've seen how you looked at each other. He can't leave here and you... I understand."

Drew wanted to shout at her. He didn't want her understanding, or her sympathy. He followed her to her car. They didn't speak for the whole journey. At the vet's surgery, Drew climbed out.

"Take care of yourself," Carrie said.

"Take care of him."

Carrie frowned at him. "Of course, we will, like we always do. We'll pick up the pieces and he'll bury himself in his work like he always does."

He shut the car door and waited until she drove off. Once inside the surgery, grateful he'd arrived out of consultation hours, he asked for Jenna at the counter. The receptionist phoned through and a minute later Jenna appeared. She took one look at him and opened her arms. He let her enfold him. He'd expected tears, but none came His heart had been damaged if not broken in the past and he reached for those familiar walls to shut out the pain.

"It's only a couple of hours since I left you two together."

"I don't want to talk about it," he said.

"All right. I haven't had my lunch break yet. Mandy, I'll be a couple of hours and back for teatime surgery. Please let Mhairi know. Come on, let's get you back to mine and maybe a drink."

He nodded. He didn't want to speak. There weren't any words.

* * * *

"Everything okay, boss?"

Duncan glanced up to see Lenny staring at him. "Shouldn't

you be with the visitors? I thought there was a party of them wanting to learn cowboy skills this afternoon."

"Umm, I came to collect another lead line. None of this family have ever ridden before, and as they're here for two weeks, we're working with the kids to get them more confident, using a couple of the ponies. To be honest, the kids are quicker on the uptake than the adults. We're out in the paddock if you want to join us."

Lenny's expression showed worry and concern, but the last thing Duncan wanted was company. "I'm going to take Blaze out. Look after Misha for me."

"But your arm…"

"Bugger my arm. I've had worse pain."

He strode past Lenny into the tack room, grabbed his saddle and a bridle and stomped back. He needed to calm himself. Blaze would pick up on his mood and he didn't want to spook her. She nudged him and he held out his hand to reveal one of her favorite sugar lumps. He loved the feel of her mouth on his palm, so soft. He patted her neck as he hooked over the bridle and buckled up, making sure the bit was secure.

"Don't you be sneaky and breathe out, young lady." Sometimes, he could swear she did it deliberately, testing him as he put on the saddle and secured the girth. He led her out of the stable, noting Lenny walking away toward the paddock. He seated himself, pulled his hat down and set off. He wanted to gallop, but this landscape wasn't made for speed although, with care, he could manage a canter in places. He set off, holding the reins in his right hand to spare his left shoulder as much as possible, but making sure he gripped with his thighs.

Blaze did everything he asked of her, letting his anger fade as the breeze struck his cheeks and threatened to remove his hat. He pulled her to a halt, brought the chin strap down and took out his canteen to swill down some water. His ride had brought him to the pasture where the Belted Galloways stood eating. Scattered in amongst the adults were a few calves, looking as gorgeous as the Highland Cows. These little creatures had black fur and white-striped middles. He let them calve and produce milk when they needed to rather than milk them every day and kept the male offspring for the round-ups and to sell. He loved them, but he was still a farmer.

As he stared down the glen, he resigned himself to being alone. The only other gay man he knew in the area was Lachie, and despite the young man's good looks, there was no attraction there. He was more like a younger brother than a potential partner. He had his suspicions about the lad in the pub, but he was younger still. Even Drew was thirty to his forty. He had to face it, he was an old stick-in-the-mud, and he doubted if joining Grindr would help up here. He could find a woman willing to put up with him. A few had shown interest, but none had attracted him enough. He wanted love, not companionship. And he wanted great sex, not quick fumbles in the darkness of a nightclub. He wanted Drew, but he couldn't have him, so instead he'd have to go on as he always had done.

"Come on, Blaze. I suppose we'd better get back. Perhaps I'll buy one of those Fleshlight things."

Blaze whinnied at him and he had the feeling she was laughing. He patted her neck. "Yep, you're probably right, old girl."

He walked her back in no hurry. As he turned into the yard, Carrie stood with her hands on her hips and a frown on her face. How long could he spend brushing Blaze down to avoid the woman?

He got an answer straight away when Lachie met him at the entrance to the stables. "Mum says the kettle is on and your presence is required."

"Who owns this place?" he mumbled, shaking his head.

"She said to tell you she took Drew to Jenna's." He put a hand on Duncan's arm. "Are you sure you're all right, boss?"

In truth, he was anything but. Most of him wanted to

jump in his car and chase after Drew, but what would be the point? Drew had made the decision for them, and Duncan's head told him it had been the right thing to have done. If they'd stayed together, they would have made love... He halted, shocked at his own thoughts. Made love, not had sex. *Oh, hell.* Men didn't cry. How many times had his grandfather said those words? Better to end things now with a clean break. He gazed straight ahead. "I'll live. I'd better go and face the music."

He patted Blaze's rump as Lachie led her away, then turned to amble, as nonchalantly as he could manage, back toward the house.

Chapter Thirteen

Early October
London

If Drew never saw another model again, it would be too soon. Although his company wasn't one of the big players, they'd found some space in Milan, London and New York to show off their collection and had been favorably received, resulting in a major store making overtures to him and Joy to work for them. At first, Drew had thought the guy wanted to get into his pants, but after they'd chatted over a drink in the hotel bar, he'd offered Drew his card, so maybe he was legit. Drew had to admit he was tempted — after all it would mean creating his designs without worrying about finance.

Meanwhile, on the side, his lace-wear line for men was going from strength to strength. He had more questions roaming around his head than answers. He needed to sit down with Joy and discuss the pros and cons. Giving up running everything for himself didn't seem like such a bad idea after so much stress. A knock on the door distracted him from his worries.

Reluctantly, he dragged himself from the sofa and ambled to see who had disturbed him. Peering through the spyhole, he wasn't surprised to see Ben and Jonty on his doorstep carrying pizza and wine. He opened the door then returned to the sofa without words and let them follow him in.

"You look like shit," Ben said, handing the wine to his partner, Jonty, who immediately disappeared into the small kitchen.

"It's good to see you, as well," Drew replied, running his fingers through his hair and pushing his glasses up his nose as he collapsed back on the sofa. "I've hardly stopped for the last month."

"We know," Jonty said, coming into the room. "So we've brought pizza, garlic bread, onion rings and enough wine to ensure a good time." He sat on Ben's lap in the armchair, dangling his legs over the side.

"No offense, you two, but I could do without the PDAs, as well." Jealousy reared its ugly head as visions of the Scotsman he'd left behind weeks ago filled his memory.

"Why won't you admit you're missing your cowboy?" Jonty said, wrapping his arm around his partner.

"Because there's no point."

"Then you need to get out there and get over him rather than sitting over your drawing board doodling Stetsons and snapping at everyone. I'm surprised Joy and the team haven't left."

Yes, he had been like a bear with a sore head, but so much rode on these shows. Would they get orders? Would anyone famous pick up his designs? Did he care? *What the fuck?* He sat up and rubbed his eyes. He *was* tired. Several people had expressed interest and there was that offer. In this business, beggars couldn't be choosers. He'd wanted this all his life, hadn't he? He was a whisker away from getting real notice. Of course, he cared. But did he care enough?

"I'm too tired for clubbing and who would want anything to do with a grouch like me? I've bigger bags under my eyes than the suitcases I've been dragging around for weeks."

He opened the lid on one of the pizza boxes and grabbed a piece. The saltiness of the melted cheese covered with posh ham, mushroom, onions and black olives danced on his tongue.

"When will Jenna be here with her bridesmaids?" Ben asked.

Drew studied his friends. Ben, immaculately groomed and dressed as always, with his dark hair gelled back.

Wearing proper trousers and a white shirt without a hint of a crease, he was a complete contrast to his partner Jonty who lolled across Ben's lap in skinny jeans ripped at the knees and a tight T-shirt meant to show off his sculptured torso. His bright-red hair was as usual attempting to escape from whatever styling product Jonty had used. They made an interesting pair.

"We can hit the town when they come and show them the sights," Jonty said excitedly. "Like an early hen night."

"They're here the weekend after next, so I need to make sure the dresses are ready. I expect I'll have to take them in, as usual. And I'm not sure Carrie is ready for the sort of venues you two visit."

"Oh, come on, what woman doesn't love a gay club? I swear some nights there are more straight women at these places than gay men. Anyway, we have some news of our own."

Drew blinked a few times then worked out both men had proffered their hands. "What the… Are those what I think they are? When did this happen?"

"Ben took me out for my birthday, got down on one knee and proposed. It was so romantic, so what else could I say but yes? We got the rings yesterday and ordered ones for the wedding. So how do you fancy being best man for both of us, along with my brother? We're going to do this right and have everyone there, not some quickie. I want a string quartet, and doves and thrones. Should I wear a dress, do you think? You could design me something spectacular."

Ben raised his eyebrows but grinned all the same. "Ignore him. We'll both be wearing suits."

"You are so repressed." Jonty kissed him. "But I love you, anyway. And I'll be wearing some of your stuff underneath. White lace thong and a garter maybe, or a corset instead of a waistcoat—something different. You know how much you loved the corset and the way the suspender belt curved over my arse, or so you told me as you—"

"Jonty, we're not alone, remember."

"Oh, Drew doesn't care, do you? After all, he makes those lacy numbers. What about it, Drew? You know, corsets made especially for men, and suspenders. I'm sure there's a market, and I'll model on your website if you want."

Drew laughed at the spat. "We need to drink to your engagement. I have a bottle of champagne at the back of the fridge. Let's open it and drink to the happy couple."

In the kitchen, he leaned on the counter then opened the drawer. A photograph of Duncan patting the huge Highland bull stared back at him. Shrugging, he pushed the drawer closed again, grabbed the champagne and glasses and carried them back to the living room to find Jonty and Ben locked in an embrace. He felt like an outsider in his own flat. He coughed.

Ben attempted to put a guilty expression on his face and failed abysmally. "Sorry, we'll behave. Anyway, you'll see you have to come out with us soon. There's this bloke who started working at our place as senior buyer in the women's department a couple of months back. He's a fan of your creations—I may have mentioned I knew you when he said he'd be at London fashion week. He's been pushing to get your designs in the store."

Could he be the same man he'd met? "I'm not interested in a blind date."

"I'm not saying you should shag each other stupid, although you could do with getting some fun, and he's tall, dark and handsome. I think he may have some Italian in him or Spanish—something Latin anyway. Just meet him and see what he has to say. It can't do any harm, can it?"

Drew sank into the sofa again. "Maybe not. Now, let's get this bottle open and drink and eat until we can't move."

* * * *

Drew checked himself in the mirror. He'd lost weight, and if he wasn't careful, he wouldn't have enough arse left to fill out his trousers. His memory drifted back to fresh air and huge steaks with chips and all the trimmings as made by his mother while he was with his parents. He attempted to still his shaking hand as he buttoned up the blue shirt. *It's just a drink and Ben and Jonty will be there.* He checked his watch. He still had time.

Maybe I should get Joy to come after all. He'd spoken to her, of course, before he agreed to meet Sebastian. He'd imagined the S standing for all sorts of names when the man had given him his card, but Sebastian hadn't crossed his radar—Sebastian Healy, chief buyer. He wouldn't be producing exclusive high couture, but if he was honest, he preferred the idea of making clothes for all sorts of woman, and this deal would give him a chance to do that, as well as continuing and developing his own lingerie for men company.

He stared at the dresses hanging up on his wardrobe ready for Jenna, Carrie and Mhairi when they visited. They were stunning, if he said so himself. Joy and the seamstresses he employed had done a wonderful job, and he'd had shoes covered with the same fabrics to match. It was a first fitting, and no doubt he'd have to take them in, despite begging them not to lose weight before the day. He'd be there on the morning, adjusting once more. Smiling to himself, he grabbed his suit jacket from the hanger and headed out.

The taxi dropped him in front of the restaurant—nothing fancy, just one of a chain in London. He was bang on time so hoped Ben and Jonty were already there. Striding in, with his head held high to hopefully cover his nerves, he spotted his friends at the bar with a man he recognized. So, he'd been right about the bloke from the show. Ben sprang out of his seat and hurried toward him, pulling him forward.

"Drew Sinclair, this is Sebastian Healey, chief buyer at Fairfords."

Drew held out his hand. "Nice to meet you again."

Sebastian met his gaze and took his hand. His green eyes sparkled in the neon light from the bar. "It certainly is. I wondered if you would remember me."

I'd hardly be likely to forget you. "You made me an interesting offer."

Jonty clapped his hands and glanced at them, first one then the other. "I love it when a plan comes together. Now, another round, I think, then talk and food."

Sebastian proved to be good company—both charming and knowledgeable, and if Drew knew anything about men, and he liked to think he did, interested in getting to know him more than on just a professional basis. Any other time, Drew might have reciprocated his interest, but, despite the charisma, he found his mind wandering, and above all else, comparing. The charm was *too* charming, too deliberate. He guessed Sebastian was used to getting his own way, in and out of bed. A nudge in the ribs brought him back to the table.

"So what do you think? Could you design a line of clothes for our autumn collection, catering for sizes ten to twenty-four? It's not the sort of couture you're used to, but it's equally challenging. Fairfords has always been renowned for its traditional look, and we'll still have that, but we're looking to appeal to younger women with this new line."

"I need to talk to Joy, my partner, and do some research, but I'd be stupid to turn down this chance, especially if this is going to be an exclusive label, and I can still produce my own single pieces and men's designs."

Sebastian leaned forward. "Ah yes, I'm familiar with your men's lingerie collection, but I'm not sure Fairfords is ready for those—unfortunately. Do you wear them yourself?"

Drew thought about the black lace shorts under his suit. In the past, he'd have asked if Sebastian wanted to find out, even with Ben and Jonty present, but instead he twirled the last of his spaghetti around his fork and placed it in his mouth, deliberately not answering. He was rewarded when Sebastian clearly reached under the table to adjust his trousers.

Jonty fanned himself and waved to the waitress. "Could we have some iced water please? I think we all need to cool down."

Drew leaned back in his seat, picked up his napkin and wiped his mouth. "So, let's set up a meeting for next week. You and your team can tell me what you want, and Joy and I can come up with some ideas and see what you think. I assume you've been researching, asking focus groups, checking what's out there, searching for the niche in the market, checking which colors are in and what styles are tipped for next year."

"Of course. I know my job, and I'm good at it. I'll email you with the details of when and where. I look forward to working with you and getting to know you better."

Jonty yawned.

"Come on, time to get you home," Ben said, waving his hand for the bill.

When it came, Sebastian grabbed it. "Expenses," he said.

Sebastian handed over his card and they followed behind Jonty and Ben.

"Can I give you a lift?" Sebastian asked. "We could continue our discussions over coffee at mine."

A taxi appeared and Ben raised his arm.

Drew leaned back to address Sebastian. "It's been a long day, and I've some thinking to do. If you don't mind, I'll take a rain check."

Sebastian leaned in. "So you're not saying no, then?"

Was he? Ben and Jonty stepped into the black cab. "Are you joining us?" Ben asked.

"Give me a minute." He needed to explain and addressed Sebastian. "Look, I hope this won't make a difference to your offer, but there's someone I met in the summer and he's still on my mind, and until he isn't, I'm not prepared to lead anyone on, whatever they want. I hope you can respect that." Had he blown it?

Sebastian placed a hand on his arm. "Thank you for being honest. I'd be lying if I said you didn't interest me, but I don't like to share, even with someone who isn't here. And I do want your designs. I think we'll do well together."

"Thank you for understanding. And I'm looking forward to working with you, too."

Drew climbed into the taxi and sat opposite his friends who stared at him with questioning expressions. "Well?" they both asked as the car set off.

"Well, what? You heard. We're going to work on this line."

"Yes, but he obviously fancies you, and he is drop-dead gorgeous with a cherry on the top."

Ben touched Jonty's thigh, shutting his partner up. "You're not over this Scottish bloke, are you?"

"Truth?" Drew asked. "No. Not yet. I have to get him out of my head. I said the same to Sebastian. It may be stupid, but that's how it is."

"Your heart is in the Highlands. Shit, it's like some tragic Gothic romance." Jonty clutched his partner's hand.

"Sometimes I wonder why I call you a friend," Drew said.

"Because you love me," Jonty replied. "But you need to sort yourself out."

"I will," Drew replied without conviction. But could he? Did he want to? He wrapped his arms around himself and stared out into the dark.

Chapter Fourteen

Joy sat next to him on the bench, clutching two coffees. He closed his sketch pad and placed it in his bag. He'd had the idea to people watch and check out what women chose to wear on a day like this. The schedule was tight and he needed a range of ideas to present to Sebastian before the meeting next week. Fashion worked so long in advance, picking its colors, shapes and lengths, but there were certain standard outfits every woman needed, the classic lines and shapes, from the comfortable to the special occasion. His first range would be out in a year. He needed a color scheme, a theme even, something to make the range stand out.

"Have you discovered anything?" Joy asked, handing him the coffee.

"This line needs to cater for all body types. I want everything to go together so the range can be worn individually and layered. It's got to be both comfortable and stylish, suitable for work and weekend."

"You're asking a lot of yourself. Shades of purple are supposed to be in next year. We could go with a color or two and accent with standard black, or pink." Colors and fabrics were Joy's specialty.

"Layering means we can get away with lighter material and fitted, as well as flowing. Whatever the catwalk says, women want value and style. This way, they can pick and choose from a range and not face wearing the same clothes as someone else, but know they all go. A confident woman like her," she said, indicating the woman sat opposite, "would choose to go with a fitted skirt and blouse, maybe even a corset-like waistcoat with a jacket. Another woman might want more freedom to move, more of an A line design, even with swing around the hips. Can we give all that?"

"We can try." He sipped his coffee.

"So, Jenna and the others arrive Friday for their weekend in the big city," Joy continued.

"They do, indeed. Friday night out to dinner and maybe a club. Saturday shopping, a bus tour and a show, and Sunday maybe a museum or the Tower, depending on the weather, then back home."

"And some time trying on the dresses. Sounds like a whirlwind weekend. I hope they like the finished products."

Drew swiveled on the bench. "I'm sure they will love them. They are exactly what Jenna wanted and the colors are perfect for a winter wedding. The fabrics you chose are brilliant." He stopped for a moment and considered his friend. They'd worked together since meeting at university. Joy had studied textiles. There was nothing she didn't know about the way a material moved or fell. They were a great team. But even after twelve years, her private life remained something of a mystery. She didn't tell, so he didn't ask.

"So, dinner with Sebastian at your place tomorrow, then?" She grinned.

"Stop it. Our relationship is strictly professional."

"I saw how he gazed at you. He's interested, and he's easy on the eye."

"I'll not deny that, but he is rather smooth, and maybe a tad too metrosexual, even for my tastes."

"Says the man whose bathroom cabinet has more toiletries than mine." She rose and placed her cardboard cup in the nearest bin. "Let's go to the warehouse. I said I'd pick up some samples for you to show Sebastian tomorrow."

Drew dropped his cup in the same bin and followed her out of the park. They had a long day of drawing, sketching, matching — making boards to show off — ahead of them.

* * * *

His hands shook as he clipped the sketches to the couple of boards he'd brought home from their tiny rented studio space. So much depended on this. Even now, Sebastian could reject their ideas. He and Joy had spent the afternoon attaching the fabric samples to the sketches until she'd been called away.

"I'm sorry. I can't leave her. You don't want me here, anyway, cramping your style."

"Don't be silly — just go. I hope she's all right."

Joy's mother lived in sheltered accommodation. Joy had called the warden before she left and he hoped her mother's fall wouldn't be too serious. The knock on the door surprised him as the flats had an intercom at the entrance. He opened it, expecting to find Joy had forgotten something.

Sebastian stood in the doorway, dressed in black jeans and shirt with an unbuttoned grey waistcoat. His dark hair smoothed flat, he appeared every inch the sophisticated city boy he was.

"Joy let me in. I hope that's okay."

"Yeah, it's fine. She's sorry she had to go — her mother." Drew stood to one side and let Sebastian in. He immediately strode toward the boards and stood studying them, feeling the materials, without comment.

"Would you like coffee?" Drew asked.

"Yeah, coffee would be great." Sebastian didn't raise his head from the sketches. He was still there when Drew returned with the drinks.

"These are good. I like the way they can be worn separately or together and how the colors blend. The lines allow women to choose the fit but still get a similar look. When can you have these ready for us to do some focus groups? We have regular buyers and those who have never entered our doors. It helps us get an idea before we invest in a whole line. We've all seen what happens when companies try new lines and fail. We're thinking of launching a model

131

competition as well rather than get the usual famous faces — you know, everyday women with different shapes to show off the versatility of the range."

It began to sink in exactly what Drew had committed them to. Working for himself, he had deadlines, but his designs had been one-offs and now, some time in the future, he could be walking down a street and see women wearing his concepts. He sank onto the sofa and stared clutching his coffee in both palms.

Sebastian glanced at him. "Are you all right? You've gone awfully pale."

"Sorry, it's just this will be huge for Comfort and Joy."

Sebastian sat next to him. "I've been meaning to ask about the name. I get the Joy part."

"Comfort is my middle name," Drew said. "Drew Comfort Sinclair — I use St Clair for the company. Comfort was my mother's maiden name. We liked the sound of the title and wanted our clothes to be both wearable and look good."

Sebastian placed a hand on Drew's thigh. "I think you've got something here. I've no doubt the team will approve. Your talent shines through."

If he leaned forward, Drew knew a kiss would follow, then more. He could so easily end up in bed with this man, getting fucked into his mattress. He had the feeling Sebastian liked to be in control, but having a relationship with someone he worked with was asking for trouble. The intercom buzzed and he jumped up.

"Are you expecting someone?" Sebastian asked, eyebrows raised.

"I wasn't." He pressed the button. "Hello. Who's there?"

There was a cough, which morphed into a throat being cleared. "Drew?"

It couldn't be, but it sounded like— "Duncan?" He glanced across the room. *Shit.* Awkward wasn't the word for this situation.

"Can I come in? It's started to rain."

"Yes, sorry, of course. Push the door when you hear the

noise. There's a lift on the left of the entrance. I'm on the fourth floor — flat twelve. I can't believe you're here."

He pressed the button. He had a minute or two at most. Too many questions flooded into his mind. How was Duncan there? Why was he there? Would he want to stay? They hadn't even spoken since he'd left so abruptly.

"A friend of yours?" Sebastian asked somewhat pointedly, annoyance at being interrupted writ large across his face.

"Yes, he must be down with my sister and her friends. I'm doing a fitting for the wedding and bridesmaids' dresses tomorrow. My sister's getting married at Christmas up in the Highlands of Scotland, and Duncan is the best man."

"Sounds like he's decided to visit the big city."

Drew couldn't help but notice Sebastian hadn't made any offer to leave. He jumped at the knock. "I don't know how long he'll be staying." Could he drop a bigger hint for Sebastian to go? He rushed to the door and opened it. Duncan filled the space. He wore jeans, one of his usual plaid shirts, a black leather jacket and a tentative smile, which faded when he discovered they weren't alone.

"I'm sorry. You should have said you had someone with you. I didn't mean to interrupt." He was half turned away when Drew grabbed his arm.

"No. Stay. We're discussing some new designs I've done for his store." He wanted to say that's all — there's nothing going on.

"If you're sure." Duncan stepped into the room and suddenly it seemed oh-so-much smaller. Sebastian stood when Duncan walked toward him and held out his hand.

"Duncan McLeish."

"Sebastian Healy. Drew says you met in the summer. Come to see the bright lights of the city, have you? It'll be different from the quiet of the Highlands."

Drew stood his ground, automatically comparing the smooth lines of Sebastian's outfit with Duncan's comfortable look, which included his usual boots. Both men stood about the same height, but there the similarity ended. Duncan with his wide shoulders, broad chest and strong arms seemed so much bigger.

"I've been to London before," he said. "In fact, I've been to lots of places. I spent my early years traveling with my parents. My mother was a diplomat so I got to experience life in many parts of the world."

Oh, no, the pissing contest has begun. Drew smothered a snort when a vision of them willy-waving at each other slipped into his head.

"And still you decided to live up north in the middle of nowhere. I couldn't do that myself. I'm sure Drew will concur that London is the place to be. I can't imagine what you find to do up there, and being away from shops and restaurants." He shivered and glanced at Drew as if he sought confirmation of his declaration.

"Oh, we find plenty to keep us busy and we have shops and great places to eat. Air travel puts us less than an hour away after all. And the beauty of the land is great compensation for not being able to get a skinny caramel macchiato on every corner. Anyway, I won't interrupt your *meeting* any longer. Perhaps we could get together tomorrow morning before Jenna and the others arrive, Drew? I should have called ahead." Duncan had the door half-open again before Drew managed to get a word out.

He stepped forward and glared at Sebastian. "Duncan, please stay. It's fine. You've come a long way. Sebastian and I have finished, haven't we?"

Sebastian brushed his clothes and straightened up. "I suppose so. I'll expect everything ready for the board next Tuesday. I hope you won't be too distracted."

"I take my job seriously. The designs will be finished, I can assure you, and I do appreciate your support. This opportunity means a great deal to Joy and me." Drew took Sebastian's arm and hurried him toward the door. "We won't let you down. I'll ring you Monday to finalize everything." He hoped he hadn't blown this deal. Sebastian wouldn't risk his company's best interests in a fit of pique or jealousy — surely?

Sebastian glanced once again at Duncan then his face softened. "I have full confidence in you. I love the designs, and I can tell we're going to work well together. I'll see myself out."

Duncan stepped out of his way and moved to stand in front of the sofa. Drew shut the door and leaned against, it facing Duncan, his heart beating so hard he was surprised not to see it jumping out of his chest. Nothing had changed. He still wasn't sure he believed his cowboy was standing in the same room once more.

"I missed you," he said, breaking the silence between them, if not the distance.

"I'm sorry. I couldn't stay away. I took the train down this morning. The others are flying tomorrow."

"You must be exhausted. For God's sake, sit down. Have you eaten? Do you have somewhere to stay? You can stay here."

Duncan sank down onto the sofa. "I was hoping you'd say that. I left at six this morning."

"I'll order takeaway. Pizza do you? Or I can get Indian, or Chinese, or Thai? Whatever you want." Yes, he was rambling.

"Pizza is fine. Anything except pineapple. I can't stand fruit on pizza. Would you mind if I used your bathroom to wash up and get rid of the dust from the train?"

"Of course not. Take the door through and it's the room opposite."

He unfolded himself and closed the distance between them. Drew wanted to climb all over him, feel his arms around him holding him tightly, but he needed to be sensible. His common sense lasted all of ten seconds.

"I'm so glad you're here."

"Me, too."

The kiss which followed threatened to make him disappear as he melted into those strong arms. Duncan pressed his tongue, parted his lips and probed his mouth.

Chest pressed against chest, groin against groin. Duncan pushed his thigh between Drew's legs until they rubbed against each other. He grabbed at Drew's shirt as he adjusted position and pushed his tongue forward.

"Oh, God," Drew panted between breaths. Duncan stroked his bare flesh and he gasped at the contact. He wanted Duncan on his knees. He couldn't remember being this hard in his life.

"Duncan. Stop."

Duncan's reaction was immediate. Drew studied his face and noted the dark circles and the extra crinkles around his eyes.

"What's wrong?"

"Nothing," Drew assured him. "But you're exhausted, and I don't want to have sex up against a door. I want you in my bed, and in my arse. Let's eat first after you've freshened up."

Duncan's smile took up his whole face and reached his eyes. "You may have a point. I've waited a few months, so a couple of hours won't matter. My shoulder is better now and I've been dreaming of everything I intend to do with you. Food and copious amounts of tea first. Afterward, though, Drew Sinclair, you are mine."

Chapter Fifteen

Drew was glad for something to do, something ordinary, like ordering food while Duncan stood within meters, washing off the dirt of the day. He'd needed distraction from the worries gathering speed in his already conflicted mind. He'd thought he'd ended things and walked away.

All right, he wasn't over Duncan, but he was a work in progress, and now, as he watched Duncan eat pepperoni-covered pizza, all he wanted to do was feel the weight of his body pressing him into his mattress, the sensation of skin touching skin, kisses all over and the joy of being full to the brim with another person, to have someone as part of him and to be part of someone else. Yes, it was romantic nonsense, foolish in the extreme, making no sense whatsoever. Yes, he had no idea of the future, what they might do, where they might be, what they both wanted. For now, he didn't intend to envision any further than this weekend. All those advice columns advised living for the moment, so that's what he intended to do because sometimes moments were all life gave.

"I don't have to stay."

Duncan's words penetrated his thoughts. "What?"

"I said I don't have to stay. You looked like you might be regretting me being here. You don't owe me anything."

"I shouldn't have left like I did. I bottled out of a last night."

"And now?"

"And now you're here, and although common sense tells me one thing, every part of me wants to make love with you."

Duncan swallowed, with difficulty, and adjusted his trousers. "The things you say. You make me so hard." He edged nearer on the sofa. "I've lain awake at night thinking of you. I even bought one of those things you used, but there's no heat."

Drew stood and held out his hand. "Let's go to bed."

Duncan followed suit and allowed Drew to pull him up then lead him. They undressed in silence. Drew lay on his back and waited.

"You are so beautiful," Duncan said. "Your hair is shorter."

Drew rain a hand through his blond locks. "I got fed up of it falling over my face while I worked. Are you just going to stand there and stare?"

Duncan climbed onto the bed and laid his considerable weight on top of Drew then kissed him. "I'm not too heavy, am I?"

"No, I like it."

Duncan grabbed both Drew's hands in one of his and pinned them above his head before smothering his face and neck in kisses which gradually became nips and bites. He'd have evidence of their coming together for days. He arched up, craving closeness, wanting more, loving the way their swollen cocks rubbed against each other. Duncan squeezed a nipple. Drew gasped and moaned when Duncan replaced his fingers with his mouth and sucked on the hardening nub. Drew kept his hands above his head, even after Duncan had released them, winding fingers around the bars of his metal headboard, letting Duncan set the pace and take control. He squirmed as Duncan moved between nipples, licking and biting, making Drew moan.

"You like?" Duncan asked.

"Oh, God, yes."

"I want to fuck you."

"Condoms and lube in the drawer. Hurry. If you keep pressing against me, I may come now, and I want to feel you inside me."

Duncan leaned over then sat back on his heels between Drew's thighs, his cock jutting straight out, full and heavy with his balls hanging low. He rolled on the condom and slathered his fingers with lube before covering the top of Drew's cock with his mouth and slipping fingers into Drew's arse.

"I won't need much prep," Drew said. He didn't explain how often he'd fucked himself fantasizing about this moment.

Duncan stopped sucking. "I don't want to hurt you. I still feel like such a novice."

"Stop worrying. You won't. Anyway, I want to be feeling this tomorrow. So, fuck me, cowboy."

Duncan pushed Drew's legs up and over his shoulders, leaving Drew's slicked arse totally exposed then took hold of his cock and pressed the head against Drew's hole.

Inch by glorious inch, Duncan pressed onward until he was balls-deep and he leaned over to kiss Drew once again.

"Move. Make me feel it." Drew whispered, loving the feeling of Duncan's body covering his and how his arse was so full.

Duncan almost withdrew then slammed back in.

"More," Drew demanded. Duncan lifted Drew's legs over his shoulder. His breathing increased as he pounded Drew's arse over and over, hitting his prostate every time as if they'd been doing this forever. His gaze never leaving Drew's face.

"You're so tight, so hot. I can't go slowly," he warned.

"Don't. I want it hard and fast this time. We've all weekend to slow things down." He let go of the headboard and fisted his cock with one hand, knowing it wouldn't take long, feeling the tingles in his spine, the electricity across his skin, his every hair standing on end as if each wanted to be as near as possible to the man taking his body to the heights.

"So close," he said.

"Let yourself go. I want to feel you come around my cock."

Two pumps and he spurted all over his hand and stomach, loving the sensation of his arse around Duncan's shaft. Duncan reared up, plunged in once more and heat filled Drew as he was bent double.

"That was amazing. I've never come like that before. I wanted it to go on and on."

Drew wanted to tell Duncan he should try it for himself, but he had no idea if Duncan would want to swap roles. Instead he lay there with one hand still gripping the metal. He eased his fingers apart.

Finally, Duncan leaned back on his knees, his chest heaving, and pulled out, leaving Drew empty but sated. He removed the condom, tied it off and dropped it over the side of the bed into the waste bin, before rolling back over to face Drew, who had his head propped up on one hand and was idly making patterns in the drying liquid on his torso. Duncan flicked out his tongue and tasted, making Drew's cock twitch even after coming so fiercely.

"You are incredible," Duncan said. "That was... I'm not sure what words to use."

Drew smiled as he stifled a yawn behind his hand. "You need to sleep. Tuck in behind me."

Duncan did as instructed, tugged the duvet over both of them, and within seconds, his body relaxed and his breathing slowed. Drew clutched Duncan's hand pulling around to his chest and closed his eyes, letting sleep overtake him before any regrets could find their way in.

* * * *

Had he made the right choice? Waking up with his arm numb, but not caring because it was wrapped around the man in front of him, Duncan couldn't find it in himself to regret his decision. Every day had seemed like an eternity since Drew had left. The home he'd loved for all those years now seemed empty. Yes, it was ridiculous. Craig had told him as much as he'd bent his ear back about his alcohol consumption. His bed now seemed so vast.

He smiled at the tourists, giving them his usual cowboy charm, dipping his hat to the women, addressing the men as 'sir', keeping up the façade.

Even though he'd only known Drew those few days, and no matter how he tried, no matter how many times he combed the horses, rode with the cattle, walked Misha, he felt Drew's absence like a huge black hole, sucking his happiness and contentment away. More often than usual, he took Misha up to his lake and sat staring at the mountain side as it changed from its summer colors to autumn, from green to purple and back again with the occasional brown, tan and russet from the few trees and bushes up to the tree line.

Drew stirred and pulled his hand forward. "You're thinking," he said.

"Yes, I suppose I am. I'm not sure I'm not dreaming. Being here seems so unreal."

Drew pushed back against him. "You feel real enough to me, judging by what's poking into my back." Drew turned to face him and stroked his chest, trailing his fingers lower until they brushed over Duncan's erection, and he moaned. Drew grinned then moved until they were lying top to tail. Getting to the same page, Duncan followed Drew's lead, grabbed the impressive sight in front of him and sucked on the head while Drew's tongue danced over his own needy cock. Minutes later both men lay sated from the experience. Duncan ran his tongue over his lips, still tasting Drew until he couldn't ignore the need to use the bathroom any longer.

"I've got to use the loo," he said. "And I need to shower. Can you wait?"

Drew nodded. "I slipped out in the night. You were so tired you didn't even notice. I'll go in after you. I'm not sure sharing would be a good idea—today's going to be busy. Jenna said she'd call when she got to the motel, then we're going to lunch before the fittings. How about a trip to the National Gallery before lunch and tonight a show, maybe even a club, if we're all still awake? I assume they know you're going to be here."

"They do." Duncan stared at the floor. He hadn't explained his spur-of-the-moment decision, just made a vague suggestion about seeing London and not wanting to fly.

"So, what are we? Simply good friends, or can I touch you?" Drew ran a finger over Duncan's arms and every hair rose, making him shiver.

Duncan wasn't sure how to answer. When he lifted his head and met Drew's challenging gaze, he gulped down his panic, ducked out of answering and jumped out of bed. "Sorry, need to pee." He also needed to think.

After relieving himself, he pulled down the lid and sat on the toilet, staring into space. Jenna wouldn't care, except she'd worry about her brother. Carrie would be happy he wasn't lonely, and frankly, he didn't care what Mhairi thought. Craig knew, anyway. When he weighed up everything, the truth was, it didn't matter, so why was he hesitating? His grandfather, and his prejudice, was dead and buried. He rose, checked his hair and ambled back to the bedroom. His heart leaped at the sight of Drew, sitting up bare-chested, with his glasses perched on his nose, reading.

"I wasn't sure if you'd fallen in or were just avoiding me."

"Neither." He closed the distance between them and sat on the bed. "About your question. You know I like you. I don't know how things are here, but I'm not usually one for public displays."

"It's okay. I don't expect you to snog me in the street."

"Let me finish. We're more than friends, at least I hope we are, so, yes, to the touching. I doubt the women will be shocked. Carrie raised her eyebrows when I said I was coming, especially the day before, and not booking into a hotel. I don't need to do that, do I?"

Drew leaned over, pushed his glasses up his nose and took Duncan's hand. "I'm likely to flirt with you, be suggestive, rub my thigh against yours and invade your personal space. Are you prepared? If we go out tonight, I might even want to dance with you."

Duncan shook his head. "No dancing. I don't dance. I've two left feet."

Drew winked at him. "We'll see. Now, there's a café round the corner that does amazing breakfasts and tea so strong you can stand a spoon up in it. Give me ten minutes to get ready. We can get the Tube and visit the National Portrait Gallery and Trafalgar Square, have a mooch around then meet the girls."

He kissed Duncan on the nose, sprang out of bed, shaking his perfectly formed arse as he did so, and rushed to the bathroom, leaving Duncan on the bed grinning like a fool. If life was testing him with lemons, he intended to make the sweetest lemonade and drink every last drop.

* * * *

"I love these old paintings," Duncan said, gazing at a huge portrait of Elizabeth I. "So much symbolism in them—the Tudors knew how to get messages across. Imagine what she could have done with photographs, with all the retouching they do now. You'd know about that, I suppose in your industry."

"Yeah, it still happens, but I know she controlled all images of her until the end of her life and you're right about the dresses. There's a famous one with embroidered eyes and ears on the bodice telling people she had spies everywhere, which she did."

Duncan nodded. "There's something fascinating about her. I could spend ages just trying to work out the messages in each painting."

"I'm heading into the next room." Drew strolled away while Duncan stared. He'd never been there before. His parents had taken him to the Louvre, but six had been too young to appreciate the mystery of the Mona Lisa. Now, as they wandered through the galleries, he experienced the stretch of time the portraits covered and the myriad styles. He turned and caught up with Drew in the next display area.

"It's funny, isn't it, how women have always been forced to fit their bodies into certain forms, whereas men's fashions have always fitted around them? It's one of the things I'm looking forward to, designing for women, not finding women who fit my designs."

"I can't say I've ever thought about it," Duncan replied. "My parents were always immaculate. I used to watch them getting ready for formal occasions. My father in his dinner suit, his white shirt gleaming, with my mother putting his cufflinks in while she wore the most beautiful dresses and jewelry. She suited bright colors and always wore her long dark hair up in the most elaborate of designs.

'People expect you to look your best, and we're representing our country so we do.' Her words."

He stared at the floor. His heart ached with the loss. Drew held his hand. His first instinct was to pull away as they were in public, but instead he lifted his head and smiled at the concerned face in front of him. "I'm sorry. Even now, I find myself missing them so much." He breathed in and let the air leave his lungs slowly until calm washed over him. "You must be excited about this new line. I expect it'll need a lot of work."

"It will for Joy and me. We work so far in advance, trying to reflect and channel trends. Sometimes, I come to galleries to get ideas for colors and shapes."

"Well, even platform shoes came around again, so I suppose there's nothing new. Would you mind if we got some air now, or as much as Trafalgar Square can provide?"

Drew pulled his hand free to answer his phone's beep. "They're here," he announced. "I'll text them to find us in the Square, then we can go for lunch and back to mine for the great dress-trying-on. Are you up for that?"

"I'm not usually one for drink, but I may need some if I'm

going to survive."

"I've bought in several bottles of wine for when they are not wearing the dresses. Red wine is a bitch to get out. Come on, cowboy, let's go people watch."

"More idea gathering?"

"A good designer always checks what people wear."

Duncan leaned his head next to Drew's ear. "Got any interesting lace designs I haven't seen yet?"

Drew's chuckle went straight to his groin. "Lots. I may model a few for you later. And if you're a good boy, I may let you remove them with your teeth."

Duncan covered his front with his hands, conscious of the constriction in his trousers, while Drew hurried away. He glanced around, his cheeks burning, and rushed after him.

Chapter Sixteen

They'd sat thigh to thigh, unobtrusively holding hands, for forty-five minutes, until a loud shout of "Drew" and the sight of three women waving madly and heading their way resulted in them standing up and waving back. Jenna hugged them both while Carrie eyed Duncan with a small, knowing smile on her face, as if she'd magically seen their fingers entwined.

"Everything went to plan then?" Drew asked.

"Oh, aye, like clockwork. We weren't in the air long enough to eat so grabbed something at Heathrow, got the train, dropped the bags at the hotel and came here. I don't think I've ever seen so many people in one place." Carrie did a three-hundred-and-sixty-degree swivel, taking everything in. "I expect you thought the same, Duncan. It's different here. But maybe you haven't seen much yet."

Drew pushed his hand through Carrie's arm. "Oh, he hasn't had chance to lie around in bed. I've kept him busy since he turned up at my door last night. Isn't that right, Duncan?"

Heat flushed his face and neck and he wanted the ground to open and swallow him, but he had said Drew didn't need to hide, so he'd brought this on himself. Jenna spoke before he had any chance to reply.

"How far away is Covent Garden? I always get confused. We fancy a stroll around the shops then lunch before the great try-on, although I'd better not eat too much."

Drew examined his sister from head to foot. "I'd say you've already lost some weight. I'm right, aren't I?" He swung to Mhairi, who so far had simply stared in every direction. "And you, as well? Thank goodness Carrie has more sense."

Duncan chuckled when Drew cried "ouch" as Carrie elbowed him in the ribs. "Enough of your lollygagging. I don't get much chance to shop, so lead on."

Duncan let Drew banter with the ladies and followed on behind as they tramped along the Strand, taking much longer as they passed several shops along the way. Once at the Covent Garden piazza, Duncan begged to be excused and found a chair at an open-air café just opposite the Opera House.

"Are you sure you'll be all right?" Drew asked. "I feel guilty leaving you. You won't wander and get lost, will you?"

"I'm a big boy. I can cope on my own." Was he flirting? He was flirting. Here. In public. With Drew.

Drew leaned into him. "Oh, I know how big you are." Before he could protest, Drew kissed his cheek and raced off after the women. Duncan glanced around, but not one person was taking a blind bit of notice. He chuckled to himself, found a newsagent, bought a paper, and settled down with a large, and surprisingly tasty, coffee.

The rest of the day passed in a flurry of hanging on to the coattails of three people intent on seeing as much as they could of the capital city, and seemingly buying quite a bit of it, followed by the trying-on of dresses accompanied by lots of wine. Duncan stayed well out of the way, it having been decided he couldn't see the outfits just in case he said anything to the bridegroom. He settled into an armchair and closed his eyes, surprised to be woken a couple of hours later by a hand shaking his shoulder.

"Wake up, old man." He opened his eyes to see Jenna staring at him.

"Sorry, I guess the train journey and this morning wore me out."

"Nothing to do with my brother and last night, then?"

Duncan glanced over his shoulder toward the kitchen. He

guessed Drew, Carrie and Mhairi were there.

"You know Craig and I don't give a damn if you're gay, or bi, or whatever, don't you?"

He nodded, afraid of what he might blurt out. Denying their relationship would be a betrayal, but he didn't feel prepared to say *yes, I'm having sex with your brother, but that's all it is.* He didn't find it easy to lie, but obfuscation was a different matter. By saying nothing, he might just get away with it.

"Oh, Duncan, I'm afraid how this will end for both of you. Drew tends to wear his heart on his sleeve. We talked before he left in the summer, and I think you choosing to show up like this has thrown his world completely off-kilter."

Duncan swallowed hard. "I get the feeling you're asking what my intentions are, and the truth is I don't know. I kept thinking about him while we were apart and I had to find out what this was."

"And have you decided?"

"I like him, Jenna. I think if we spent more time together, I could more than like him. He takes me out of myself and makes me laugh. I can be… What's the word I'm looking for? Pompous, maybe. I know people think my polite cowboy is an act, but it's how I was brought up — keep your feelings to yourself, don't rock the boat, smile and move on, don't fight battles you can't win. Until I inherited the ranch, I always took the easiest route and kept my head down at school and with my grandfather. Relationships are complicated and no one interested me enough to consider a future…"

"Until my brother came along."

"Until Drew came along. But he lives here and I live hundreds of miles away, and I've no idea what our future might be, if we even have one."

Jenna squeezed his thigh. "Don't give up, that's all. You never know what might happen."

"You two look serious," Drew said, as he and the others entered the room. He glanced at each of them. "Did I miss something?"

Jenna rose. "No, we were talking about tonight. Us girls are off to see *Mamma Mia!* so we'll leave you two to yourselves. I'm sure you'll find something to occupy your time."

Duncan didn't want to watch the show and it meant spending more time on his own with Drew.

Jenna continued, "You and Drew go out together. You don't want to be bothered with us. Maybe we'll meet you at a club later."

"I've never been to a gay club," Mhairi chipped in.

Duncan noticed Drew's frown. He guessed Drew might not be too keen on Mhairi treating the club as a place to stare at the clientele.

"At least then I don't have to be worried about men hitting on me when I dance," Mhairi added. Had she caught Drew's expression?

Jenna checked her watch. "Well, ladies, we'd better get a shift on if we want time to eat, then get to the show." She hugged Drew and whispered in his ear. Drew nodded as he gazed at Duncan over her shoulder. Duncan didn't hear her words.

"Thanks, sis. Maybe I'll see you later. Text me."

Jenna patted his arm. "And the dresses are magnificent. Come on, ladies. Let's get ready to hit the town."

Drew waved them off at his door while Duncan gazed out of the window. Pink and orange streaks from the setting sun covered what could be seen of the horizon in between the tall buildings. The door clicked shut. They were alone again.

"At home, I can't see any lights at night other than the stars. Here you're surrounded by them. And the traffic? Does it ever stop?"

Drew's shoes tapped on the wooden floor as he moved to stand next to him. "I suppose I'm used to it by now, after twelve years. When I was growing up, I couldn't stand the silence at home. Even when I'm working, I have to have music on. If it's silent, I end up listening for every noise. A buzzing fly can distract me. I used to lie in my bed listening for the animals outside—the foxes and the deer."

Duncan turned to face him. "What have you got planned for tonight?"

"Dinner then, despite your protests, dancing."

"I'm not exaggerating when I say I have two left feet," Duncan explained.

"Don't worry. The way I dance, you won't need to move around too much."

Duncan didn't press again with questions neither of them wanted to answer. They had less than twenty-four hours before life would divide them again.

* * * *

"You want me to give in my shirt as well as my jacket?"

"Trust me," Drew replied. "You'll be too warm. Shove it in the pocket."

"But it'll get all crumpled, and all I've got on underneath is a vest."

Drew grinned. "Yeah, I know."

Duncan's Adam's apple bobbed as he gulped and Drew grabbed his hand. "Come on, and stay close to me. This place can get full."

They made their way to the bar. "Two Godfathers, please."

"Should I ask?" Duncan said.

"Just a taste of home."

The barman handed over the whisky-based drinks and Drew led Duncan to stand to one side of the dancefloor. When two chairs became free, they grabbed them and sat. The music made chat impossible.

"Good?" Drew questioned, shouting in Duncan's ear and holding up his drink.

Duncan nodded. He stared out onto the floor. Drew noticed men giving Duncan second glances as they passed and who could blame them. He swallowed the last of the cocktail.

"Come on. Time to dance." He pulled up a reluctant Duncan.

"I think I need more alcohol first."

Drew wriggled his denim-clad arse against Duncan's groin and grabbed his arms so they were pinned around his waist. He reached around Duncan's back and held on to his hips. They stayed in that position as the music played, swaying together with Drew moving up and down, enclosed in Duncan's arms. After a few minutes, he turned to face him, pulling their groins closer. When another man twisted to rub against Drew from behind, Duncan growled, sending shivers down Drew's spine as the man backed off and apologized. Drew buried his face in Duncan's neck and kissed him then smiled as he clocked the dancers appearing in the cages behind them.

"I'd love to see you dressed like them," he shouted into Duncan's ear. He nodded and Duncan swung them around, keeping hold of him. His eyes widened as he took in the outfits of the cage dancers—silver G-strings, high-heeled boots, chaps and topped by Stetsons as they wove around the tall poles, shaking their arses.

Duncan stared open-mouthed as they gyrated around and up and down, creating a vast variety of shapes and poses.

"They're amazing," Duncan said, as Drew found himself being pulled closer. "The athleticism is incredible. They must be fit to get into those positions."

Drew leaned in. "You must be the only one here not staring at their arses. Let's get another drink."

Duncan nodded and let Drew pull him through the growing crowd.

After a few more drinks, they took to the floor again. Lacking room to move, they simply rubbed up against each other. Duncan grabbed under Drew's arse and lifted him while they kissed and spun around. Drew crossed his legs and held on.

"Take me home," he shouted. "Take me home and fuck

me into the mattress." Drew wished they were nearer. The journey back to his flat took forever. As soon as they were through the door, Duncan picked him up in the same way he had at the club and carried him to the bedroom then threw him down on the bed. Neither man waited and, within a minute, Drew lay there naked with Duncan standing above him, sporting an impressive erection. Drew's mouth watered in anticipation. He whistled and wiped his forehead.

"Duncan McLeish, you are one gorgeous hunk of a man."

Duncan gave him a slight smile and twisted his hands around as if uncertain what to do next.

"*Momentum interruptus*?" Drew questioned.

"What?" Duncan asked.

"You look like a rabbit caught in a car's headlights." Drew moved until he was sitting on the edge of the bed. He opened his arms and Duncan inched forward until Drew could press his face against his stomach. He kissed above Duncan's belly button.

"Don't worry. I won't lick your navel."

"It tickles," Duncan said. "And not in a good way. The kissing is good, though. Ohh." He lurched upward as Drew took hold of his balls and caressed them. Duncan's shaft stiffened. Drew licked his lips and with his other hand took hold and bent forward to probe the slit with the tip of his tongue. Duncan groaned.

Drew let go to open a drawer and pull out a condom and lube. He rolled the rubber over Duncan's erection, then covered it with lube and sat back with his knees up and apart and a smile on his face.

"Fuck me," he said.

"But we haven't…"

"Dunc, we've spent the last few hours rubbing up against each other, smelling each other's sweat and kissing. I've had all the foreplay I can take and now, I want you inside me. I want to make memories. Fuck me. Bite me. Hold me tight. I don't care. I want to know where you've been." He pulled his legs higher, exposing himself further.

Duncan climbed onto the bed, held his cock against Drew's entrance and pushed in slowly, but in one go. The burn was glorious but didn't last long.

"I feel so full." Drew wrapped his legs around Duncan and pulled him forward. He raked his nails down Duncan's flesh, making him rear up and slam in once more.

"Fuck."

"Is it wrong I love making you swear?" Drew asked. He also loved making the mild-mannered cowboy fall apart. He turned his head to one side, offering his neck. Duncan didn't need to be asked twice.

With teeth and tongue, he left his mark on Drew's neck and shoulder then down his chest. Every time he pulled out, Drew hauled him back in because he couldn't stand the emptiness. When Duncan hit his prostate, he opened his eyes to see Duncan rising up over him. He reached his arms over his head and grabbed the rails of the bed head.

"Yeah, cowboy. Just there. Fuck me. Make me come."

Duncan lifted Drew's arse and held him there. Every thrust filled him. His body lit up. Every nerve and every fiber absorbed in the task of chasing the orgasm still tantalizingly out of reach. He wanted it and he didn't. He loved being made to wait. He loved how his body teased until he couldn't hold off any longer. Feelings gathered in his spine, in his balls, a surge of sparks met and exploded when he took hold of himself with wave after wave that he wasn't sure would end.

"Drew," Duncan cried as he came a few seconds later, and when his arms failed to hold him, he fell panting onto Drew's chest.

"Bloody hell." he managed between pants. "I've never..."

"Me, neither," Drew managed. He stroked Duncan's hair with one hand and wrapped his arm around his back not wanting to let him go or leave his body while they remained as one. How far away everything else seemed at this moment. Nothing mattered — only them. There was no city, no ranch, no company, no situation forcing them apart. They were here, and together, and, for those precious few minutes, until the real world came crashing in, nothing else mattered.

Chapter Seventeen

The beeping of Drew's phone woke him. It took a few seconds to recognize the source of the noise and that he couldn't move because Duncan's arm was wrapped around his waist. Drew wriggled, reached out and managed to get his fingers on the glass and hook it close. Duncan murmured behind him, sending warm air onto his neck. He swiped the phone and read the message from Jenna.

Will we see you today?

He glanced at the clock, then rubbed his eyes unsure he was seeing properly. Nine already. No wonder his bladder screamed at him. He tapped out a reply.

Maybe not. Is that OK?

The answer came immediately.

That's fine. Skype tomorrow. I want details.

I don't think you want all the details.

Ha bloody ha. Take care of yourself, as well.

Duncan stirred again. "What time is it?"

"Nine. I need the loo and a shower. We fell asleep before we wiped yesterday. I suspect we're both crusty."

"I could join you in the shower." Duncan kissed the back of Drew's neck. "You okay?"

"I'm good. I've got to go. Join me when you're ready. Then we're going for a full breakfast. Jenna isn't expecting us, so we have the rest of the day. We could go somewhere or stay here. Whatever you want. I've got to go."

Drew hurried to the bathroom, relieved himself and brushed his teeth. He wanted to taste good for kisses in the shower. He turned on the water and stepped into the enclosure. A minute or two later, Duncan opened the door.

"Oh, God. Have you seen? I'm sorry, I got a bit reckless last night." He caressed the line of small bruises down Duncan's chest. His neck was similarly marked.

Duncan placed his hand over Drew's and clasped his fingers then brought them to his lips and kissed each one. Drew's knees shook, threatening to drop him. He clutched Duncan's shoulder.

"What you do to me, Duncan McLeish."

"What you do to *me*." Duncan ran his fingers over his chest. "I wish I could stop them fading, have them tattooed on." He moved forward, pressing his body to Drew's chest, pushing him against the cold tiles. The water streamed around them. Duncan took hold of Drew's cock and held it with his own. He kissed Drew, pushing his tongue past Drew's lips until Drew groaned, then dropped his hands to his sides, letting Duncan take control, afraid his brain might short-circuit from too many sensations. Finally, the need to come again overwhelmed them all. He closed his eyes while Duncan pressed kisses to his neck and shoulder.

"I'm close," Duncan whispered. "Come with me."

Drew concentrated everything on his cock, thrusting into Duncan's hand. His breath hitched and his climax slammed into him taking his breath away. At the same time, Duncan bit into Drew's neck as he came spilling more warmth between them. Duncan kissed him again and Drew moaned into Duncan's mouth, barely able to hold himself up. He let Duncan's strong arms do the work. *Bloody hell.* This man might be the death of him, but at least he'd die happy. He attempted to catch his breath. What the hell were they going to do?

* * * *

"Can we go to the zoo?" Duncan asked over the large breakfast they'd ordered in the café. "The weather's fine, so I'd like to stay outdoors. I can't believe how much warmer it is here."

Drew thought it a strange choice but said nothing. Somehow, he'd imagined they'd spend the day in bed. "I've never been," he said. "I've lived here twelve years and there are so many places I've yet to visit."

"Do you mind? I can't stay in all the time, even with such a gorgeous distraction." Duncan smiled and Drew's insides turned to mush.

"The zoo it is then. We can walk through Regent's Park. The colors will be wonderful." He swallowed tea from the huge mug. "What time do you have to leave?" Not that he wanted to know.

"The sleeper train leaves at eleven-thirty from Euston. I'll pick the car up from Glasgow and drive home from there. We've got twelve hours."

Drew grinned. "We'd better make the most of them then. According to the website, they feed the tigers at twelve, or we could go to the otters. They've a new lion enclosure, too, and there's the penguin feeding, the meerkats, lemurs and pygmy hippos. I don't think I've ever seen a pigmy hippo."

"Me, neither. I hope I can still move after eating all this." He burped. "Sorry. But you were right about this place. How do we get there?"

"Tube to Regent's Park then we can stroll along the Broad Walk. At the end, we turn left to get to the entrance."

"A stroll sounds great. If we want to see the tiger feeding, we'd better get a move on."

On the Tube, Duncan discovered he didn't like escalators, but at least it wasn't crowded.

"Thank goodness we're out of there. I don't know how

you stand it."

"Just get used to it, I suppose." Drew spun around then pushed his arm through Duncan's as they ambled down the Broad Walk. "I can't remember the last time I walked through a London park and actually took in my surroundings. The trees have so many colors."

Duncan glanced in all directions but didn't withdraw his arm.

Drew noted his actions. "No one cares. And if they do, fuck them. We're not the only ones."

"I'm sorry. I'm not used to PDAs but it's nice being just like this together. Nothing will beat the Highlands, but the trees are beautiful and it's good to stretch my legs and get some air, even if it isn't as clean here. Was that a lion roaring?"

Drew listened. "It could be a tiger. Imagine living around here and hearing the animal noises at night. Beats the sound of foxes or deer."

They reached the end of the pathway, turned left and walked a few steps farther. At the entrance, there was a small queue of families out for a Sunday trip in the autumn sunshine. They paid their money and checked the map to find where the tigers were kept.

"I've read about the zoo," Duncan said, pointing the way. "They do great work here with conservation of species, but I wish we didn't need them."

Drew watched the huge Sumatran tiger chewing on the meat. "They are magnificent creatures. I was surprised when you wanted to come here. I didn't think you'd like seeing the animals in captivity."

Duncan leaned on the rail. "In a perfect world, I'd rather they weren't, but I recognize what's necessary, just as I do being a farmer. And zoos are nothing like they used to be, well, not ones like this. Let's have a wander."

They headed past the gorillas and other smaller animals and on toward the penguin beach.

"When I was six and my parents were in South America,

they flew in a small plane over to Tierra del Fuego and we saw King penguins in the wild. I've always loved them. There are gay ones in a zoo in the US. They gave them an egg to hatch and wrote a kids' book about it. The chicks are so cute. I wanted to bring one home."

Drew smiled, imagining Duncan as a small boy being exposed to such wonders. "You know what they say — lots of animals display homosexual behavior but only one displays homophobia."

"Yeah, we could learn a lot from them."

"You must have had an interesting childhood," Drew said, trying to change the subject which had become gloomy rather quickly.

"Until I was eight and sent to school, I thought everyone lived the same way. We lived in Argentina and Chile. I doubt I appreciated the scenery then."

"Have you ever thought of going back?" He wanted to kick himself the moment the words left his mouth.

"No, I've never been able to… Let's just say, flying isn't my thing." He walked on and Drew hurried to catch up.

The penguins waddled around and swam in the pools. As if they knew the time, they gathered on the near side of the area waiting for their fish. Children and their parents watched with glee as the birds dived to get their meals.

They spent the rest of the afternoon taking in as many of the other animals as they could in the time — lemurs, giraffes, lions — until they arrived at the indoor section and Drew baulked at the spiders.

"Come on, they can't hurt you," Duncan said, grabbing him by the hand.

"No. Not a chance in hell. All those hairy legs."

"But I've got hairy legs," Duncan replied, laughing. "and you don't seem to mind them."

"Yeah, but you've got two and you don't skitter around like they do. I can't stand them, or moths — in fact, most insects. The cottage we lived in was full of creepy-crawlies. Jenna got a moth in her ear once. She wasn't fazed, but I

159

slept with cotton wool in my ears for weeks, just in case."

"They say you swallow around six spiders in your lifetime," Duncan said.

"That's apocryphal. Or it had better be." Drew shivered. He glanced at his watch. "Let's get a taxi home. We haven't got much more time together and I'm hungry again. Maybe it's watching the lions taking apart their meat. We can pick up some Chinese around the corner from my block."

Duncan grinned at him. "Sometimes I don't know whether the innuendo is intended or not."

Drew spun around and grabbed his hand. "Stick around long enough and you'll find that's part of my charm." His heart felt lighter as Duncan didn't pull his hand away and let himself be dragged through the zoo to the exit.

* * * *

Lying on the sofa, stuffed with pizza, and with Duncan's arm around him pulling him in closer, Drew sighed. He lifted his gaze to the bedroom door. They had about three hours before Duncan had to leave. Drew had offered to go with him to Euston, but Duncan had protested.

"I don't want to say goodbye at the station with people around." And Drew had agreed. For the last couple of hours, they'd done anything but talk about the elephant in the room. Right now, they were watching *Antiques Roadshow* and speculating on whether a painting was worth a fortune or not, and even if it was valuable, how they wouldn't give it wall space.

"Perhaps we should have gone to the Tate," Duncan said.

Drew slipped out from under Duncan's arm and picked up his coffee. He sipped it savoring the taste. "We need to talk, Duncan."

"I know we do, but I'm not sure what to say." He leaned over with his elbows on his knees and his head in his hands.

"You must have come down here for a reason," Drew said.

"I missed you. You appeared out of nowhere and turned my world upside down in a matter of days, and I wanted more. I couldn't get you out of my head. I even bought one of those contraptions, I told you. I thought about going to Glasgow, but I couldn't. You made me want the impossible, even for a couple of days. I've no idea what makes you so special, so different."

Drew gripped his mug with both hands. "Thank you, I'm flattered I'm sure."

"I'm sorry that came out wrong. I'm not good with words."

"You're the son of a diplomat. Don't give me the shy-cowboy crap you spout to the visitors. I deserve more, don't I? Which brings me back to what the hell are we going to do? Long-distance love? Seeing each other a few times a year like some Highland version of *Brokeback Mountain*. I'm not sure I can do that. And you came here, Duncan. You came after me. I was attempting to move on from you." *All right, perhaps that was a slight exaggeration.* "You turned up on *my* doorstep."

"*You* didn't push me away."

Drew placed his mug on the table, stood and walked over to the window, his hands balled into fists. He stared out at the lights, which the night before had seemed so romantic and full of possibilities.

"I ought to punch you. What am I, Duncan? Am I someone you can fuck and forget? Is that what this is? Am I just another of those fucks you've had in Glasgow and told no one about?" A feeling of déjà-vu swept over him. He didn't want this to end the same way as last time.

Duncan rose and joined him at the window, wrapping his arms around Drew from behind and resting his chin on Drew's shoulder.

"We've had a grand total of a few days together, but I have feelings for you, Drew. Yes, I chose to come here. I needed to find out…"

"What?"

"I don't know exactly. Whether I'd imagined it all. Whether it was real."

"And did you find out? Is it?" Drew's stomach fluttered, waiting for an answer. Either would break his heart.

Duncan turned him around so they were facing and kissed him hard. Drew closed his eyes and lost himself as the kiss deepened and they moved each way, changing angles, open-mouthed, tasting each other until Duncan broke off and peppered Drew's face and neck with more kisses. So close Drew could feel Duncan's erection pressing against his thigh, knowing his own cock had reacted in the same way.

"Does this answer your question?" Duncan asked.

"Oh, hell. You can't leave your ranch, and my life and career are here. I'm on the brink of something big, something which could make my name, and there's Joy to think of. I could fly up sometimes, though. It's not far by plane and the others know about us — or those who matter do."

"I used to care what people thought, but I don't know what to think anymore. Do long-distance love affairs work? That bloke the other day obviously wanted you. If I hadn't appeared, would you have slept with him?" He paused. "Sorry, that's none of my business."

"It's okay, I like you being jealous and no, not then. Maybe in the future. I don't know, Duncan. Would you have given in and gone to Glasgow to have some quickie in a club or a hotel?"

"I told you. I couldn't. When I closed my eyes, all I saw was you. I don't think that's going to change anytime soon."

Drew clasped Duncan's hand and led him to the bedroom. "Make love to me, Duncan. Touch me, hold me, take me apart."

Duncan's Adam's apple bobbed as he gulped for air. He pulled Drew's T-shirt over his head and undid his jeans, letting Drew step out of them and his briefs. After Duncan stripped off his own clothes, he and Drew stood facing each other. Duncan fell to his knees, lifted his head and gazed at him. Never, whatever happened, would Drew forget those eyes staring at him. He rested his hands on Duncan's shoulders to steady himself while Duncan smoldered.

Bloody hell, have I slipped into some romantic parallel reality. Smoldered?

He nodded and, with his gaze locked, Duncan enclosed Drew's cock in his mouth right to the base then pulled slowly back, sucking as he did and running his tongue along the vein underneath.

"Shit. Have you been taking lessons?" Drew asked.

Duncan's face flushed even as he took hold of the base of Drew's erection. "I may have done some research. You can learn a lot online."

"Show me," Drew demanded, lowering his voice.

Duncan wrapped his strong, calloused fingers around Drew's cock and stuck out his tongue to lick the bead of pre-cum from the tip before covering it and sucking fiercely.

"Yes," Drew said, his breath already fractured as his world centered and he let himself succumb to the feeling. For the next few minutes, Duncan licked, mouthed and fisted Drew's cock like he'd recently gained a PhD in blow jobs. When he slid his other hand to cup Drew's balls, every nerve ending sizzled and Drew tried in vain to prolong the sensations, naming in his head as many designers as he could think of.

"I can't... I'm gonna..."

Duncan gazed up at him but didn't pull away. Drew couldn't stop the gathering and leaned on Duncan's shoulders as his orgasm ripped through him, leaving his knees weak and his heart pounding so loud he was certain Duncan would hear it. Duncan continued his ministrations until Drew had nothing left then sat back on his legs and licked his lips.

Duncan stood and moved toward him until his crotch nudged Drew's face. If he'd written his message in fifty-foot letters across the sky, his meaning couldn't have been clearer. Drew got his breathing under control and undid belt, button and zip before reaching in and taking hold of Duncan's erection.

"Someone is happy to play out," he said. "I'm not sure I can equal your ability."

"Try," Duncan growled. Drew didn't argue and went straight to work.

* * * *

"I've got to go," Duncan said, a few hours later. "I need to call a taxi."

Drew wrapped his arm across Duncan's chest and pulled him closer. "We still haven't worked out what we're going to do."

Duncan sat up. "I've no idea. We have Skype and you could fly up when you've time or…"

"We leave this as a satisfying experience and get on with our lives. Is that what you want?"

Duncan shook his head. "It's the last thing I want, but I don't see how we can make this work. Long-distance relationships. You know. And, as I said before, Sebastian seemed interested in getting to know you better."

"He was," Drew said, reaching for his sweat pants and vest before pulling them on.

"He lives here and I don't. Our lives are so far apart. I don't see how we could have a future. You'd get fed up of me and my old-fashioned ways."

Drew's heart fractured. He didn't see how, either. He pushed away the thought that he would have to see Duncan for the wedding. Maybe he could avoid Duncan, or at least being alone with him. Duncan's nudge brought him back into the room.

"I shouldn't have come. It was selfish of me, but I wanted to see you again. We had so little time, and you've got to admit, we're good together."

"Yes, we are, but sometimes there isn't a way." He waited while Duncan dressed then zipped up his bag. A tear ran down his cheek and he wiped it away before Duncan saw it.

"I'm going to leave. Don't get up. I'll see myself to the door."

Drew didn't expect a final kiss especially as he'd wrapped his arms around himself, knowing his body language screamed *don't touch*. He didn't think he could bear it. Duncan said nothing before he walked out of the bedroom door. What could he say? When the outer door clicked, Drew turned and buried his face in his pillow.

Chapter Eighteen

Duncan stared out of the French doors of the kitchen while hugging his early morning tea — not that he could see much in the dark. Misha sat at his feet. He turned at the noise behind him.

"How bad is it?" he asked, when Lenny came in and stood in front of the Aga, warming his hands.

"There's around six inches so far. As soon as it's light, we'll check on the cattle. At least the forecast was right and we brought them closer yesterday. The Michaels family loved helping with the round-up. Lachie's out feeding the dogs. I noticed Oscar and Grouch asleep in the living room."

"You know cats. Have you heard from your mum?"

"She says she'll try and get here later. It's due to pass over soon, and it's not enough to affect the power." He glanced up at the banging on the doors. Lachie stood shaking snow off his coat.

"Better let him in, I suppose," Lenny said.

Duncan poured them both large mugs of tea from the pot. It had been over a month since his visit to London. He'd spoken to Drew via Skype a few times, but all it did was leave him frustrated. Drew was full of talk about his new clothes line. Sebastian's name had come up a few times, and afterward all Duncan wanted to do was punch something. Instead, the last time they'd spoken, Duncan had allowed his feelings to get out of hand.

"I work with him, Duncan. There's nothing going on. How many times do I have to say it?"

"I bet he wants there to be."

"He might well do, but I've made it clear I'm not

interested."

"Maybe you should be. He's suave and sophisticated, unlike me. He lives in London. You have a lot more in common with him." He'd desperately wanted Drew to disagree, but instead all he'd done was shrug and say he had to leave. They needed to talk face-to-face, not over a machine. Neither of them wanted to let go, knowing the wedding would bring them together, but equally neither of them had any idea what they'd do after that.

He'd been out of sorts ever since, growling at everyone, wanting no one's company except Misha. Blaze hadn't been taken out so often in ages, despite the weather getting colder and the days shorter. The others hadn't asked any questions — even Craig and Jenna had kept their thoughts to themselves.

"I'll get over to the stables," Lenny said.

"I've fed them," Lachie confirmed, "but they need cleaning out. I turned the heaters on, as well, so it'll be warmer when we return. Give me a few minutes to warm up again and I'll be over. Will you be joining us, boss?"

Physical work would take his mind off things. "Yes, don't worry I won't leave it all to you. We need to check the water troughs as well and get a few bales up to the cattle."

Lenny swilled his mug, patted Misha and disappeared out of the doors. Lachie stared at him as if he expected Duncan to say something.

"What?" he asked, glaring back.

"Mum, Craig and Jenna are worried about you."

"I'm fine," he lied.

"You're not. You haven't been fine since you saw Drew in London. You've been even worse for the last few days. You even snapped at Misha yesterday and you never do that. You can talk to me, you know."

"There's nothing to say." He crossed his arms and made to get up. Lachie placed a hand on his arm.

"You might be my boss, but I hope we're friends, as well. You and Drew?"

Duncan pulled his arm away. Yes, it was petulant of him, but he couldn't help himself. He didn't want anyone's pity. He didn't want to talk about his fears out loud. He had no right to stop Drew seeing Sebastian if he wanted. He had no claim over the man, after all. "There isn't a me and Drew. There's no future in it. And when you boil it all down, we had six days together."

"Six days can be enough. Sometimes all it takes is six hours, or even six minutes. Dad says he knew the moment he met Mum, and it's embarrassing what they're like together, even after over twenty-five years. There's a reason Lenny and I couldn't wait to get our own place — the noises they make would frighten the dead."

Duncan couldn't help but grin. "Good for them. At least someone is having fun."

"So is it all over? Have you had a row?"

"There's this other bloke sniffing around. He's everything I'm not, and he's there. It's only a matter of time before Drew sees he needs to get over me. He said as much. I shouldn't have gone there."

Lachie nodded. "I get what you're saying, but what about when he's here at Christmas?"

"I don't know. I'm terrified, either way. After the wedding, there'll be no reason for him to be here again. It's bloody hopeless. We'll probably end up in bed together then have to part again. That's the reality, even without Sebastian."

"I suppose he had to be called something like Sebastian, didn't he?" Lachie's face split into a grin.

"Stop trying to make me laugh. It's not going to work."

Lachie placed his hand on Duncan's arm again. This time Duncan didn't remove it. "Do you love him?"

Did he? How did he tell? "I think so. I don't know. I've never been in love." Duncan threw up his hands, hitting his mug, which fortunately didn't fall off the table. "There's no point to this discussion. I may as well want to fly, and I can't even do that in a plane." He needed to change the conversation. "Enough of me. What about you? Have you thought any more about telling your mum and dad?"

"Not yet, but I told Lenny and, as I suspected, he said he already knew. He'd seen me snogging the biker, but figured I'd tell him when I was ready."

"I assume he was fine with it."

Lachie grinned. "Oh, yeah. He said all the more women for him, and did I know the bartender at the Highlander was gay? He said he'd have a word if I was too shy."

Duncan snorted. "Typical Lenny. One day, Mhairi might give in to his advances, but she did enjoy the bright lights of London, and, with her qualifications, she could get a job anywhere. And talking of your brother, we'd better get out to the stables or he'll be complaining. I'll get my coat and meet you out there."

Misha danced around in the snow as Duncan tramped over toward the light in the stables. He kicked his boots on the wall to remove the snow and slush before entering. It would be a couple of hours until the first hint of light came over the mountains. The snow fall had already lessened. A couple of hours shoveling would warm them all up and the tack needed sorting.

There was always something to do. A vision of Drew lying in his bed in his warm flat popped into his head. The rut he'd fallen into seemed to get deeper and deeper. He couldn't go back to how it had been, but forward planning was just as impossible. He pushed through the stable doors, strolled to Blaze's stable, fed her the carrot he'd brought and stroked her nose as she crunched. Once she'd finished, Blaze nickered and nudged him.

"No more carrots, girl." He patted her neck. Misha barked as she played with the other dogs and Lenny shouted at Lachie to put his back into it. This was his world and he loved it but... Blaze shook her head and he picked up a shovel.

* * * *

Drew sat, staring into space, not concentrating on the task in hand. It had been a hectic few weeks. The design lines he'd come up with had been finalized and he and Joy had spent weeks hammering things out with the team from Fairfords.

"You're not used to working with anyone above a size six to eight," Joy said impatiently.

"I know, but I want to. It's more of a challenge."

"Well, real women, like me, have curves, and Fairfords want this line to cover sizes ten to twenty-four. Take the woman over there."

Drew glanced over at the dark-haired woman now talking to the advertising team.

"Some designers would have apoplexy if they had to dress her. Actors who aren't a small size have been turned down by designers, but you've got to admit, she's beautiful. She has such a perfect hour-glass figure she shouldn't have to hide in big clothes. Women have thighs and hips and arses and bingo wings. At least your designs give women a chance to show off, as well as feel comfortable. That's why the every label works — every woman, every day and every night. I hope they pick her. She'd be stunning in the colors we've chosen. I'm going to have a word with Sebastian."

Drew yawned. Insomnia had been his constant friend recently and allowed him to get more work done. Ben and Jonty had given up trying to get him to go out and he couldn't bear being around their touchy-feely happiness as they planned their wedding. The Skype conversations with Duncan had been awkward, to say the least. And he still had no idea what the hell he would do when faced with seeing Duncan in person at Christmas. The chat he'd had with Jenna the day before hadn't helped.

'He's like a grizzly bear. He even barked at Misha. Carrie says he's not eating and Craig's worried about him.'

'What d'you want me to do?' Drew felt got at. It was hardly his fault. *'He came here and ended my attempt to get over him. I was even thinking of dating someone else, someone handsome and*

successful, who still wants me to have dinner with him, I should point out.'

'But you said no.'

'Of course, I said no. I'm still hung up on this bloody annoying Scottish cowboy, and I don't know how to change.'

'If you love him…'

'For fuck's sake, Jenna. Just because you're all loved up with Craig, it doesn't mean you can bandy that word around. Half of me hopes the snow is so bad at Christmas I can't get there.'

'Don't you dare. You are going to be at my wedding come hell, high water or six-foot snow drifts, but you need to think about what you want. You deserve to be happy, but so does he. You have to decide what matters the most.'

But it has to be me. Duncan can't leave his home. I'm the one who has to give. He glanced over to where Joy was speaking to Sebastian. When the woman broke into a smile, Drew guessed Sebastian had agreed with Joy. His partner strolled back to him.

"Looks like she's happy," he said, nodding toward the woman with the hour-glass figure.

"She is. She's a single mother. Her bastard of a husband left her for a younger and thinner model last year, and a friend told her to try for this."

"Good for her."

Joy's gaze followed the woman as she practically skipped out of the room while another group of five entered from the other side. Could he give this up now he was on the brink of getting more notice? Could he juggle both his lives? They kept saying how the world was getting smaller, and how many chances did life give you that you could afford to throw them away? Was so little time enough to base a life-changing decision on? Maybe Christmas would sort out his feelings. He idly sketched another corset for his men's range of leather and lace.

"Hmm, pretty and sexy," Joy said, looking over his arm as he drew. "Have you warned Jenna she'll need to practice with her corset before the wedding?"

"I sent her up an example yesterday so she'll have a few weeks to get used to wearing it. The one built into her dress isn't as restrictive, and I'll be there to lace her in, after all. This is one of the men's range I'm thinking of adding to my *Hold With Style* collection. I need to do more research, though. Ben and Jonty have promised to try some on for me as long as I let them take me out. Jonty wants to wear one as a waistcoat for their wedding. At this rate, I'm going to become a wedding clothes designer by accident."

"I went to a young designers show at the weekend. There were some amazing corsets on display there with one worn by a male model. All a bit out there as you'd expect, but this guy—the designer—shows real promise. His fabric choice was incredible. I got his name when he explained he wanted to find a mentor in the industry. I think he'd be a great fit for us and get us connections with the university. Should I contact him?"

Drew pondered if he could be bothered to mentor, but he'd been lucky at university and he could do with some positive karma. "Why not. What's his name?"

Joy dug in her bag and pulled out a piece of paper. "Idris Fox—he's Welsh. I'll give him a ring later and set up a meeting."

A loud cough from the other side of the room diverted them. Sebastian stared and nodded at the group.

"I guess they're the size sixteen to eighteen models," Joy said. "Maybe we should pay more attention."

Drew rose and ambled over to Sebastian, taking the seat next to him. "Sorry, Joy has a student who needs a mentor."

"Sounds like a good idea. All work and no play makes Drew a dull and exhausted boy."

Drew could almost feel the caress of those eyes as Sebastian swept his gaze down his entire body. Although he'd never pressurized him, Sebastian hadn't hidden his interest, either. He turned back to consider the female models without further comment.

"We're going to get them in your prototypes now and ask

them to model and walk. I would appreciate your input—and Joy's."

Drew beckoned Joy over.

"Um, would you like to grab dinner after this to celebrate—no strings or expectations?" Sebastian said.

Drew thought for a moment before replying. He did like Sebastian and they got on. They also had a lot to talk about. "Sounds good," he said before concentrating once more on the woman walking down the catwalk and noting that the top she wore could use more shaping at the bust before it flowed out over the hips.

Chapter Nineteen

Drew threw himself onto Ben and Jonty's sofa and buried his head in his hands. "I can't believe I did that."

His friends sat with side of him on the leather monstrosity, as he called it. Ben had hinted it gave them a touch of leather when…and was easy to clean. He'd stopped him right there.

Jonty handed him a large brandy. "To be fair, you haven't told us what you did. And as it's after midnight, and you were on a date with Sebastian, you have to admit *that* could be anything."

Ben rubbed his hands together then put one arm around Drew's shoulder. "Come on, tell Uncles Ben and Jonty. You know we should have one of those names — you know like Sterek, or Janto, or Destiel."

"We'd be Jen or Bonty. I think not." Jonty put his hand on Drew's thigh. "Come on, spill the beans. Did you sleep with him? Or did he have an odd-shaped penis? Or did he want to do something kinky? I have to say he looks the sort with those dark, brooding eyes."

Drew sat up and swallowed the brandy in one go, letting the warmth roll down his throat until it hit his stomach. "If the pair of you'd shut up for a minute, I'd tell you."

Both men made locking signs on their mouths and sat in silence.

Drew sighed, letting the air out of his body as he slumped. "I didn't sleep with him."

"Well, that's good, isn't it?"

Drew frowned at Ben. "We went back to his place. I had a couple of drinks. I was nervous. We made out a bit on the sofa. He kissed me and I let him."

"Was he any good?"

"For fuck's sake, Jonty, let the man speak. He didn't pressure you into anything, did he?"

"Do I look like some naïve teenager? I may not be huge, but I can handle myself. I needed to try someone new, to see, you know, but it was awful."

"Did he have BO? Or was it bad breath? I haven't noticed myself. I had a boyfriend years ago—awful." Now it was Jonty's turn to stare at Ben.

"Way before we met, hon," Ben assured him.

"Can I continue?" Drew asked.

"Sorry. Not a word."

"I put my hand down his pants and pulled out his dick."

"I told you. He did have a weird cock."

Drew jumped up. "For fuck's sake. It was perfectly ordinary, but I froze. I couldn't do anything. I got up and ran out of the place just leaving him there."

Jonty gasped and put his hand to his mouth. "With his cock hanging in the wind? Now that's cruel."

"What? Should I have just given him a hand job then politely left?" Drew shrugged.

"Duncan?" Ben questioned.

"Of course, it's bloody Duncan. Last time we spoke ended badly, so I thought… And I have to see him in a few weeks. I am so fucked."

"Or not," Jonty said, turning a chuckle into a cough.

"Not helpful," Ben said, glaring at this partner.

"I can't go forward and I can't go back. I'm stuck in this limbo. The clothes line has gone into production ready to be in the shops next summer for the autumn collections. I've worked so hard and got everything done in record time. All the models have been chosen. They've done focus groups and the line has gone down well with all sorts of women. My men's lingerie line has outsold any of my predictions and I've employed more seamstresses in the Manchester factory." He paused for a moment.

"What?" Jonty asked.

"I have something to ask you both. I've had this idea. How would you feel about coming in with me? You know, forming a company. We'd make a good team. Our skills complement one another's, and Joy loves you. I think we could make it work for all of us." He didn't mention the other part of his idea.

"I don't know. We'd need to talk about everything." Ben nudged Jonty. "What d'you think?"

"You should call him," Jonty said.

"Duncan?" Drew replied, confused.

"No, Sebastian. Or at least text him an apology."

For a moment, he'd forgotten. "D'you think?" Drew wasn't sure.

"Just say sorry. You did tell him about Duncan, didn't you?"

"Sort of."

"Oh, Drew. Come on, sit down. I'll make us all cocoa." Ben rose and left him with Jonty.

"You are so lucky," Drew said, taking his place once more next to his friend.

"Yep. Ben is the best thing that ever happened to me."

"Should I text him?"

"Couldn't hurt."

Drew pulled out his phone.

I'm sorry. It's not you. I'm still hung up on someone else. I shouldn't have. I'm sorry. Can we talk?

"There. Not perfect, but something. If I was him, I wouldn't answer."

"About the offer to work with you? Did you mean it?"

"Sure. We'd complement each other. Me the designer, Joy the fabrics expert, you the pattern cutter, and Ben the buyer and finance man. We'd make an awesome team."

"Would we work on everything — all your lines?"

"We'd need to talk, but, yes, ideally. I've been thinking

about it for a while now."

Ben came in from the kitchen and placed the mugs on the table in front of them. "I heard what you said and I'm in. I love my job, but there are so many restrictions, and I have no say in anything. I'd have to move to get a more senior position. This is so exciting."

"There would be a lot to discuss," Drew warned. "It would all have to be done legally."

"Of course. We all need to be protected. You know, Austin, my brother is a business lawyer. He'd help us work things out," Jonty said.

Drew held up his mug. He pushed away his worries. Ben and Jonty lifted their cocoas and they clashed them together.

"To us," Drew said.

"To us." Maybe there was some light at the end of the tunnel after all.

* * * *

He was early. Sebastian hadn't responded to his text, but then he didn't deserve a response. Drew tapped his toes and kept his head down over his phone, hoping no one would engage him in conversation. When the door opened, he looked up automatically and his gaze met Sebastian's. If Drew hoped to see some sign of forgiveness in the other man's face, he was disappointed. Instead, he poured himself a coffee and took a seat as far away as possible. Drew tapped out the message on his phone.

Can we talk after this – please?

Sebastian checked his phone.

My office

Drew glanced at him and nodded.

The meeting seemed to last forever as they decided with

the firm's in-house team which images they intended to use for the ad campaign. Drew checked every photograph, pleased to see how each piece worked with the models. While the team talked slogans and scripts, his mind drifted elsewhere, so when Melanie Townsend, the women's clothing chief, called an end, he was jerked out of his own head back into the room. Sebastian hurtled out of the meeting.

"The clothes are gorgeous," Melanie said, before he had chance to move. "We may need some changes before everything is finalized, but we're confident we've picked the right women. Now, we need a star to bring them all together, and we've a few ideas, people we've worked with before."

"That's good. I like how the women are different ages as well as sizes. It's been a great experience trying to produce a line which allows as many women as possible to choose how they dress and what makes them happy. I look forward to producing further collections. Now, if you don't mind, I'm afraid I must go. I've a meeting with Sebastian."

"He was the person who first sung your praises and pushed for you. I've always respected his views."

Drew's stomach lurched and not in a good way. He mumbled a "me, too" and fled from the room to the gents'. He removed his glasses and rubbed his tired eyes, then stared at his blurry reflection in the mirror and chided himself for being a coward, but he didn't want to do this.

"Grow up. You're heading for thirty, not thirteen. Go and apologize."

Minutes later, he knocked on Sebastian's door. At the shout of "come in," he swallowed hard and entered. Sebastian kept his eyes on the computer screen for a few minutes while Drew waited, not sitting down as he usually would have, knowing this was Sebastian's way of asserting himself. Drew clasped his hands behind his back.

"Sorry, I had to finish before I forgot what I wanted to say. Sit down."

Drew took the seat, which allowed the desk to separate them. Had Sebastian written his thoughts down as some sort of prompt?

"Can I say how —?"

Sebastian raised his hands to stop him and Drew halted immediately. "I don't need an apology. I'm a grown-up, Drew. You'd been honest and told me about this other man, and I'm guessing he's the reason you left me high and dry."

Drew nodded and waited for Sebastian to continue.

"I think maybe you and I shouldn't see each other socially. I don't want to be your way of moving on. I'm worth more, but I did know what I was getting into. I can't deny liking you and wanting to get to know you better, but I'm not sure you're ever going to be over this guy."

Sebastian's face suggested it was time for Drew to speak. He wiped his sweating palms on his trousers then clasped them together on the desk. "What I did was wrong. And you're right. I used you and you didn't deserve that. In other circumstances, things might have been different."

"Please don't try and reassure me by telling me I'm a nice man and there's someone out there for me."

Drew attempted a smile. "I wouldn't dare. I'm not a complete idiot. If it's any consolation, my friends Ben and Jonty were appalled, and I had the hangover from hell the next day."

Sebastian frowned — Drew had forgotten he worked with Ben — but said nothing about his confession. He leaned forward.

"So, what about what's his name?"

"Duncan? I'm not sure. I'm due to see him at my sister's wedding in a few weeks. She's marrying his best friend and Duncan is best man. I did the dresses for her and the bridesmaids. We haven't had much time together —"

"Sometimes you don't need time." Drew was grateful Sebastian had interrupted his babbling. "Anyway, what does he do up there in the Highlands?"

Grateful to be on firm ground, Drew continued, "He owns

and runs a ranch, you know like the one in *City Slickers*. Tourists stay there and learn cowboy skills and he has cattle and other animals. He inherited a run-down estate and turned it into a profitable organization."

Sebastian nodded then winked as he tipped his head to one side. "Does he wear a Stetson?"

"He does." Heat rushed into Drew's cheeks. "He has chaps, too, but I haven't seen him wear them yet."

"You know the world is a smaller place. How long does it take to fly up there?"

"Longer in the airport than on the plane," Drew agreed. "I've an idea how I can."

Sebastian glanced at his watch. "Let's get lunch. There's a great place across the road. You can tell me all about it."

Drew hoped that someone waited out there for this man. "Sounds good. I could do with some carbs."

Sebastian looked him up and down. "Yeah, you could. I usually like more meat on my men. Did I mention the manager has been giving me the eye?"

Drew laughed as he followed Sebastian out of the door, happy that, even if he'd lost a lover, he might have gained a friend.

Chapter Twenty

Drew stamped his feet on the mat. The recent snow had melted, leaving the ground slushy. Immediately, he was enclosed in his mother's arms while his father stood behind, waiting.

"You're looking thin. Have you been eating properly? Rory, put the kettle on and get the fruit cake I made."

Drew pulled back. "You brought cake?"

"Of course I brought cake. One has no marzipan, just as you like it, and the other is iced as Jenna likes it. I wasn't coming up here without my Christmas cakes. The mince pies are already in the chest freezer at the big house. Duncan is such a nice man. Your father brought a few birds from the estate, as well, and there's my venison sausage rolls and pigs in blankets."

"You know your mother, son. No one cooks anything as well as she does."

Drew glanced around the cabin. He hadn't been in one when he came in the summer. "It's nicer than I expected," he said.

"Duncan says each one is individual. There are two bedrooms here, both en-suite. Normally, I'd say you can stay with us, but Jenna is staying here before the wedding. The dress you made is beautiful." She reached over and cupped his cheek. "I have such talented children. You know I'm proud of you both, don't you?"

Drew swallowed, pushing down the lump in his throat. "We know how lucky we are."

"So, you'll be fine up at the big house?"

"I have stayed there before, Mum."

She rubbed his chin. "You could do with a shave."

Drew wasn't going to say he'd left his stubble deliberately after Duncan had shared how much he loved to feel the scratchiness against his skin.

"Where's your suitcase, not to mention your sister?"

"It's in Jenna's trunk and she's checking on one of the horses. Beulah stumbled in the poor conditions and has developed a limp. She'll be over when she's finished."

"Thank goodness it's only a fetlock and she hasn't had to put her hand up some poor animal."

"Rory, there's no need to be coarse."

"I saw her deliver a breech calf in the summer. She was awesome," Drew replied grinning. His mother shook her head and tutted.

His dad pulled him into a hug. "Any chance of some tea now, love?" he asked, over Drew's shoulder.

Drew sat on the sofa while his parents settled into the two armchairs. The kitchen, dining and living area were all one with a high-beamed ceiling and tartan fabrics everywhere. The wood burner glowed orange and he reached to warm his hands.

The door opened. Jenna entered, removed her thick coat and took the seat next to him. "Tea. Yes, please. And cake."

"This is my cake," Drew said, pushing back his glasses as they fell down his nose. He really did need a new pair.

"Mum, tell him to let me have some cake."

"But hers has got stuff on it."

His mother sighed. "One slice won't be a problem. And pouting isn't a good look on you."

"All right, then. But just the one slice. How's Duncan and the horse?" He hadn't seen him yet.

"The horse will be fine with appropriate rest and liberal application of liniment."

"I wondered what the smell was. I didn't like to mention anything in case it was a new perfume Craig liked." The dig in his ribs caught him off-guard and he yelped.

"Remind me how old you two are again," his mother said.

Jenna grinned. "And Duncan is Duncan, nice, kind, handsome. He wanted you to know your room is ready and Craig will be staying at the house, as well. The forecast is mixed, but most of the guests are here already. Granny says you'd better get over and see her and Great Auntie May."

Their grandmother had a cottage on the estate she'd been given by the Laird. Like his parents, his grandparents had lived on the estate all their lives.

"What about Uncle Scott?"

"He rang. The weather's bad, so he's decided not to come. He promises he and Alain will be over in the New Year. But Craig's parents and grandparents are here and Craig's hoping his brother, Cormac, will get here in time." She hugged herself. "I can't believe it's my wedding the day after tomorrow. Christmas Eve. I'll wake up on Christmas Day a married woman."

"Poor Craig. Still, after so many years, he knows what he's getting."

"I can uninvite you, you know. I've got the dresses already." They had been delivered by special courier days before Drew had flown up. Jenna had picked him up in Inverness.

"Yes, Mum said, but you need me to fit them for any last-minute adjustments. Right," he said, after scoffing the last bit of cake. "I'll be off to see Granny and Auntie May, then I'm up to the house."

"We'll be over later. Carrie has made her beef stew and dumplings for us all after the rehearsal."

Drew swallowed hard. He'd forgotten. "I'm not needed, am I?" Three pairs of eyes glared at him.

"If I've got to be there, son, so have you."

"Yes, Dad." Maybe he could get some time alone with Duncan before the rehearsal if Craig made himself scarce, but then Carrie would be there and Lachie and Lenny most likely. "I'll get Granny and May's presents out of the boot."

"I dropped your case at the house. Duncan said he'd put it in your room, the one opposite his like last time. Craig is next door to you."

They stood. "I'll come and open the car to get the parcels."

Once outside, Jenna clicked and the boot opened. "I told Duncan you wanted to talk to him."

"You didn't tell him anything, did you?"

"Of course not, but, Drew, this is huge. You are sure, aren't you?"

"I don't think I've ever been more sure of anything in my life."

She hugged him. "I'm so happy for you and him. He's been moping around and biting everyone's heads off."

"All I've got to do is get him alone and ask him. He might not want me here."

"As if. Granny is over there." Jenna pointed at the next cabin slightly nearer the house. "Give them both a kiss from me and tell them I'll see them tonight. I've got to get back for teatime surgery, then I'll be over with Mhairi and Sandy."

Jenna jumped in the Land Rover and waved as she drove up the narrow track to the house. He shivered and hurried the hundred yards to the next cabin.

His granny was making tea when he arrived, knocked and entered. She placed the teapot on the table. Drew noted it was the one she had at home. No other teapot poured like hers did. His Auntie May also sat at the table. Now in their eighties, both women had constitutions of the proverbial ox, except for their arthritis.

"There you are, bonny lad." His granny hugged him to her ample bosom and told him to sit. "My, you're pale. Isn't he pale, May? You need building up. Not enough good air and food down there. Those bloody fancy restaurants don't serve real meals."

He kissed his aunty. "I'm fine, Granny." They had the same conversation every time. "I can't stay. I'm due at the big house, but I'll see you later for the rehearsal and dinner afterward. I've just had tea and cake with Mum and Dad."

She took one step back and stared at him. "There's something about you that's different. I can't put my finger on it, but I will."

"Oh, Granny. You and your hunches." Sometimes her unerring accuracy scared them all. He'd need to be careful around Duncan.

"The young man in the house seems a good sort – solid and dependable. He reminds me of your grandfather with his dark hair and those dark eyes. I believe you met him in the summer and he visited London with Jenna."

He fought the blush and failed. His granny, still as sharp as a tack, missed nothing.

"Yes, we did, Granny, and, yes, he is handsome."

"You'd better get off and see him, then, and not waste time with us old ones."

Drew grinned at her and not for the first time marveled at her seemingly psychic powers. "I will. Jenna said she or Craig will come and pick you up later. The ground's slushy after the recent snow and rain."

Once out of the door, he took a big breath to calm his nerves and tramped the half a mile to the house. Dark clouds hung over the tops of the mountains, obscuring the weak sun and hastening the dark. The day before had been the shortest day, after all. At least, from now the days would get longer, but here, in winter, it didn't feel like the light ever fully got going some days.

His suitcase stood at the bottom of the stairs when Drew pushed through the door. Gorgeous smells of food emanated from the kitchen and he followed the scent.

"He's over in the stables," Carrie said. "He's missed you." Typical Carrie – straight to the point.

"And I've missed him. Are Lachie and Lenny there, too?"

"They're around, but I told them to make themselves scarce when you came. They're setting up in the indoor arena, putting boards down for dancing. Tomorrow, we're all going to be busy. I'm hoping the girls can get over to help. It's supposed to be cold and frosty, but no snow until New Year, so fingers crossed. I hope those heaters work. Still, as long as we get the registrar here, we're fine. Duncan said he'd get the sleigh out if needed."

"I'd better get myself over there then."

He sidled through the door to the stable block and ambled to Blaze's stall. "Hello? Duncan?"

Nothing. Maybe he was over at the arena, as well. Once outside, he jogged past an outbuilding.

"Drew? In here." He opened the door to find Duncan wiping down the most magnificent sleigh. Misha lay at his feet. His heart did a fandango and his stomach performed somersaults which would have won a gold medal in any gymnastics competition. He stood, fixed to the spot, staring at the man dressed in jeans, cable-knit jumper and padded jacket. Neither of them moved until finally Duncan closed the distance between them, wrapped his arms around him and kissed him like there was no tomorrow.

Drew let himself melt into both the kiss and Duncan's arms. If he'd have lifted him up, bent him over the sleigh and taken him right there, Drew wouldn't have objected. He wasn't sure if the kiss or the cold made him shiver right down to his toes. They changed angles and met once more, open-mouthed. Drew pushed his hands under Duncan's coat, feeling his back, pulling himself closer, until, needing air, they pulled apart.

"I'm sorry," Duncan gasped between breaths. "I couldn't help myself. I shouldn't have."

Drew placed a finger on his lips. "I'm not complaining, and I didn't fight you off."

Duncan allowed himself a slight smile. "No, you didn't, but I wasn't sure where we stood."

Drew glanced around. "In an outbuilding, next to a Christmassy-looking sleigh."

"Don't make fun of me, Drew."

He stared into Duncan's worried but gloriously handsome face. "I'm not." He clasped Duncan's hand. "Can we go back to the house? I need to unpack, and I've something to tell you."

"All right." Duncan's voice was barely a whisper, but he didn't let go of Drew's hand as he led him across the yard and through the front door. Duncan put Misha in the front room by the fire, telling her to sleep, then hurried up the stairs. When the bedroom door closed behind them, Drew kissed Duncan. And, as much as he'd have loved to have both of them stripped naked immediately, he wanted to talk first. He sat on the bed and patted it for Duncan to join him.

"I'm glad you didn't say we need to talk," Duncan said. "Every time I've heard those words in a film, it's not good news."

Drew took a deep breath. "I get we've only known each other —"

"Five months is quite long," Duncan interrupted.

"Yes, but we've only —"

"Been together for days."

"And on Skype."

"Yes, all right. Could I get a few words in?"

"Sorry. I'm nervous," Duncan said.

How could a man with those shoulders and thighs manage to make himself appear small? Drew had no idea, but Duncan held himself waiting, not even breathing, with his hands clasped in his lap. Still, his leg shook as he tapped his toe, waiting for Drew to speak.

Drew turned to face Duncan and laid his hand on his knee.

"If you had the choice, would you like me to live here?"

Little lines creased between Duncan's eyebrows and on his forehead. "I don't understand. Is this some sort of trick question?"

Drew pried Duncan's fingers apart and took Duncan's hand in his. "I mean, would you like me to move from London to here? It's quick, I grant you, despite the five months, and I couldn't do it straight away as there's a lot to work out first, but I think we have something here, and I don't want to be without you." He hadn't mentioned love, but being with Duncan again had left him in no doubt that love was in the room with them, surrounding them.

Duncan shook his head vigorously, and Drew's heart sank.

"You don't want me—?"

"No. I mean yes. I'm sorry I'm sounding like an idiot. I wasn't saying no."

"But you shook your head," Drew protested.

"I wasn't sure I'd heard right. Did you just say you'd leave London and come up here to live? With me? You'd do that? You'd come up here to the back end of nowhere? What about your job and the clothing company? How?"

"I'm not saying it's going to be simple, but I've asked Ben and Jonty to join with me and Joy to form a company. They'll help with the business side, as well as design. Jonty's always been interested in developing his skills. He can tell a person's size by looking at them and has a great eye. Ben will look after the finance and organization, liaising with Fairfords when I'm not there, leaving me to do the design work. With the Internet and easy access by plane, I can be down there in a couple of hours when needed. The clothes business will be busier at certain times of year when we're designing for the seasons, and I'll need to spend more time away then. There'll still be one-off designs for certain clients, and my men's lingerie business, but I have a great production manager in Manchester where they sew the garments, and again, I can get there quickly enough. I'll need to set up a distribution warehouse around here."

"You could operate from the ranch. There's a farmer in Yorkshire who did exactly the same to diversify. Everything is done on the Internet, and we have the space. You could get couriers to pick up from here, or take parcels to Fort William. Getting jobs locally isn't always easy. I'm sure some of Carrie's girls would be interested, and I've more outbuildings which could be adapted. I'm thinking of building a couple more cabins for next season, too. Diversification is what it's all about in farming these days. And I've been offered four more alpacas."

Drew allowed himself a small smile. "We could do this," he said.

"Are you sure, though? As you said, we haven't had much time together, and it's a huge sacrifice to make. Everything could go belly-up. There's not much to do around here, and you can't get coffee on every corner."

"I can buy a coffee maker," Drew said. "And I don't need the bright lights. I'll miss Joy and Ben and Jonty, but there are compensations. After all, I'll get to sleep with you every night. We could have a trial run for a while before I consider moving the business to see how it goes. Sometimes the stars align." They both burst out laughing. "Don't ever tell Jenna I said that. I'll never hear the end of it."

"Do they know? Jenna, or your parents?" Duncan gazed at him.

"Jenna does, but not my parents." Drew gazed back. "Do you know there are little green flecks in your eyes?"

He pushed Duncan onto the bed and climbed on top of him, then ran his hand under the chunky jumper, touching skin. His cock filled out in anticipation. He moved with intent, rubbing their groins together, not caring they were both still fully dressed.

"Kiss me," Duncan said. His voice hit every button Drew possessed as he obeyed Duncan's command and leaned forward open-mouthed, pushing open Duncan's mouth with his tongue as Duncan wrapped his arms around Drew's back and held him in place while making the most delicious groaning noises.

They stayed, rutting against each other, kissing and nipping. Somehow Duncan managed to get his hands into the back of Drew's jeans and briefs, touching his arse and raking his nails on his flesh. Drew bucked and pressed down again, feeling his orgasm gathering and not caring if he came in his pants, even if it would spoil the lace.

"Don't stop," Duncan moaned.

"I've no intention of stopping." They rubbed against each other like well-oiled machines, perfectly aligned.

Duncan lifted his chin and threw his head back. "Oh, yeah. That's it." Drew didn't hear the rest of the words as his orgasm exploded into the confined space and heat flooded his clothes. Both men lay panting until Drew kissed Duncan's nose then pushed back his glasses, which had been in danger of falling off.

"Wow," he said. "I can't remember the last time I came fully dressed." Drew pulled at his jeans. "But can I suggest we get out of these clothes and into the shower?"

"Sounds like a plan."

They sat up and stripped off their clothes. Now naked, Duncan opened the door and dashed for the bathroom only to see Craig's face as he reached the top of the stairs.

"Shit. You could have warned me."

"Sorry," Duncan said, pulling Drew after him. "The bathroom is busy."

Laughing, Drew let himself be pulled through the door and they fell against it, holding their sides.

"You know I can never unsee that, don't you?" Craig shouted through the door. "I'm going to need a stiff drink."

Duncan reached down and took hold of Drew's semi-hard cock. "Looks like he's not the only one needing something stiff."

Duncan kissed Drew's forehead. "Let's get in the shower. I'm bloody freezing."

"When we first met, Jenna told me I had to be good around you, as you didn't swear," Drew said, as the hot water cascaded over their bodies.

"You have totally corrupted me, Drew Sinclair."

Drew reached down and cupped Duncan's balls. "If you ask nicely, maybe I can corrupt you a whole lot more."

Chapter Twenty-One

The next morning, a hammering on the door woke them from their slumbers. Drew untangled his legs, allowing Duncan to move.

"Hang on," Duncan shouted. He winced. "I think I might walk a little strangely."

"I'm surprised Craig didn't hear you as I pounded that rather gorgeous arse of yours."

"Shush," Duncan said, feeling the heat rush into his face.

"Can I come in? Are you decent?"

Duncan covered over the damp patch they'd made and he'd ended up sleeping in some time in the early hours of the morning. How they'd survived not getting caught taking sneaky kisses the night before, Duncan wasn't sure. They'd managed a brief fumble in the straw as a preamble with the excuse of checking on the animals at one point and ended up pulling out bits, hoping no one would notice them, focused as they were on the bride and groom.

Duncan pulled on some briefs, let his friend in then returned to sit on the bed. Misha darted in behind Craig but sat, waiting to be fussed. To his credit, Craig didn't bat an eyelid seeing Drew bare-chested sitting up leaning against the headboard. Duncan scratched Misha's ears absentmindedly.

"Thank goodness," Craig said, plonking himself down on the ottoman at the end of the bed. "It's madness down there. My mum, your mum, and Carrie are organizing all the food for tomorrow and supervising the girls and Lenny and Lachie as they set up everything over in the arena. The tables and chairs they hired arrived with enough bunting to sink a ship as well as the extra heaters. The flowers have just been delivered. Lenny is sorting the music while Lachie gets the local lads to help with the regular work and the horses. Your mum was all for coming up here and getting you out of bed, but I said I would."

"Thanks," Drew replied. He breathed a sigh of relief.

"So, is this a proper thing now — you two?"

Duncan turned toward Drew. "We've decided to give it a go. To see if we can do this. Drew's going to move up here and test things."

"I don't know if you're being incredibly brave or amazingly stupid," Craig said. "But I'm glad for you. It won't take the others long, you know. Carrie and the boys are curious after the visit to London. Jenna told them you'd been so tight-lipped."

"I needed to be sure," Drew said. "There's still a lot to work out, but we want to try."

Duncan leaned over and kissed Drew as if it was the most natural thing in the world. "Will you be my date for the wedding?" he asked.

"I'd love to, but I'd better speak to Mum, Dad and Granny and Aunty May first. For everyone else, we can simply dance together."

Craig laughed. "Carrie's already told me to get out from under her feet. It seems all I need to do is make sure I'm dressed tomorrow and stand in the right place. I'd better get myself out of here. I've surgery for a few hours and some home visits. I'll be glad to get out of the madness."

Drew grinned. "'Twas ever so. We'd better get dressed. I'll see Mum first."

Duncan grabbed the pair of jeans he'd carelessly thrown over a chair the night before. "And I'd better check on the animals. Christmas or weddings, the animals get fed. I need to check the water troughs aren't frozen and take up some extra feed to the cattle. I'll meet you back here at half past eleven, Drew. That should give you time."

* * * *

Drew entered the kitchen and tapped his mum on the shoulder. Duncan and Craig had already left, giving the impression he and Duncan had risen from their beds separately. "Can we talk?" he said.

His mother cupped his cheek. "Are you all right. darling?" She searched his face.

"I'm good, Mum, if starving."

"Give me five minutes and I'll be with you. I'll bring coffee and toast through to the front room. Ned, is that everything now?"

The harried-looking landlord nodded. "All we'll need to do is heat some food tomorrow and everything will be right. I'll be getting off now. I've a pub to open."

Drew didn't hang around, either. There were already far too many bodies in the space, as well as piles of food, surely more than enough to feed the thirty or so guests due to be there.

Oscar and Grouch had already taken the sofa, so Drew sat in one of the armchairs and warmed himself next to the fire. Oscar jumped from his position and straight up onto Drew's lap.

"Good boy." Smoothing the cat's luxurious coat gave him something to do with his hands. A few minutes later, his mother came in carrying a tray with a cafetière, mugs and a rack of toast. His mouth watered at the smell. Automatically, she poured him a coffee and buttered a slice of toast.

"Now, what is it you need to say?" she asked, before biting into the toast and moaning as trickles of melting butter escaped her mouth.

"You know when I was here in the summer to do the dresses?"

"Yes, of course, I do." She glanced at her watch. Drew pushed away his annoyance and bit back any snide comment about keeping her from her tasks. He decided to cut to the chase.

"I met Duncan then and we got together, but we didn't think there was any future in it. Then he came to London, and we talked over Skype, and well, I've decided to leave London and come and live up here most of the time with him. We realize we haven't known each other for long, but we want to try. If it doesn't work out…" He stopped, conscious that his mother was still chewing her toast and not saying anything. "Mum?" he questioned.

"Yes, Drew?"

"Did you hear what I said?"

"Of course, I did. I'm not deaf. You and Duncan are together and you're going to move up here."

"And?"

"And what? You're a grown man. I'm sure you've worked out all the business connotations and I like Duncan. I'm surprised he's your type, or you his, but attraction is a strange thing, as is love. I trust you to make the right choices for yourself and I want you to be happy. Does Duncan make you happy?"

Drew sat confused and uncertain how to reply, but when he thought about it, his mother's reaction was typical. When he'd announced his intention to study design, and relocate to London, she hadn't queried his decision. When he'd announced he was gay, she'd simply said she'd always known. She didn't pry into his life or criticize his choices, and she'd never said *I told you so*, either. Sometimes her seeming lack of interest had annoyed him, but she'd always said people could only learn from their own mistakes. Even if she thought this was a disastrous decision, she wouldn't say.

"So you're all right with this?"

"Darling, I'm thrilled and I'm pleased you told me. Does Jenna know?"

"Yes."

She smiled. "That's good. I've always been proud of the way you two support each other and I'm proud of you both. I should warn you your dad will think you've lost the plot, giving up the life you said you always wanted for a cowboy who lives in the Highlands of Scotland. You've got to admit, it's a touch ironic. Would you like me to tell him?"

Drew shrugged. "I should tell him myself and Granny."

"No need, at least with your granny. She may be an old lady, but there's nothing wrong with her gaydar, or whatever you want to call it. I'll bet any money she already knows. It used to scare me when I was younger, but now I take it for granted."

Drew furrowed his brow as his mother rolled her eyes. "She did say I looked different yesterday."

"There. This time, I will say I told you so. Your granny has an instinct for these things. She knew about your father and me. She told me the day I met him I'd marry him, and I laughed like a drain. I'd been determined I was going to the bright lights of Glasgow to work in some fancy restaurant. But she was right, and I found new dreams. Last night, she whispered in my ear you two were an item. She thinks Duncan is handsome, by the way. Her exact words were 'he fills a pair of jeans in a pleasant way', but the idea of a long-distance relationship, or you ending up hurt, worried her. She'll be thrilled to hear you have plans. She's always wanted you to find the right man, and she says he's the right one for you, just as Craig was the right man for Jenna, even if it did take them ages to get around to the wedding. Oh, and you might want to close your mouth, darling. You don't want the wind to change and you stay that way."

The chuckle welled up in him until he couldn't prevent it emerging. He snorted then laughed before crossing the room and hugging his mother tightly. She patted his back.

"Now I'll be able to visit both my children at the same time." She glanced at the clock on the mantel. "I'd better get moving. We've lots to do. Why your sister had to pick Christmas Eve to get married, I don't know. If you see Duncan before this afternoon, get him to come over to cabin four. Carrie, Joanna and I are decorating the place for tomorrow night, but don't tell Jenna or Craig. She's working today, then coming over here to stay tonight while Craig is staying with you two."

"Craig's gone off to work and I'm not sure when he'll be back as he's got visits to do. I think he wants to stay out of the way, anyway. Duncan's out with Lachie and Lenny checking on the animals. I'd better go and speak to Dad."

"Such handsome boys those two and a credit to their parents, but so different in personality," his mother said brushing a few crumbs from her clothes. She glanced down. "Damn, that'll need the cleaner run over it now."

"Morag, we could do with a hand when you're ready." Drew recognized Carrie's harassed-sounding voice.

His mother stood. "I'd better get going. Food doesn't sort itself, I suppose. You go off and find your man and leave your father and granny to me."

"If you're sure." Drew kissed her and sat back into the armchair sipping his coffee, trying not to worry about the prospect of turning his life upside down.

* * * *

"I might have guessed I'd find you here." Drew wrapped his arms around Duncan as he combed Blaze's withers and mane.

"Everywhere else is madness," Duncan confirmed. "My indoor arena is now a wedding venue with tables and chairs and decorations all over the place. Lenny and Lachie have taken the feed up to the Highland Cows and checked on the others. They have the other lads shoveling compost. Carrie, your mum and company have set up flowers, and were sorting enough food to feed an army when I passed through the kitchen. I'm beginning to have second thoughts about hosting weddings."

The words 'not even ours' sprang unexpectedly into Drew's mind, but he didn't say them out loud. The very thought shocked the hell out of him.

"I told Mum," he said, perching on a bale of hay.

Duncan spun round. "About us?"

"Yep. It's official now."

"What about your dad?"

"I said I'd tell him and Granny, but Mum said she'd do it and that Granny's sixth sense had told her, anyway. Maybe we weren't as discreet as we thought last night at the rehearsal dinner."

"And your mum? She's all right with this? She didn't say you'd be mad to leave London and live in the back of beyond?"

"Mum trusts my judgment. She also believes in allowing her children to make their own decisions and mistakes — not that this is a mistake."

Duncan sat next to him. "Are you sure? It's such a big decision. I know you said you'd be able to get to London if you had to, but it's not like you can be there in a few minutes."

Drew threaded his arms through Duncan's and kissed him. "It's a matter of priorities," he continued. "I've tried living away from you and I missed you. Who can tell if things will work out? If you don't take a chance once in a while, you miss out on so much. Who'd have thought there was a market for lace panties for men? And yet here I am, making money and working out how to transfer distribution to here. I'll have Ben, Jonty and Joy in London for emergencies and I can video conference even to show off designs. I'll make it work." He kissed Duncan again. "It's a pity there's nowhere we could go now to get away from everyone. And no, I'm not up for a quickie in the tack room."

Duncan grinned, dipped into his jeans pocket and waved a key in front of Drew. "I've already thought about that. Lodge five is empty until later. Craig's uncle and aunty won't be here until around four, so we have a couple of hours if you're up for it, and there's something I want you to do."

Duncan running his hand along Drew's thigh before

letting it land on his now bulging crotch clearly revealed Drew was up for anything. "Oh, yeah," he said with eyebrows raised. "I can't wait to find out what you have in mind. Do you think we can get there without bumping into anyone?"

Duncan took his hand. "Only one way to find out."

Checking both ways, they hurried across the yard and around the front of the house, skirting the lodges and ducking under windows until they reached their destination.

"Take your boots off," Duncan said. "We don't want to have to clean mud from the carpet." He fiddled with the key in the lock until they hurried inside and threw themselves on the bed.

Drew immediately straddled Duncan then bent over and kissed him, pushing his tongue between Duncan's lips while raising his arms over his head and holding them. He shifted his hips, grinding into Duncan.

Drew let go of Duncan's arms to pull his jumper and shirt over his head, revealing his pale skin. Duncan lifted himself to peel off his own sweater then laid his head back on the pillow. Despite his fears, he wanted to enjoy every minute of this. Drew's regrown fringe flopped on his face as he leaned over and took Duncan's nipple between his teeth, bit then licked. Duncan bucked and groaned under him.

"So, cowboy, what did you have in mind. You've obviously been planning this afternoon's delight." Drew eased back. A hint of green lace appeared just above his belt.

"I want you to take off your jeans, but leave on the briefs."

Above him, Drew visibly shivered. "God, I love it when you get all growly and masterful." He quickly did as Duncan had said and repositioned himself. "Is this what you wanted?" he asked, running his hands over the emerald-green lingerie which covered only the top half of his glorious arse.

Duncan gazed into Drew's beautiful face, noting practically none of the blue remained in his eyes. He needed to say it.

"I want you to fuck me."

Drew's eyes widened as he took in Duncan's words and he ran his tongue over his bottom lip. He ground his arse over Duncan's groin, making Duncan's cock throb and harden even more.

"If you want to, that is."

"Oh, I want to. I didn't like to ask. I wasn't sure..."

Duncan placed a finger on Drew's mouth. "I wasn't sure myself. I nearly asked you this morning, but here we can be alone, even for a few hours. There's no one to hear or interrupt us. I need to feel you inside me. I trust you. I know you'll make it good for me."

Drew swallowed. "No pressure then. Well, if I may say so, one of us is overdressed."

He lifted one leg over and scooted to the end of the bed to remove Duncan's jeans and briefs, leaving him totally exposed. Drew slowly crawled up the bed toward him until he reached Duncan's cock and encased the tip in his mouth. Duncan lurched up, wanting more. Drew lifted his head and shook his finger.

"Now, now, who's an eager cowboy? We need to get you all prepped and ready for this, don't we?" Drew clutched his cock over the manties with their leaf pattern lace. "Shit. Condoms? Lube?"

Duncan nodded toward his jeans. "In the pocket."

Drew grinned. "Should I be offended you thought I'd jump in the sack at a moment's notice?"

"I hoped you would. Have I—?"

"Shut up, you idiot. I can't think of any better way to spend the afternoon than inside you, except maybe, you inside me. If we have a second wind, perhaps..."

Duncan reached up and dragged Drew down to kiss him again. Drew peppered Duncan's face, neck, collarbone and chest until Duncan could stand no more and pushed him back.

"Oh, God, look at you so hard and needy." Drew swiped his tongue over the tip of Duncan's leaking erection again and took hold of Duncan's balls. He continued licking, sucking and stroking while Duncan groaned and squirmed under him, unable to do anything else. Drew loved to tease.

"How d'you want me?" Duncan asked.

"Doesn't matter to me, although I'd prefer to see you."

Duncan sighed with relief. "Me, too. I want to see your face when you come."

"Pull your knees up and apart," Drew said.

Duncan lay back, knowing his arse was totally exposed, but caring not one jot. In a short amount of time, it wouldn't be his fingers in there, like when he'd practiced before, but Drew's. It would be Drew stretching him, getting him ready, touching him, making his body hum with the expectation of being filled.

Drew leaned back on his knees and stared. He didn't move at all.

Duncan felt butterflies in his stomach. Had Drew changed his mind? His throat had dried, making swallowing tricky. "Drew? Are you all right?"

Drew shook his head. "Sorry, it's just I can't believe how lucky I am." He picked up the lube, opened the packet and squeezed some on his finger.

Duncan tried to relax. The websites he'd checked out had advised him to bear down and let the other person in.

"I know what to do," he said. "Come on, I want this. I want you."

Drew pressed a finger against Duncan's hole then worked it in past his sphincter muscle.

"I've been practicing," Duncan admitted. "More."

Drew stared at him. "God, that's so hot, imagining you lying back like this, fucking yourself."

Duncan had nowhere to hide. Heat flushed into his face and he covered his eyes. Drew pulled his hand away.

"Don't. You never need to feel embarrassed with me even

if you want to ride me wearing chaps and a Stetson and yelling yee haa." He leaned forward and kissed Duncan's nose then winked. "I don't suppose there's any chance of that on your birthday?"

"Maybe the other way around," Duncan replied grinning. "After all, it is *my* birthday." He'd almost forgotten Drew's finger buried deep inside him. When Drew added a second, the burn hurt at first, but once he made himself relax, he only wanted more.

"You feel so good," Drew said. "I can't wait to feel all that heat around my cock."

He moved his fingers and Duncan jerked as his nerve endings lit up. "Crivens!"

Drew grinned. "Good, isn't it?" He hit Duncan's prostate again.

"Enough. I want you. I can't wait any longer." He reached inside the lace pouch and eased out Drew's cock. It stiffened at his touch. "I need this inside me."

"Are you sure? It'll—"

Duncan pressed a finger to Drew's lips. "Enough. I know you'll be careful. Just go slowly to begin with, and…leave the panties on."

"Kinky bugger," Drew said, grinning.

His words sent heat rushing into Duncan's face once more, but this time, he simply grinned back. "It's your fault. You shouldn't look so sexy in them."

Drew withdrew the fingers, leaving Duncan empty. "Here," he said, tossing the condom packet for Duncan to catch. He opened it. Drew maneuvered up the bed until his cock was tantalizingly near to Duncan's mouth. He rolled the condom down and slathered lube all over before passing the rest to Drew, who took his time caressing Duncan's entrance. Duncan squirmed, pressing down, wanting to experience that feeling of fullness again.

"Please," he said, dragging out the word. He pulled his knees as far apart as he could manage.

"Lift." Drew grabbed a pillow. "It'll make the angle

easier." Drew placed the support under Duncan's arse then positioned himself. Duncan tried not to brace.

Drew's cock pressed at his hole. He gave Duncan a questioning glance. Duncan nodded. To begin with, he wasn't sure he'd take it all. Drew wasn't wide, but he was long and the stretch burned so much he wanted to yell.

It won't last forever. And it didn't. He breathed through the pain, which subsided to nothing, leaving him feeling full. He opened his eyes to see Drew smiling, but the smile hadn't reached his eyes.

"It's good," Duncan said to reassure him. "Move. Make me yours."

Drew leaned over and kissed Duncan. "You are mine. This arse is mine to do with what I like."

Duncan raised his arms and wrapped his fingers around the bars of the headboard then pushed down until Drew's balls nestled against his arse. "Now, fuck me."

Drew took his time and built up speed gradually until each thrust hit Duncan's prostate and his balls slapped hard against Duncan's arse. Duncan groaned and gasped and eventually begged for more. Every so often Drew would lean over and kiss him or suck a nipple, sending tingles of sensation through his body. Somehow, this only increased the connection he felt and he never wanted it to end.

"I'm getting close," Drew warned. "Touch yourself. I love watching you come."

Duncan took hold of himself, knowing his orgasm gathered. He arched his back, needing more of Drew, chasing the climax that waited in the shadows. Sometimes, he came slowly, feeling the gathering of every nerve of the blood rushing, but this orgasm hid, making Duncan work for it.

Finally, Drew lifted himself on his hands, and with one final thrust, came. Warmth rushed inside him and he longed to feel nothing between them. He fisted his cock until his orgasm burst out of him, in wave after wave of release, even after Drew collapsed on top of him, his cock still inside. Duncan wrapped his arms around Drew's back, not wanting to let him go, not wanting to be empty again, while only the sound of Drew panting with his head lying on Duncan's chest filled the room.

"That was incredible," he said, stroking the back of Drew's head. Drew gazed up at him.

Duncan couldn't stop the words coming out of his mouth. "I love you, Drew Sinclair."

Drew grinned. "I love you, too, cowboy, but you're going to have to let go of me or the people in this cabin will get quite a shock."

Reluctantly, Duncan let him go. Drew withdrew, removed the condom and tied it off. He leaned over the bed and took the plastic bag from the bin. "We'll have to take this with us," he said. "And now we need to make the bed and spray some air freshener or something. This place smells of us, and gorgeous though that is..."

Duncan rolled over onto his side to watch Drew dressing. "Promise me we'll do this again," he said.

"Oh, hell, I've created a monster," Drew replied, shrugging on his jeans. "Perhaps we'd better wait until tonight, though, for a repeat performance. Don't forget we're hosting the boys at the house while the girls get together, and I've got to make sure Craig doesn't drink too much. He's collecting the pizza after work."

Scotland the Brave chirped on Duncan's phone. Drew tossed his jeans over to him and he dug in the pocket. He might have guessed.

"Talk of the devil. Hi, Craig. Yes, everything is fine."

Drew sat back on the bed and stroked Duncan's nipple. "Stop it." He slapped Drew's hand away.

"Stop what?"

"Sorry, Craig, didn't mean you."

"Are you two at it again? Please tell me you're wearing clothes."

"Craig wants to know if we're wearing clothes," Duncan said, grinning.

Drew leaned into the phone. "Duncan has socks on. Does that count?"

Duncan glanced down. "Knew I'd forgotten something. How can I help you, Craig?" He pressed loudspeaker.

"I rang about tonight. I've ordered the pizza and garlic bread."

"Should you be eating garlic?" Drew asked.

"Jenna loves it," Duncan said. "He's safe there."

"Please tell me you two won't be making PDAs all night?"

"We'll try to behave," Duncan said.

"I'm promising nothing," Drew interrupted.

Craig groaned. "I'll see the pair of you later, then, and do get dressed."

At the sound of the call ending, each of them shook with laughter. Duncan glanced at the clock. "I suppose we'd better get back before we're missed."

Drew's ring tone sounded and he picked up his own mobile. "Hi, Jen. I'll be over in a jiffy." He shifted back to Duncan. "She wants to check the dresses with Carrie and Mhairi. Yes, Duncan's here and yes, I told Mum about us so you can mention it. She's parked outside Mum and Dad's lodge. I'll see you in a few minutes, sis."

Duncan kissed him. "Go on. I'll sort out here and remake the bed."

"Don't forget the condom," Drew said, pulling his jumper over his head.

"I won't. Now, get off and see your sister while I go and set up in the house. I'll see you soon enough."

Drew grabbed his coat then opened the door, letting the cold rush in. "Bloody hell, it's cold out there." He turned and stared. "Love you," he said, leaving Duncan without a chance to reply. He moved to sit on the edge of the bed, picked up the pillow and hugged it. He'd get his chance to say those words back again soon enough.

Chapter Twenty-Two

"For goodness sake, Jenna, stand still, will you?" Drew rubbed his eyes, forgetting the plastic gloves on his hands.

"Has the registrar arrived yet, Mum?"

"Yes, she's up at the house drinking tea. Now, stop fussing and do what your brother says."

Drew mouthed a thank-you at his mother who'd already dressed, collected the buttonholes from the house and checked on the venue.

"Everything is as it should be. Carrie has events in hand with her girls. I told her you'd be over to make sure her dress fitted perfectly, Drew. Now, darling, drink some champagne." She handed a glass to Jenna who swallowed it then burped.

Drew reached out to take a glass. Morag swatted his hand away. "You had quite enough last night, judging by the state of the groom, and him a doctor as well. At least your boyfriend had some sense. Your father tried to claim he'd eaten a bad pizza. I warned him to stay off the whisky, but as usual, he didn't listen. Whoever bought the Glenmorangie... I left him in our bedroom moaning something about the world coming to an end. *Men.*"

Drew stood back. "There. Now I only need to adjust the ties and you're ready." He moved around and adjusted the corset ribbons.

"Fuck, Drew. Give me room to fit in some food later."

Morag tutted.

"Sorry, Mum."

"That's all right, love. It's your wedding day, after all." She stood and gazed out of the window. Glimpses of weak winter sun glinted through the glass. "The frost has started to melt. Do you still intend to wear those boots for the ceremony? The others have beautiful heels and you'll be in those great galumphing things."

"Yes, Mother. I can't walk in heels and they *are* white. Craig knows what he's getting. He's seen me first thing in the morning. I didn't want a painted face or some dodgy hairstyle. This is me. I'm a vet in the Highlands, used to having my hands in places most people would rather avoid. This is our wedding, our way. No fuss, no stupid over-the-top ceremony, just our families and a few friends, with straightforward simple food and dancing. Are you done, Drew? I can barely breathe."

"Don't worry, sis. I can adjust them later to allow you to eat in your body weight in sausage rolls. There. Now," he said, moving to stand next to his mother. "Take a look for yourself."

Jenna moved in front of the full-length mirror Duncan had brought from the house.

"Oh, my. You look stunning. Your dad will burst with pride accompanying you down the aisle."

Jenna grinned. "I hope not." She turned and hugged Drew who wiped the first tear of the day away from his face, thankful he'd chosen waterproof eyeliner.

The door creaked behind them.

"Wow. Look at you three in your finery."

"Dad," Drew said. "How's the head?"

"I'll be fine, son. Wouldn't say no to a cup of tea, though. Where's the camera?"

Morag fussed over her husband's dress, checked his jacket, shirt and kilt, and attached the single white rose to his lapel. "Let's try and do something with your hair."

"Dinnae fuss, lass. No one's going to be looking at me with these two in the room. How I produced such beautiful children, I'll never know."

Drew rolled his eyes at Jenna and waited, knowing what would happen next.

"Ouch. What was that for?" He rubbed his arm where Morag had punched him.

"I think you'll find I had something to do with your two children," Morag said, hands on hips.

His father winked at him. "Oh, yes, how could I forget I'm married to the most beautiful woman in the world?"

"Hmm," Morag said.

"Will this make things better?" He dug into his pocket and produced a ring box. "It's a few days early for our anniversary, but I wanted you to have it today."

Jenna threaded her arm through Drew's. "Did you know about this?" he asked.

"I helped him pick it out."

Morag opened the box to reveal a beautiful ring set with sapphires and diamonds. She covered her mouth with her hand. "It's so beautiful."

"So, today, my two best girls will get rings, and I'll be the happiest man alive. Maybe someday I can dance at your wedding, as well, son."

The group hug brought tears to all their eyes. *I hope so, Dad. I really hope so.*

"Right, enough of this. You and your mum need to get over to the house and check on the bridesmaids. Leave me with my daughter, so she can be unfashionably on time. I'll do us both some toast. And before you say anything, we'll wrap ourselves in towels. Now get off."

Drew helped his mother over the boards to Duncan's Land Rover. The sun hung low in the sky even at midday and he reached for his sunglasses. More cars had parked in the large yard and trails of footprints could be seen along the boards to the indoor arena. Drew pulled up in front of the house, where Duncan waited at the door with Misha at his side. Drew had left him undressed, but now, wearing full Scottish highland dress, Duncan took his breath away.

"Carrie and Mhairi are upstairs waiting for you both. Craig is already over in the venue with the other guests. The food has been set out and the girls have changed.

Lenny and Lachie have sorted the animals and the music and seated everyone. So, all are ready. You look lovely, Mrs. Sinclair."

"Thank you, Duncan. And you look handsome, too, which my son might have mentioned if he wasn't currently catching flies. Close your mouth, son."

Unable to resist, Drew strode up the steps and kissed Duncan there in front of his mother. "You are so fucking me in that outfit tonight," he whispered. Duncan blushed.

"You're pretty hot in your outfit, too. I hope you're wearing something suitable underneath."

"Wouldn't you like to know?"

The cough reminded Drew they weren't alone. "Sorry, Mum. Come on inside."

Thirty minutes later, with everyone sitting waiting and final adjustments made, Drew sat in the front row next to his mother, waiting for Jenna and his father to arrive. At the head stood the registrar, a nervous groom and Duncan. Hundreds of lights twinkled like stars from the ceiling, adding to the faux candle lights on each table.

Maybe *Flower of Scotland* wouldn't have been everyone's choice for walking up the aisle, but when the music began, everyone stood. The gasps as Jenna made her way on her father's arm pleased Drew. He'd done a good job for them all. The colors, white, purple and green, suited Mhairi and Carrie, despite the age difference between them. Across the aisle, Lenny couldn't keep from staring at Mhairi. He turned to face the front again when the registrar spoke the opening words.

"We are gathered here today to witness the marriage of Craig Douglas Mackie and Jenna Lyndsay Sinclair..."

The civil service didn't take long. Drew spent most of it staring at Duncan's back. He'd never thought about marriage, not even after same-sex marriage had been made legal, believing it wasn't for him, but perhaps, some day, he might stand next to the most handsome man in the room. Duncan glanced back and caught him staring. This time heat rushed into his cheeks, so sure was he that Duncan had read his mind.

"You may kiss the bride."

The cheers from the guests woke him from his musings as Craig and Jenna held hands and strolled down the makeshift aisle to the rear of the room where tables had been set out. Carrie hurried to supervise the revealing of the buffet, and the catering staff hired for the occasion began to take the warm food from the heated cabinets.

"If you could all grab your chairs and take them to the tables," Duncan stood at the front in his best man role before following the bride and groom to sign the marriage certificate.

"You did an incredible job with the dresses." Drew swiveled to find Craig's parents standing behind him.

"Thank you. I had to make sure my sister looked her best on her big day."

Craig's mother glanced from side to side then leaned in. "Craig told us about you and Duncan. We're so glad for him. He's been like another son to us. We hope you'll both be happy."

The newly formed lump in his throat stopped his first attempt at a reply. He coughed. "Sorry. And thank you. I hope everyone will be so welcoming. We'd better get moving for the speeches. Duncan's been practicing half the night."

"That much?"

Drew realized the implication in her words and decided discretion was the better part of valor. He coughed loudly and stared at their backs as they laughed and nudged each other, carrying their chairs to the top table. Craig's parents explained the laid-back nature of the man himself and why Jenna loved them.

"I see you've met Craig's parents," Duncan said. Drew wanted to lean back into the man behind him, but waited until Duncan took a lead with his own actions.

"Yes, I think Craig's told them about us."

"I asked him to."

"Really?" He faced Duncan, who looked devastatingly sexy in his formal Scottish attire. Duncan took his hand.

"And you're sitting next to me on the top table."

Drew couldn't help letting his mouth drop open. "Are you sure?" he questioned.

"Well, you are the brother of the bride and the partner of the best man."

Drew noticed Duncan made no attempt to lower his voice. A few heads swung in their direction as the two men their way to their seats. Maybe there was the odd nudge, but Drew didn't intend to let it bother him.

"I said I wasn't going to hide," Duncan said. "If anyone has anything to say, I'm sure they will after a few drinks. Now, I have a speech to give, so shall we take our places, get it over with and let everyone tuck into the food?"

"Sounds good to me."

* * * *

Duncan wasn't one for speeches. He reached into his sporran where Drew had tucked the paper that morning— after he'd given Duncan a blow job in the shower which had left him weak at the knees. He smiled, hoping he'd never get enough of the man sat next to him, who was giving up so much to be with him. He still wasn't convinced Drew had made the right decision, despite his protests to the contrary. Could he manage all aspects of his life from the Highlands? Would he come to resent Duncan? He'd thought about pushing Drew away for his own good, but this had been Drew's idea and Drew was a grown man, with a business brain, as well as a talent so beautifully on display today. A sharp pain woke him.

"You're on. Dad's finished," Drew whispered. "You were miles away."

"Just thinking of you, on your knees," Duncan replied, without blushing.

He stood and unfurled his paper.

"Craig and Jenna are two lucky people," he began. "Lucky to have found each other in this big wide world and lucky to both be heroes. They save lives but don't boast about it. I know this because Craig helped save mine. I won't bore you with my past, but when Craig came to my school, I was a lot smaller than I am now. Craig rescued me from bullies and became my best friend."

"When Jenna first came here, many farmers thought this young chit of a girl would be useless, but from the first time she saved my old dog Misha, then performed a difficult delivery with one of my cows, I knew she'd do. I introduced the pair, so if you want to blame anyone then blame me. I—"

A door burst open and in stepped a large man in a great coat. Craig stood.

"Cormac?"

"Large as life and absolutely knackered. I said I'd get here. Sorry to cut it fine, but at least I haven't missed the food."

Cormac made his way to the table and hugged his parents and brother, leaving Duncan unsure whether to continue. Out of the corner of his eye, he noticed Lachie staring at the man now removing his coat to reveal a casual outfit of jumper and jeans. Duncan had to admit Cormac presented a handsome package. He struck the glass in front of him and all eyes turned back in his direction.

"I'll propose the toast then. Let's raise our glasses to Mr. and Mrs. Mackie."

Everyone lifted their champagne flutes. Craig quickly said his piece, thanking everyone, then the eating began.

"He's certainly handsome," Drew said, placing his plate on the table a little while later.

"Sorry? What?" Duncan leaned back in his seat, his food still untouched.

"Cormac. You were staring. A person could get jealous."

Duncan sat up. "No, sorry. I wasn't..." Did he break a confidence? "It's Lachie. Have you noticed he hasn't taken his eyes off Cormac since he arrived? And Cormac is showing signs of interest, judging by the way they're talking over there."

"But Craig and his parents are with them, as well as Jenna."

"Exactly, Lachie seems...out of place."

Drew frowned. "I'm assuming paternal concern here." He bit into a piece of quiche and swallowed too quickly, nearly choking.

Duncan slapped his back. "I know Cormac of old, and Lachie would be just his type."

"I'm sure Lachie could protect his own honor. He's a big strapping lad, after all." Duncan checked in each direction and leaned closer to Drew's ear, resisting the temptation to suck on his ever so tempting lobe and hear Drew groan in a way that shot straight to his cock. This wasn't the place for a hard-on even under his kilt. "Lachie's gay. He told me a while back, and Cormac has a reputation for taking any opportunity presented to him. There was some bother with him getting some girl pregnant while shagging her brother at the same time. It turned out she wasn't, but the other side of the world seemed a better idea than facing the slightly dubious family."

Drew leaned forward on his elbows and chewed on a stick of satay chicken while staring over at the group. "Well, I'd say Lachie's showing signs of interest, but he's a grown man, so if he fancies some fun where's the harm? I mean he's not a virgin, is he?"

"No, but he doesn't have much experience, and he's not out. Sorry, I'm sounding like a stick in the mud, and you're right, he's old enough to make his own mistakes. I doubt he's looking for love, and Cormac undoubtedly has the experience."

Drew patted his arm. "Eat up and we'll keep an eye on things. Time for dancing soon, and after the time at the club, I'm not listening to your excuses."

"But you know I'm not much of a dancer?" Duncan said.

Even after the first occasion, he dreaded showing off his inability to move next to Drew.

"Come on, you managed last time, and I seem to remember a certain person fucking me into the mattress. Maybe we can have our own Christmas party later and make all the noise we want as Craig will be with Jenna over at the lodge."

"You've forgotten Mhairi, Carrie and Sandy will be there," Duncan reminded him.

Drew leaned closer. "So, we'll have to be quiet while you slide inside me."

Duncan shivered as his cock stiffened. "Damn!"

Drew dug his fork into a canapé and lifted it to Duncan's lips. "You owe a pound to your swear jar again."

"I blame you."

Across the room, the first few bars of *Waiting for a Girl Like You* sounded and Craig and Jenna rose for their first dance. Everyone watched for a minute before being beckoned onto the floor. Drew stood and put out a hand to Duncan. "Are you ready for this? All you need to do is stand there. I'll do the rest. By the time I've finished, you'll be glad we're both wearing kilts and wanting to drag me to the stable for a quickie."

Duncan gulped. "I want to already but shouldn't we let them have their moment? I don't want to upstage them."

"Craig and Jenna insisted we start as we mean to go on and get it over with." The hair on the back of Duncan's neck stood up. He had no idea of his emotions as fear and excitement intermingled.

"Come on."

Duncan took Drew's outstretched hand and let himself be led to the area set aside for dancing. Everyone not already dancing was staring at the bride and groom so no one noticed them at first as he took Drew in his arms and moved from foot to foot with Drew's head on his shoulder. Holding Drew in his arms felt absolutely right. A few people stared, then nudged, then smiled. Craig patted him

213

on the back as they danced past. Duncan wrapped his arms around Drew and pulled him closer, letting the rest of the world disappear until he was rudely awakened from his daydreams by a slap on his shoulder.

"Why, Duncan, you sneaky bastard. If I'd known you batted for both teams, I'd have made my own pitch. And who's the lucky fella?"

Duncan turned to see Cormac standing behind him. "This is Drew, Jenna's brother and my —"

"Boyfriend," Drew said, holding out one hand while taking hold of Duncan's with the other. "It's nice to meet you. I hear you've been away for a while."

"Yes, Australia, but I've been offered a job in Glasgow, and I wanted to see oor Craig get wed, so I came straight here. I hope there's room for me somewhere." Duncan followed his glance across the room to Lachie and bit back a comment. Lachie could make his own mind up and he didn't need Duncan speaking for him.

"Maybe we can get a dance in later, but now I need a drink, or I'm likely to fall into my food. My body clock has no idea what day it is let alone what time. Catch you later, Dunc. Looks like this wedding's going to be more interesting than I expected."

Chapter Twenty-Three

Drew pulled Duncan closer into the shadows and leaned back against the wall outside the arena. "We should go back in. It's freezing," he whispered into Duncan's ear before sucking on it again.

"Or we could go over to the house. I'm so hard under this kilt and it's all your fault. Or it could be the cold." He turned his head at the door opening.

"Just up here. We have rooms over the stables."

"It's Lachie," Duncan whispered. "No prizes for guessing who's with him." He pulled out of Drew's hold. "Maybe I should…"

"Do nothing. Lachie is a big boy who can take care of himself and getting off at weddings is a tradition. I was hoping to get lucky myself with this sexy cowboy. He has dark hair and brown eyes the color of melted chocolate, wide shoulders and an arse that's so biteable."

"Damn, you should warn a guy before you grab him." Duncan squirmed as Drew palmed his cock through his briefs.

"Wanna feel mine? I'm wearing something special underneath this kilt." Drew grabbed his hand letting Duncan feel the lace cupping his cock and balls perfectly. "They're your favorite color, too."

"Please, you need to stop, or I'm going to come right now."

"I could drop to my knees here," Drew offered before sucking on Duncan's bottom lip. He groaned, his senses on overload.

"I don't suppose they'd notice us gone, would they? We

could slip over to the house for a while. Everyone knows where they're sleeping tonight and it's not snowing. Oh, God, I'm leaking so much."

"Come on, then. I want you inside me. I intend to ride you so hard."

Duncan's stomach fluttered and his nerve endings tingled.

"Are you okay? You shivered."

"Only with anticipation. Come on, I've got the perfect hat for you to wear, cowboy."

* * * *

"Should we go back? It's ten already."

Drew sat up and stared at him. "Really?"

"I am the sort of host, after all, and we've been gone a couple of hours now. I can't help feeling guilty. It's not like we don't have tomorrow, and the day after, and the day after that." He couldn't have stopped the grin spreading over his face if he'd tried.

"All right, but I'm putting on my jeans and the thickest jumper I possess."

Back at the venue, Duncan glanced around the room. Lenny and Claire moved to the music on the dance floor with Jenna and Craig next to them. Carrie, Sandy, Drew and Craig's parents and a few others, all sat around a table, sipping what appeared to be tea. Their chances of returning without comment were nil.

"We weren't sure we'd see you before tomorrow," Drew's dad said. "Pull up a couple of chairs. Are either of you two fit to drive?" He held up a glass. "We'll need a lift back to the lodges."

"I'll be fine," Duncan said. "I haven't had much."

"Have you seen Lachie anywhere?" Carrie asked.

Duncan glanced at Drew, who shook his head. "He'll be checking on the horses or feeding the dogs. You know what he's like — so dedicated."

Carrie stood. "I'll going to make cocoa back at the house.

Would you give me a hand with the flasks and plastic cups, Duncan?"

How could he refuse? That Carrie planned to interrogate him was obvious from the look on her face. He swallowed hard, knowing he had no choice.

"Of course."

In the kitchen, Carrie busied herself while Duncan patted Misha and gave her a few biscuit treats, then found the large flasks they kept for group picnics in summer. Finally, he sat at the table and waited for the inevitable.

"He's with that Cormac, isn't he?"

Duncan nodded. There didn't seem to be any point in arguing. "How long have you known about him?"

"He's my son, so all of his life. Cormac's not the first. There was a German guy last season, and, I suppose, there have been others. I can't help but worry, though, just as I worry about you. Both of you tend to jump in with both feet. Drew's making a big sacrifice to be with you. It worries me and Drew's parents, too. I'm the nearest you have to a mother and I love you like a son. I don't want you to be hurt."

Heat rushed into Duncan's cheeks at the thought of people discussing him. "It's his decision. He's sorted everything out with his job. It's not going to always be easy, but what relationship is? I love him, Carrie. I didn't expect to. He's so different from me, but opposites attract, I suppose, and we seem to work. I see him and my stomach flips. I'll do whatever it takes to make this work. And as for Lachie, he's still young. Maybe it's time he got away from here and saw more of the world. Cormac starts work in Glasgow in the New Year so… But then again, tonight may be a one-off. Not everyone falls in love at first sight. It took me more than twenty-four hours."

He picked up the flasks. "Come on, let's get these over to the others and have a night-cap."

When Duncan returned, he found Drew talking to his father. Drew beckoned him over. He checked each side, then, finding no one, he tried his best to amble nonchalantly while his stomach tied itself into knots. Finally, standing in front of the man he loved and his father, he came to a stop. He didn't have to wait for long.

Strong arms used to an outdoor life pulled him in and hugged him. Over the other man's shoulder, Drew grinned. The slap on his back winded him and he coughed.

"Let him go, Dad."

Rory Sinclair stepped back, keeping his hands on Duncan's arms. "Welcome to the family. Morag and I want you to think of us as your surrogate parents. You don't have to call us Mum and Dad unless you want to, but we wanted to say an official welcome and we insist you come over to visit us soon. Morag has albums of baby photos to show you."

"Fuck, not those, Dad."

"Language, Drew."

"I can't wait to see them, Mr. Sinclair, and you are welcome to stay in one of the lodges anytime you both want a change."

Duncan tried not to wince at the slap on his arm. "We'll be sure to take you up on your offer, laddie. Now, who's for a wee dram in their cocoa?"

Cormac appeared a few minutes later as the group cupped their drinks while Jenna and Craig continued to sway to the music.

"Sorry to disappear—jet lag. I needed a lie down for a few hours."

Duncan glared at him, hoping he'd got the message, and spotted Carrie giving him a look that would have felled Goliath if he'd been glancing in her direction. Of course, Cormac had no idea who she was. Duncan kicked his ankle and nodded toward the flasks set out on the food table. At least Cormac got that message.

Duncan waited while the Cormac turned the tap and filled another plastic cup then leaned against the table watching his brother. "Aww, see the pair of them. Oor Craig landed on his feet with that one. Will you and Drew be tying the knot now you can?"

"We haven't got that far yet." He swallowed a mouthful of cocoa, wishing he had added some whisky. "Where's Lachie?"

"Asleep, I would imagine. I'm only standing because my body thinks it's midday. That boy has hidden depths, a talented tongue and thighs which wrap around and pull you in. He said he'd told you, and you never thought—"

"He's not my type."

"So I see." Cormac glanced over to where Drew sat with the others. "Who'd have thought you'd go for a skinny city boy?"

"Have you always been this much of a dick, or is this something you've picked up abroad?" Duncan clenched his hands into fists.

"Look, Lachie knew what he was doing, and he dragged me to his lair, not the other way around. He's a grown man and I like him. All right, I have a reputation, but he was up for it. You need to give him credit for taking what he wanted, and stop acting like his father."

"His father's over there, the big man next to the woman in the matron of honor dress. He's the local bobby and he doesn't know Lachie is gay."

Cormac raised his eyebrows. "Oh. Am I likely to get my lights punched out?"

"Maybe you should say goodnight and go back to the house across the way. You can kip in the front room. You'll find the cats in there and a throw over the back of the sofa. Misha, my dog, might come and investigate who you are, but she'll be fine. I'll tell them you're tired."

"Thanks—I owe you. And Drew is gorgeous, by the way. I've no idea what he sees in an old curmudgeon like you."

"Me, neither. I'm just grateful he's willing to give up so much to be with me. Maybe one day, you'll be lucky enough to find love with some mad person ready to take you on."

Cormac grinned. "You never know."

Duncan ambled back to the group. "Cormac's gone back

to get some sleep."

Sandy leaned across. "Was he with Lachie? It's all right, son. You can tell me the truth."

"Yes. He said he left him asleep."

Sandy nodded. "I think it's time we retired to bed."

Carrie nodded. Lenny and Mhairi, arms wrapped around each other, got up and said good night without any further comment.

"I'd better get those two to their lodge first, then I'll take everyone else."

An hour later, everyone had been deposited in their accommodation for the night and Duncan sat waiting for Drew to finish in the bathroom. When he appeared wearing a teal-blue satin kimono with a pattern of embroidered dragons, Duncan's cock leaped once more.

"Bloody hell. You look stunning."

Drew beamed then undid the belt and let the kimono hang open to reveal a reindeer-shaped pouch complete with antlers and a red nose. He flung a Santa hat at Duncan, who placed it on his head. Drew sashayed toward him and sat on Duncan's knee.

"Hello, Santa. I've been such a good boy."

"Are you sure?" Duncan asked, lowering his voice.

"Why, Santa? What do you have in mind?"

Duncan checked himself. Had his mind let the thought of spanking Drew's fine arse then kissing it better slip in? He swallowed in an effort to wet his dry throat as his cock hardened. Could he really go again? He stood with Drew in his arms and dropped him unceremoniously on the bed, joined him and pulled Drew on top so they could kiss each other dizzy.

After a few minutes of kissing lips, noses, eyes, chin, and grinding their groins together, Drew lifted his head.

"I'm going to come in my pants and get Rudolph all sticky if we keep this up."

Duncan placed his hands on Drew's arse and pulled him closer, moving so they rubbed together once more. "This is how we did it the first time and Rudolph will get over it."

"I need skin against skin," Drew insisted. He lifted himself and somehow managed to release their leaking erections from the confines of their briefs as they slid against each other once more.

Drew bit and licked along his shoulder and his neck, making Duncan groan and thrust upward. "So close," he whispered.

"Me, too." He shifted the angle. "Oh, yeah, there."

Warm liquid spilled between them as Duncan's orgasm hit and Drew thrust his tongue, fucking his mouth. Duncan rolled him over and kissed Drew hard before lifting his head.

"Sorry, am I squashing you?"

"A little," Drew replied. "I hope we weren't too loud."

Duncan felt the heat rush into his face. He'd forgotten other people would be there. He'd be red-faced in the morning. "I'd better get a towel to clean up." He rolled off Drew who grabbed him.

"Stay—we can shower in the morning if we're crusty." He shimmied out of his briefs and Duncan did the same before wrapping himself around Drew. Waking with him would be the perfect present on Christmas Day.

What seemed like minutes later, Drew opened one eye to see Duncan creeping around. The clock said five after six and he groaned. "Bloody hell, it's Christmas."

Duncan leaned in and kissed him. "Welcome to my world. Animals need feeding and mucking out all year round. You stay there if you want."

Drew stirred and swung his legs over to sit on the edge of the bed before rubbing the sleep from his eyes. "No, if I'm going to be a rancher's husband, I'd better get used to the early morning." He paused, waiting to see how his words would impact. Duncan halted, buckling his belt for a moment, but that was all.

"Give me a while to get clean, and I'll be down."

"There's still plenty of hot water. I heard noises downstairs, so someone is up."

Drew hurried his shower and dressed for the outdoors. On the stairs, he overheard voices in the kitchen. Obviously Carrie had beaten them both out of bed. When he walked into the kitchen, she placed a mug of coffee in front of him. Cormac sat opposite with Duncan laying a bowl of food on the floor for Misha. Drew glanced out through the French doors to the seating area.

"Shit. Snow. That wasn't in the forecast, was it?"

"No," Carrie replied. "It's lower than they expected it to be. Lachie and Lenny have already eaten and taken the quad bikes up to the Highland Cows. They've taken fodder and hot water for the troughs if they're frozen. Sandy is with the horses and the cats have been fed."

"What would I do without you?" Duncan asked. "Did everyone get away before the snow set in last night?"

"Except for the family and Mhairi, who's stuck here for now. I've made enough porridge for an army, so tuck in."

Drew sprinkled salt on his porridge.

"Having second thoughts about being a rancher's husband in the Highlands?" Duncan asked.

Drew grinned both at Duncan's words and at Cormac's and Carrie's expressions. Neither asked anything.

A few minutes later, breakfast eaten and coffee and tea swallowed, Drew followed Duncan and Cormac across the snowy courtyard with Misha jumping and barking excitedly.

"When I left Oz, it was over thirty degrees. I'll need a new coat and boots. It's a good job we're the same size," Cormac said, wrapping his arms around himself.

In the stables, Sandy whistled as he worked. He looked up when they entered. "I've done five of them. D'you want to finish off and Cormac and I can go and check on the cattle? Lenny and Lachie said they'd go there first to feed them."

Cormac wrinkled his nose. "Cattle? Oh, God, they'll smell. That's the good thing about being a marine specialist. The sea doesn't smell." He glanced at Duncan. "Oh, well,

Sandy. Come on, then."

Drew finished mucking out and feeding, building up a sweat even in the cold. "Now what?" he said, collapsing onto the chair in the tack room.

"We'll need to get the others over to the house. I've put halters on Mutt and Jeff for the sleigh. I thought we'd collect them in style."

Excitement flooded through Drew's veins and he almost clapped. A sleigh, a real sleigh with bells and everything in the snow like out of some film. "Jenna will love it, but will we get Granny and Aunty May on it?"

"We might have to make a couple of trips. Come on, let's get the horses in place and we can go and wake them up."

"Should we do Craig and Jenna last? It is their honeymoon, after all."

The sleigh took some maneuvering, but finally, with the horses attached, they slipped down the pathways to the lodges. First they collected Drew and Craig's parents then the old ladies, who Duncan lifted onto the seats with ease. Pride surged through Drew along with a frisson of excitement that the strength of the man was his as well.

"I wish I'd seen you play Santa. I bet you looked great."

"We'll have next year," Duncan said, smiling. Drew threaded his hand through Duncan's arm.

They sang carols on the way back to the main house, drank more coffee then, having left everyone cooking Christmas lunch, they returned to collect the newlyweds.

Drew rapped on the door while Duncan jingled the bells. Jenna poked her head around and blinked. "You brought the sleigh." She turned. "Craig, it's snowed and Duncan has brought the sleigh. It's perfect."

"Are you dressed?" Drew asked. "Carrie's made porridge and everyone else is up at the house."

"Five minutes," Jenna said. "We're a bit tired."

Drew smiled. "I bet you are."

"Shut up. I bet you two just went to bed with a cocoa, didn't you? And we are married. Any more and I'll spill what you've got planned for Duncan's birthday."

Drew glared at his sister. He'd arranged three days away at a place where Duncan wouldn't have to get up early or muck out cows and horses.

"And before you ask, I'm not telling you." To his surprise, Duncan didn't argue.

Sixteen people filled the house. Carrie threw most of them out of the kitchen while she sorted dinner. They opened presents and drank too much eggnog until all mucked in, helping set up the huge table in the dining room. When everyone was seated with full plates, Drew glanced around the table at all the smiling, laughing people, but especially at Duncan. He produced a piece of mistletoe from his pocket and held it over Duncan's head.

"It's a Christmas tradition," he said.

Duncan reached into his pocket and pulled out more. "I know," he said, before kissing Drew as the group whooped and clapped.

"Happy Christmas."

Epilogue

Several months later

"I can't believe how well it's gone." Drew twirled, taking in the displays, knowing his designs would be in every store throughout the country.

"Seems weird launching an autumn range at this time of year," Duncan said, moving from foot to foot.

"That's how it's done, darling." Jonty appeared out of nowhere with Ben in tow, carrying champagne. "You have to give people time to buy. I have to say everything looks gorgeous. I can see them flying off the racks. I did have my worries about whether we could manage this company, but St Clair and Co. Designs have hit the ground running. We're already ahead on the next collection, even with you living in the back of beyond."

"Thank goodness for modern technology," Drew added, raising a glass. Joy slipped under his arm.

"What's the matter?" Drew asked, seeing her face.

"I'm still not sure about one of the fabrics and whether it hangs right."

Drew turned to Duncan. "This is par for the course. This woman is a genius, but she's never satisfied."

Over on the other end of the store, the five models stood with cameras flashing in front of them. Many fashion magazines carried shoots of the range and the TV adverts had hit the screens the night before. Sebastian strolled toward them with others from the store management. Duncan stiffened beside him.

"Down boy. He's found someone else to chase, some

merchant banker in the City worth a fortune, who's much more interesting than little old me."

"Impossible," Duncan said.

Drew kissed his cheek. "Right answer, and you'll get your reward later. I hope the girls are all right back home."

"They'll be fine. They've been trained how to receive and pack the orders and you checked the website this morning. Who'd have thought lacy pants for men would be so popular?"

Drew stared at Duncan then winked at the others. He leaned in and pushed his free arm through Duncan's. "Well, you should know, cowboy. You sure like me wearing them."

Duncan's face turned red within seconds and he shuffled even more, keeping his gaze directed at to the floor.

Jonty pushed him, laughing. "You well and truly walked into that one. Should I say I'm wearing a gorgeous pair in fuchsia?" He leaned in. "Ben has a thing for them, too, and I can't wait until the corset designs are finalized. Those waistcoats are to die for. You and Joy were inspired."

"Idris helped," Drew added. "That boy will go far."

A loud cough emanating from the other side of the space caught their attention. Sebastian stood, smartly suited and booted, in front of the small crowd of fashion writers and photographers with other store employees.

"Thank you everyone. We're extremely excited to launch the new autumn range exclusive to Fairfords stores. This Every Woman range by St Clair and Co. will do what it says and provide beautifully designed and made clothes for women of all sizes and ages. I'd like to introduce the lead designer, Drew St Clair, and his team."

Drew walked forward while the cameras flashed. He thanked everyone then hurried back to Duncan's side.

"We can leave now," he said. "And tomorrow we'll be back in the Highlands with the horses and cattle and everything you love."

"I've been so worried you'd miss all this—the city and

the people — how busy everything is, and your friends."
Duncan clasped Drew's hand and they strolled into the lift.

The doors closed behind them and Drew pressed Duncan against the wall then kissed him, his cock shooing to half hard even from this contact. The doors opened all too soon and several women waited and stared.

"Sorry, ladies," Duncan said.

"Can't say I blame you. He's gorgeous," one younger woman agreed.

Drew grabbed a startled Duncan's hand. "And I'm all his."

They rushed through the store to the busy street outside. Drew stared at the hundreds of strangers dashing along pavements and across roads while the Underground spewed even more. He thought about riding up to their lake, of lying in Duncan's arms as they had the first time, of the birds singing, the cattle lowing and Misha dancing around, ready to play. He sniffed the air, taking in the fumes and recalled the smell of the gorse and the new grass which had been all around them as they'd made love. He'd discovered a passion for the outdoors which had surprised even him.

"There's a train back tonight," he said.

Duncan grinned. "And we've a few hours to spare before then. We could take in a museum, if you want."

Drew winked. "There's nothing in this world I'd prefer to stare at than you. We could wash off the dirt in the huge bath at the hotel and lounge around in those toweling robes then get room service."

"Have I ever mentioned I love the way you think, Drew Sinclair?"

Drew's heart wanted to fly out of his body. No one had ever gazed at him the way this man did. "You may have done. Now, time's a wasting and I'm feeling dirty."

Duncan raised his arm at an oncoming black cab. "Taxi," he yelled. "You're a bad man, Drew Sinclair."

Drew pulled him into the back and squeezed Duncan's

thigh, trailing his fingers 1 higher. "When we get there, cowboy, I'll show you *exactly* how bad I can be."

Choosing Home

Excerpt

Chapter One

"Morning, sir, and welcome to Moray Lodge How can I help you?"

Seth Pritchard tried not to grimace. He hated feeling so weak, but spying the chair in reception, he made for it and sat, stretching out his leg in the hopes that taking his weight off it for a moment might help — it didn't.

"Are you all right, sir? Can I get you anything?"

Seeing the concern on her face, he raised his stick in explanation. "Sorry, I think the plane ride and drive from Inverness may have been a bit much. I'm Seth Pritchard. I've booked the cottage for six months, and I need the keys."

"Of course, Mr. Pritchard." She returned to the desk and pressed a few buttons on the laptop in front of her. "Here are your keys. My name is Caitlin, and you'll see me around the place. If you need anything, press one on the phone in the cottage and it will come straight through to here. To get an outside line, you need to press nine. The cottage has a reasonable mobile signal, depending on your service provider. There's a file with all the instructions on the coffee table in the property. I hope you'll enjoy your time with us."

He stood and pain shot through his leg once more. "Thank you," he managed, taking the keys from the beautifully polished surface of the reception desk.

"Do you need any help unloading your car, Mr. Pritchard?" Concern clouded her features. "We're setting up for lunch, but I could send someone over later."

As she spoke, a couple entered the area and stood waiting.

"I'm fine," Seth said. He knew he sounded tetchy, but he'd had enough sympathetic looks to last a lifetime. "Don't worry. I'll have a rest then get myself sorted later."

He limped outside past the couple and around the back of the hotel to where he'd left his new car next to the small cottage. After opening the driver's door, he sat with his legs on the ground and breathed in. The smell of the sea made him feel better. It was different here, cleaner somehow, but also more pungent than the Bristol Channel. He turned his face up in an attempt to capture any warmth from the bright sunlight, then he closed his eyes and listened to the waves crash onto the rocks. The sun disappeared behind a cloud and he shivered in the cold February breeze. At least it wasn't snowing.

He leaned over and pulled his shoulder bag from the passenger seat. His suitcases could wait. All he wanted to do was wrap a heat pad round his knee, take two painkillers and lie down.

The lock needed jiggling, but once he'd mastered the technique, Seth entered straight into the open plan living room-come-kitchen. The space was surprisingly large, painted in neutral colors, with windows on two sides. Although he'd seen photographs on the Lodge's website, they often gave no idea of size and scale. Happily, he noted a desk under one window where he could work. He dropped the bag on the sturdy piece of furniture, sat on the chair and stared at the view. It was beautiful. The winter sun made patterns on the constantly shifting water. He guessed there would be frost in the morning after another bitterly cold night. The current high-pressure system locked over the country would keep things dry and sunny, but cold.

Seth removed his laptop from the bag and gazed at his surroundings while automatically rubbing his knee. One door led off the main room, which he supposed could only be the bedroom. He tucked a hot pad in his pocket, then, bracing himself, he stood once more and pressed his stick to the floor. At least the carpet provided purchase to cross safely. Laminate floors were a nightmare if the stick got wet, and he'd almost fallen more than once when he'd forgotten to wipe the rubber ferrule at the end. He opened the door to the bedroom. The furniture inside consisted of a large, high bed, which would make life easier, a chest of drawers, a triple wardrobe and an armchair. He liked the shades of blue in the bedding, carpets and curtains. His injury made him assess every piece of furniture, something he'd never considered before the accident, to make sure he could get off it without too much pain. The open door to the bathroom revealed it contained a large shower at one end as well as a bath.

Finally, he sat on the edge of the bed, took out the hot pad and wrapped it around his knee. He downed a couple of painkillers, then swung his legs around to lie on what appeared to be a comfortable bed and closed his eyes.

* * * *

"Shit. What the hell?" It took him several moments to remember his location. The alarm clock told him he'd been asleep for nearly three hours.

"Hello, anyone here?"

"Yes," he shouted. "Give me a minute." Seth pulled the

wrap from around his leg and moved carefully, testing his knee before he stood up. The first step after sleeping was always painful. He moved it gingerly. It was stiff still, but bearable. He grabbed his stick and went to meet his visitor.

He entered the room to find a tall, dark-haired man in jeans and a jumper standing with his back to him, scanning the view out of the kitchen window. He turned and Seth took a sharp intake of breath. The man facing him smiled, showing straight white teeth and dimples on either side of his face. Heat rushed unbidden to Seth's cheeks and his body stirred in response to the way his visitor scrutinized him from bottom to top, then he moved forward and put out his hand.

"Hi, I'm Zac McKenzie. I own the Lodge. Caitlin told me you'd arrived. I hope everything is all right for you."

Seth noticed the quick glance at his stick, but he had no intention of explaining why he needed it. He'd come up here to put a few hundred miles between him and his past. No one knew his current location and he intended to keep things that way. He doubted anyone other than his mother would be worried, but after so long in a hospital bed, he couldn't face his mother fussing around him, or the piteous looks and tedious teasing from his stepfather and brothers. He knew it was his fault, what had happened to Anna, cosmic karma for all the lies, so he'd made his plans and had left his family a note.

More books from
Alexa Milne

Book two in The Call of Home series

You can never escape from yourself.

Book three in The Call of Home series

Can these two men overcome the events of their pasts and find truth and comfort with each other?

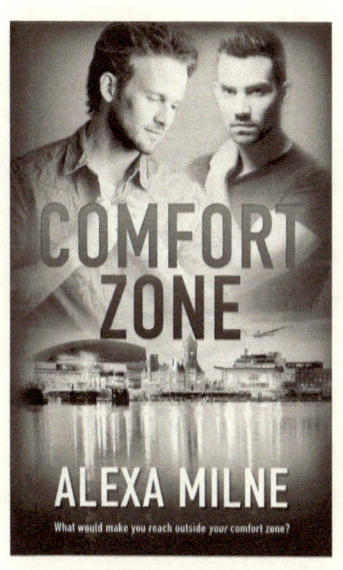

What would make you reach outside your comfort zone?

Sometimes keeping hold of love is just as hard as finding it.

Sometimes keeping hold of love is just as hard as finding it.

About the Author

Alexa Milne

Originally from South Wales, Alexa has lived for over thirty years in the North West of England. Now retired, after a long career in teaching, she devotes her time to her obsessions.

Alexa began writing when her favourite character was killed in her favourite show. After producing a lot of fanfiction she ventured into original writing.

She is currently owned by a mad cat and spends her time writing about the men in her head, watching her favourite television programmes and usually crying over her favourite football team.

Alexa Milne loves to hear from readers. You can find contact information, website details and an author profile page at https://www.pride-publishing.com/